SIMPLE MACHINES

ALSO BY IAN MORRIS

When Bad Things Happen to Rich People

The Little Magazine in Contemporary America
(Editor, with Joanne Diaz)

SIMPLE MACHINES

A NOVEL

Ian Morris

GIBSON HOUSE PRESS

CHICAGO

DISCLAIMER

There does exist in Lake Superior a chain of islands of roughly the same size and geographical location as those described in the book. However, none of the characters or events I have described are intended to reflect anyone who lived there or anything they may have done.

GIBSON HOUSE PRESS
Flossmoor, Illinois 60422
GibsonHousePress.com

ISBNs: 978-1-948721-00-4 (paperback); 978-1-948721-01-1 (Mobipocket); 978-1-948721-02-8 (epub); 978-1-948721-03-5 (PDF)

LCCN: 2018938457

Cover design by Christian Fuenfhausen.
Text design and composition by Karen Sheets de Gracia
in the Bembo, Signyard, Kirkwood, and Steelworks typefaces.

Printed in the United States of America
22 21 20 19 18   1 2 3 4 5

♾ This paper meets the requirements of ANSI/NISO Z39.48-1992
(Permanence of Paper)

FOR
MARY

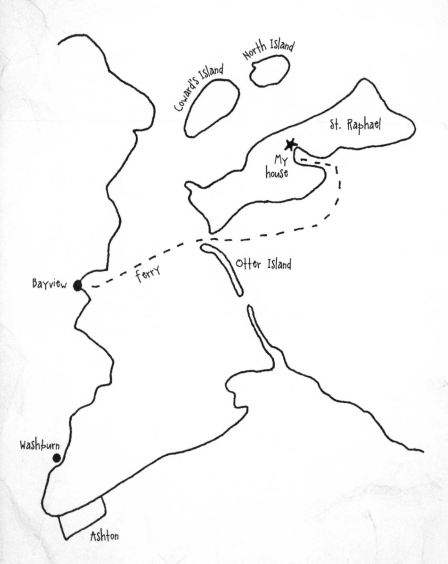

PART I

AN ISLAND
IN THE TAIGA

THE BLUE CANOE

We called it "Godspeed the Warriors" and we did it every year on graduation night. It was a peculiar ritual, where the seniors got together, in the hour before sunset, with canoes and paddles in a cove beneath the high bluffs on the southern shore of Lake Superior and rowed across the shallows to Otter Island. Our observance of this rite went all the way back to World War I, when the people of the peninsula bade a patriotic adieu to four brothers from Ashton who'd joined up. Folks had heard about what went on over there and expected, no doubt, that some of the Olson boys would not be coming back.

The year our turn came around was the first hot day of the season. We were sweaty, high, and sun-weary from two hours that morning getting roasted like heretics in our black robes on the soccer field behind the gym. For the rest of the day we had drifted from one crepe-papered back yard to another, drinking champagne from the Kroger.

The local newspapers back in 1918 recorded that the pageant lasted three days. There was a parade, Indian dances and foot races, a professional baseball team, and on Sunday the first Godspeed. It had been the idea of Alfred Bigelow, the mayor of Ashton, to capture the military spirit of the moment by recreating another savage battle, one fought on these waters centuries ago between the Ojibwa of the island and an invading party of Sioux.

Whatever happened to the Olson boys? True to the fears of the locals, none of them made it back home. None of them died in France, either. The war was over before they reached the front lines. They lived through the war (and for years afterward as far as anyone knew) but didn't come back home. And so Godspeed became for the grown-ups about going away and for us kids about the chance to never return.

After the Armistice was signed—an event also recorded in the local papers of that year—no one wanted another pageant, but they liked Godspeed the Warriors, and so it was kept and performed every year on graduation day. Since kindergarten I had watched from the bluffs with Grey Reed and the other kids my age, jealous and admiring of the seniors, who looked as grown up as we ever thought we'd want to be, and counted off the years until it would be our turn. Now that day had come, and we stood on the shore next to our boats.

Grey Reed was shirtless, with his hair leather-strapped into a ponytail. He stood surveying the water in front of us and the island beyond it, and flicked a caterpillar off the prow of the canoe, which was wood and twelve feet long and belonged to Callie's stepdad, Ray, until Grey offered to take the thing off of his hands and hauled it out from behind the barn on the Dobbses' property where it had sat hull-up across two sawhorses for so many years that the sun and the elements had stripped the wood bare of paint. Grey had refitted the ribbing in the hull and the benches and laid on three coats of polyurethane marine paint, indigo blue (because he said he'd seen his share of red canoes). When he was done, Callie said it was "pretty," which was a hard word for her to part with, since she'd made no secret of how much she resented the time he put into the job. Ray Dobbs admired the work Grey had done so much he told him he wanted the boat back.

Nobody needed to be told what to do: carry boats to the water, line them up in even rows, and wait for the signal to begin, which was three blasts of a whistle. When it came, we flipped our boats over and waded into the rocky shallows. The water was frigid and snatched at our ankles as we launched the canoe, which glided across the surface of the lake like an eager mallard, until the three of us jumped in at the same time and the hull groaned and settled among the waves. At the bow, Callie sliced the water in easy, shallow J-shaped strokes. Grey steered, and I sat without paddle on the center bench. "Riding cargo," Grey called it.

Somewhere in the history of Godspeed the idea had become to tear across to the island as fast as you could. Coming up on our right, Kurt Rossmeier and Randy Storer—two-thirds of the first line of the Norsemen varsity hockey squad—slashed at the waves with their paddles. Grey and Callie maintained their measured pace. None of the three of us, least of all Grey, was in any hurry for the maiden voyage of the blue canoe to come to an end.

The water churned as dozens of other canoes plowed past us, making the whole spectacle seem more like a water ride at Great America than like the actual historical event that this ceremony was supposed to recall.

Callie stretched her paddle over her head with both hands and twisted her hips, baring the copper skin of her lower back. "God," she said, "it's good to be out of that dress." She was talking about the black velvet number she had worn to graduation, which had looked stunning, no question, on a tall and slender girl, but wasn't a wise choice to wear under a graduation gown on an early summer scorcher. "Dolores picked it out," she said. "I only wore it because I thought my dad was coming." However, her father hadn't arrived from La Crosse like he said he would. Now she was barefoot and wearing the blue fake-satin shorts that Dolores bought her in Duluth on an otherwise perfectly good spring afternoon.

Our original plan was to stick together, Grey and Callie and me. We were going to go down to school, the three of us, and Grey and I were going to room together and Callie would live in a girls' dorm nearby with some girl from Oostburg or someplace, who we would talk to or not, depending on how we felt. Then Grey went and flunked AP English. Walt Smalley, our principal, only let Grey go through graduation on the condition that he make the credits up in summer school, which Grey had no intention of doing. Instead—jacked by his success with Ray's canoe—he was going to make boats. So now Callie was staying behind, too, and she was going to take classes at the Catholic college in Ashton.

The shadows cast by the birches on the bluffs at our backs stretched far ahead of us into the channel. Grey steered us clear of traffic, until even the slowest of the other boats had passed us up, then we idled just off shore until everybody else beached their canoes and had nothing to do but stare at us as Grey and Callie put their paddles to the water and we glided in on the waves.

Otter Island is basically a sand bar, a narrow spit of land, jutting two miles into Superior to the northwest from a point above the mouth of the Mulberry River, separated from the mainland by two hundred yards of shallows. The otters that gave the island its name are gone, victims of the timber trade, which stripped the shoreline of trees, and of the lumberjacks, who spent the hours they weren't laying waste to the forests drinking whiskey and blasting their furry ilk off the rocks with Colt revolvers. Here the Sioux raiding party swam the shallows and ambushed two Ojibwa boys from St. Raphael. Then the Ojibwa came swiftly by canoe to cut off the enemy's escape to the mainland. The result was a slaughter, with knives and fists and bows and rocks.

None of us knew much about that battle but we laid up our boats—like the Ojibwa did—on the beach that stretched northwest along the leeward length of the island.

Standing on a granite boulder among the dunes was Craig Hauser, senior class president (elected, after three defeats, in a pity vote). Fidgeting at Craig's right was Delva Cleary, our diet-pill-hoarding class treasurer, at his left Mimi Keegan, vice prez, busting out of her letter sweater, her knees pink with sunburn. Behind them the flames from the bonfire already poured upward. "Three lines," Craig called from his rock through the cheerleaders' megaphone. "Form up." And we did, wandering to the back of the third ribbon of teenaged impatience that stretched from the beach to Craig's rock to the fire beyond.

And there we waited. When you got to the head of the line you received a brown paper bag, stapled on the top and stamped with the red image of Odin, the bearded, broad-sword-swinging Viking who was the Ashton mascot. Inside the bag was a long black candle, a Dixie Cup, and a smudged sheet of carbon paper with a diagram that looked like this:

though anyone who needed a drawing to tell them what to do with a candle and a cup had no business being let loose on the SAT with a sharpened no. 2 pencil.

Our grandparents performed this ceremony with torches, maple boughs as long and thick as your arm, wrapped in rags, and doused in kerosene, and, man, I bet there wasn't a kid there who didn't wish we still did. But the school board had long ago ruled all this a safety menace. For us it was kitchen candles and Dixie Cups decorated with Hanna-Barbera characters. On mine was a Flintstones barbecue scene: Dino swiping a drumstick the size of an acoustic guitar, Fred chasing him, arms reaching, chubby legs a blur, while, on the other side of the cup, next to a Weber grill made from rock, Wilma, Barney, and Betty watch and laugh from the picnic table that Bam Bam is holding above his head, Pebbles at his feet, a bone in her hair.

Following the defeat of the Sioux, the story goes, the Ojibwa built a fire in the sand. So each year we build a fire in the sand. One of the warriors, it's said, held a Sioux lance to the flame and waved the burning shaft above his head. We do the same. After we pushed the base of candle (a) though the bottom of Dixie Cup (b), as the last rays of the sun reflect copper on the windows of the waterfront houses across the channel on St. Raphael, at no one's command, we gathered together, closer and closer, until we were standing in a lazy huddle about twenty feet from the water. And when it was dark and, on this night it is utter dark, because of a new moon (a condition that is not required by the traditions of this ceremony, only a lucky coincidence, like the absence of rain), we held our wicks to the bonfire as the glow rose on our faces.

We were summoned alphabetically. Craig boomed Melissa Aaron's name into the megaphone louder than he had to since she was standing right next to him. Holding her candle above her head, she said, "I'm not deaf, dork," and began walking, to general laughter, northward toward the far end of the island, as we sang "Never Again Our Ashton." After she walked ten steps Troy Anderson followed after her. He counted off ten paces. Then came Camille Atkins. And like that, we proceeded, one after the other, walking into the dark as all of us sang

> *By Hiawatha's shining banks*
> *Where the black bear roams*
> *Shall we ever give our thanks*
> *To the guardians of our homes.*

Grey saw me looking at him and shrugged. We never showed much of the old school spirit, but this was Godspeed the Warriors. Even if you weren't inclined to sing along, the weight of history forced the words to your lips. Callie sang too, rolling her eyes when the voices rose up at the chorus. Then it was her turn to go and she went, tugging at the belt loop of Grey's shorts as she did. We watched her walk until only her T-shirt was visible beneath the candle, and then it was Alvin Deere, obscuring Callie with the relative brightness of his flame. Grey's turn didn't come until after we had sung our way through the song a second and then a third time. "How much would you give me to fuck this up?" he said as he went, leaving less than a dozen of us.

Two more times through the song and no one was left but myself and Darrell Young, who was nursing his candle and keeping an eye on Chip Walter, the last to leave ahead of him. I counted off Chip's ten steps. Then eleven. I told Darrell, "Go." He did. Then I followed him. I walked my ten paces. Which was as far as I went. I was supposed to stop then and yell out "Zwiggy," the signal that we'd reached the end of the line. This came from—the story goes—Arnold Zweig, the name of the last boy to carry a torch back at the very first Godspeed. The word echoed down the line. When it reached Melissa Aaron, the last chorus of the Alma Mater was sung. We turned to the west, then to the east, holding our candles as high as we could above our heads, waved them to the north and then to the south, to the north again and sang the fight song,

Fight Ashton, fight, fight, fight
Fight, fight, fight
For the old red and black.

Then it was my turn again: holding the candle above my head, I walked north toward the far end of the island, along an alley of light formed by the candle flames on my left and the reflection of those candles on the water on my right. I walked too fast at first. My candle sputtered and almost went out, and I had to slow down until the flame returned. Tilting the cup backward to shield it from the breeze that even a slow walk created, I kept on, past Chip and Darrell, Candace Vukovich and Sissy Talbott and on down the row. The sand cooled under my

feet. I heard Darrell kick up a twig and cuss and was relieved
that the procession was forming up the way it was supposed to,
each of the kids I passed falling in ten steps behind the last in
line, until we looked (I'd always thought when I watched this
from the bluff) like a thread of light being sewn through the
dark fabric of the sand.

Grey was tracing the sand with his toe when I came even
with him. In his right hand he held the candle propped against
his hip. This was not a day he would remember fondly: having to
walk across the stage, shake Walt's hand, and get handed a
diploma case they both knew was empty. Dolores, Callie's
mother, made sure he didn't forget it, either. Pecking him on the
cheek and then saying, "Here come the college kids," when
Callie and I walked up behind him. As much as I hate to admit
it, I was happy to hear Grey had flunked a course, after the way
he used to ease through classes without opening a book, turning
in all his work at the last minute. I liked the idea of him sitting
in summer school, while I spent a lazy summer contemplating
my brilliant future.

That was when I thought he would go to summer school.

But true to his style he would do his best to turn that defeat
into a victory, coaxing the town council into letting him lease a
boat hangar for his business, getting his dad to write a story
about it in the paper, and going around acting like he never
wanted to go to college in the first place. Like anything having
to do with school was positively juvenile.

Up close, the line of candles looked ragged—arms held at
different heights, some candles out of step with the others, some
candles burning out, having to be replenished by a neighboring
flame. There was Alvin Deere standing as straight as anyone,
when only the week before he was saying that his uncle and the
tribal elders were going to boycott because they thought
Godspeed made them out to be savages. Grey had agreed, and
said that the fact that they didn't go through with it showed that
Alvin and his uncle didn't have any guts after all.

Two candles after Alvin came Callie, slouched at the hip like Grey, though holding her candle higher. Her lips were fixed in the same steady frown she wore the first time I'd ever seen her, at the ferry dock, on our first day of seventh grade, trying to wrestle her binder back from Terri Gustafson.

I was moving faster. I looked over my shoulder to see if Darrell was keeping up, and I saw the blur of his flame close enough so that I didn't have to slow my pace. I wanted this to be over. I passed Cammy Atkins and then Betsy Aaron and then ahead of me was only the beach and the darkness. To my right the candle lit only as far as the tops of the dunes that hid the windward side of the island from view, to my left, dim reflections of the flame flickered across the incoming waves like heat lighting. The candle split the darkness ahead of me. I looked again at the sand to my right and saw the projected image of the scene from my cup on the sand. Magnified by the distance of the projection, Dino enlarged to the size of a city-stomping Godzilla stalked down by a hulking, hate-inflated Fred, his arms raised and fingers curled in predatory intent.

If I had looked over my shoulder again I would have seen the procession following behind and Betsy Aaron's candle growing smaller, as the line doubled back upon itself until it was no longer moving in two directions at once, but became one line, moving in one direction, north, with me in the front.

Then just as we had when the procession began, we turned to the west and waved our candles and then to the east and sang the Alma Mater for our last time as students. And when the song was over, I blew out my candle, which was the signal for Darrell to blow out his and then Chip, and so on. I turned to the south and watched the candles going out all the way along the line, until the last was gone, and I was left standing in the dark, as far away from where we began as you could get.

WHEN THE LEVEE BREAKS

Darrell yelled, "You coming, Zim?"

"Yup," I said.

But instead I sat down on a toppled tree trunk half buried in the sand and gazed out over the water toward the gloomy form of St. Raphael. All along the channel, lights were coming on. Looking across the water, I could make out the Chinese lanterns on the terrace of the country club where Grey's parents and Callie's mom would be sitting on the redwood lounge chairs by the putting green. Drawing a line due west, I looked for the sliver of yellow light from our bathroom window, the one place in our house that you can see Otter Island from. I'd pestered Pop to watch from the window. He'd said he would, but I doubted him. For me to get a clear view from the bathroom I had to stand between the wall and the toilet and stick my head into the window frame. Add to that the fact that Pop was three inches shorter than me and would have to stand on his toes or even on the toilet seat. How long could I expect him to keep that up? Even if he had been inclined to watch, which he wasn't.

The water between St. Raphael and the mainland looks close enough to swim—though I'd recommend against trying. Of course, even as I say this I'm remembering that Grey and I swam the channel once, when we were twelve. I think we did it only so we didn't have to live our lives wondering if we could.

We'd tied life vests to our ankles by the straps so we wouldn't drown and set out at noon, when the sun would keep us warm. At least that's what we thought.

When we actually put our plan into action we were in trouble almost from the start. The life vests acted as a drag, and the water froze us more than the sun kept us warm. Eventually we crawled onto the beach so exhausted that we slept in the sand until late afternoon. Still we could have called the stunt a success if we'd remembered to bring ferry money. As it was we had to beg Pete to let us ride back for free, which he did. Then he went straight to the newspaper office to rat us out to Mr. Reed, who told my father, on the reasoning that Ernst Zimmermann would have been madder if he found out from anyone else. Which might have been true, though he whacked me pretty good just the same.

Right now, I didn't know what time it was. My watch broke the week before and I hadn't bought another because I figured Pop would get me one for graduation. It was early enough that the adults figured to still be sucking the liquor off their ice cubes, though it had been a long day for them, too, their tempers and the sun making for a hot one all around.

Dolores had found out at breakfast that Callie wasn't going down to the university because of Grey. She was already pissed off because Ray was out of town, which meant that she and Callie's natural dad would be attending the ceremony, each of them alone, which was sure to get some people talking. The Reeds were not content either. They were parents of the sort who would let their children learn from their mistakes (Grey being, to this point, much more eager than his little brother Todd to acquire knowledge in this way), but the possibility that Grey might miss out on college altogether was more than they were willing to sit around and watch. Yet the Reeds and Dolores stood smiling as we had filed down the rows to the tune of "We May Never Pass This Way Again."

I fished a wilted Marlboro out of a pack I'd worn in the waistband of my shorts all day. (It was bad that we smoked so much. I don't anymore, but I won't chastise my younger self for his foolishness. I really never had a chance. Pop smoked four packs a day. Ma used to smoke and still may, as far as I knew. I even remember Aunt Berthe, the family saint, walking around the Chicago house with daughter Hilde on her hip and a Pall Mall hanging from her lower lip.) The music from the bonfire was louder now, but I couldn't make out the song, only the throbbing bass. I gawked up at the smudge of the Milky Way from horizon to horizon. Orion was gone until fall, leaving behind a less familiar sky. For all the nights I spent looking at the constellations, I could not tell stories from the stars, like the ancient people did. Maybe television was to blame. Instead I looked for movement, a shooting star or satellite or the hovering lights that each time promised to be a UFO but always turned out instead to be an airliner. Then a voice behind me yelled, "Don't do it!" I started and turned toward the silhouette of a girl against the rising red tint of the bonfire on the crest of the dunes. "Did I scare you?" she said.

It was Ashley Sitwell.

"No."

"Yeah, I did. Thinking about ending it all?"

"Not until now."

"Funny."

Ashley was a senior the year before and went to school in California. She was a swimmer with a swimmer's body: broad, boxy shoulders, narrow hips, a solid, square ass, knotty blond hair with a chlorine-green tint—not bad looking, if you looked at her a certain way. And once, at a boat party, I'd looked at her just that way. For that act of imagination I'd had to take her to prom. Afterward we'd skipped the all-night party at the Marina Hotel (I think because her father owned the place and she didn't want him to see his daughter fishing below the limit) and parked her Gremlin down by the lake. Before Ashley, I'd been with three other girls, but it had never been like that. Maybe owing to the fact that I didn't like her very much, and I was pretty sure she felt that way about me, I could let my curiosity about the endless possibilities of position and stamina take over. We became a regular secret thing.

"When did you row over?" I asked her.

"Just now. Got another of those?"

"One." I held out the pack and we sat down on the trunk.

Ashley studied the parenthesis-shaped cigarette that she pulled from the pack and coaxed the filter to her lips. She snatched the half-smoked cigarette from my fingers, used it to light hers, then she kept mine and handed the bent one back.

"I didn't want a whole one anyway," she said. This wasn't like her. The Ashley of the previous summer was vain, but basically shy, the kind of girl who only wore new white sneakers like the ones she had on after they'd gotten scuffed a bit around home and were less likely to attract attention.

"What'd you come out here for?"

"Old time's sake," Ashley said. "I'm back for the summer. Thought you might want to go steady."

I glanced past her shoulder.

"Have to ask Grey first?"

"Like hell," I said.

She inhaled the smoke of the cigarette through clenched teeth like you do when you're trying to hide the pain of a wound. "Grey's not going down to school."

"Where'd you hear that?"

"Smoke signals," she said, trying to blow rings that collapsed on each other and disintegrated in the still night air. "I think that Grey's the kind of person people tell stories about."

"I bet he'd agree with you."

"You're jealous."

"No, I'm not."

"Sounds like it."

"I'm not."

"I wouldn't envy him if I were you. Grey was always going to stay. Now he's got an excuse." She flicked the cigarette toward the lake, pushed my knees together, and moved much closer. "Anyway, why should you care? You're getting out of here. That's all that counts."

She tried to kiss me, but I ducked. "I got to ask you something if you promise not to make fun of me."

"What?" she said. She was laughing already. Then she saw that I wasn't kidding and tried to stop herself, which only made her laugh more.

"Forget it."

"No, really," she said, pinching my cheek, "Ask. I'm sorry. You're so serious."

"Is it hard? I mean is it, you know, difficult?"

"Is what hard?"

"College."

She stared at me for a second and laughed square in my face. "You're scared."

"I am not."

She pushed the hair out of my eyes like I was a little kid or something. "No, it's not hard. I mean it's hard to get good grades, if that's what you want to do, but that's Stanford. You're going to a state school. You're the scholarship boy."

"Cut it out."

"I'll tell you what your problem is."

"What's my problem?"

"Your problem is you feel guilty," she said. "You feel guilty because something good happened to you and you don't think you deserve it. You're better than these people. We both are. I didn't know that either until I went away, but I do now." She traced her finger down my chest. "Now, come on. Don't you like me?"

"Yeah, I like you," I said and pushed her hand away.

She got up and knocked the sand off her jeans. "I'll tell you what you should be afraid of," she said. "You should be scared that you'll never find any place better than here."

Walking back toward the music, we approached the bonfire, which threw flames fifty feet in the air, geysers of sparks streaming skyward. Above the roar of the fire, a Led Zeppelin tune throbbed from ruined boom box speakers. The kids were dancing around, stomping the sand, clapping their hands to their mouths like Indians. I looked for Grey and found him, sitting cross-legged, beating on a rubber trash can like a tom-tom.

"Where you been?" he said.

"Out by the water."

"Ashley find you?"

"Yeah."

He laughed.

"What?"

"Nothing."

"Where's Callie at?"

Grey nodded at a circle of girls near the fire, passing a stack of snapshots. Callie stood with her back to us, craning to look at each picture in the flickering light of the fire.

"There's beer over in that tub," Grey said, pointing back toward the dunes where a single kid squatted on a boulder. I walked over and saw that it was Alvin Deere, perched on a rock taking in the whole crazy scene, the fire reflecting on his glasses.

"Man," I told him, "you look like an album cover."

This didn't please Alvin. He stared for a long time before he said, "You splitting soon?"

"Nah," I said, "I came over to get a beer."

I looked back toward the fire. Grey was hunched over his drums and Callie was lost in photographic memories, Ashley was lurking, and I figured if I stayed I was only going to get more of what I had already got.

"Okay." Alvin hopped off his rock and walked me through the shadowy dunes to an aluminum canoe already half in the water. "I came over with Warren"—Warren being his step-brother, or cousin, I was never sure which—"but he don't want to leave," he said.

Alvin did all of the rowing. In fourth grade, Grey and I went over to Alvin's house after school. It was the first time I ever rode on the school bus. The bus was for the reservation kids. We drank Tang and played Major Matt Mason, making an alien landscape of Mrs. Deere's plastic-covered davenport and lime green shag. We went back two, three days a week and blasted around the hostile voids, until the visors broke off all the space helmets and the wires broke in the legs of the action figures so that they would not hold a pose.

"When you leaving?" he asked, when we were far enough away from the fire and the music that I could hear the sound of his voice.

"End of August."

"So like three months and you'll be going back the way you came."

"I guess."

"Yeah, well. Was only a matter of time, hey."

"What's that mean?"

"It means you're not from the island. You got no right to stay."

"My dad came with me. He's not leaving."

"I wasn't talking about him. Nobody said he's going anywhere. You go with that Sitwell girl?"

"What'd she tell you?"

"Nothing. I don't talk to her. She's trouble."

"Preaching to the choir."

"Let's hope you hear it."

"Hey, Alvin, remember when we used to play Major Matt Masons?"

He took a long time to answer. "Yeah, I remember."

"How come we don't hang out anymore."

"Major Matt Mason is pussy."

"No, I mean—"

"Dude," he said, "I know what you meant."

BIBLIOGRAPHY

This is how everything happened: In the seventh grade, I wrote a report for Mrs. Furst's Social Studies class about the ferry that travels between Bayview and the island of St. Raphael. The paper won an award from the Chamber of Commerce. They gave me a plaque and a twenty-dollar US savings bond. I got my facts from a book I found in the library by G. Harris Montgomery called *A History of the Bayview Ferry*. Everything I wrote in the paper I took from that book except for the couple of dozen words I didn't use. I put my own words in their place. Like when the book said:

> Prior to 1933 there was no scheduled ferry service between the mainland and St. Raphael. It was up to anyone wishing to travel to the islands to provide their own craft or to pay an enterprising fisherman to transport him.

I wrote:

> Before 1933 there was no regular ferry between the mainland and St. Raphael. Anyone wanting to travel to the islands would either have to take his own boat or pay somebody to ride them over.

I'm sure I understood on some level that using another person's words for your own purposes is against the laws governing schoolwork. And reading what I wrote for yourself, you're probably not sure what's harder to believe: that I didn't get caught or that the judges at the Chamber of Commerce thought that crap worthy of an award. But I did win, and anyone who wants to know more about the Bayview ferry is free to read either my paper or Mr. Montgomery's book. All I wrote were the facts as I learned them, and you can't fake a fact.

The next year I entered another paper in the State Scholastic Merit Awards, this one about Michel Cabot, the founder of the town of St. Raphael. That won an award, too, this time for a hundred-dollar savings bond, a luncheon in Madison, and a photograph with the governor (a man no taller than me!). Over the years that followed I wrote several more, on topics of local historical interest, the St. Raphael Lutheran Church, the ore trade, and the Battle of Lake Erie, each of them bringing home no worse than an honorable mention. I came to think I had a future in history.

The big payoff came my junior year when Grey's father Jack Reed told me about a scholarship the University of Wisconsin was giving for historical papers and further told me that he thought that papers about Indians were the kind of thing that the people who award those scholarships like to read about, so I wrote a paper about the common ancestry of the Ojibwa and Menominee. They made me wait three months, but the news was good.

"A scholarship!" said Aunt Berthe calling long distance from Chicago. "A scholarship, Karl, isn't it marvelous."

"You honor us all," said Agnes Reed, Grey's mother.

"Do you have to go to college to get the money?" said Pop.

"Yes, he does," Jack Reed said, "and you should be grateful for it. Do you have any idea what college costs?" This was a little like asking a Bedouin if he knew the price of a fishing net. Pop had no idea what it cost to go to college and didn't see why anyone should care.

Jack, as if to prove the point, ran a story in the *Star* under my picture: "The young man who knows more than any of us about where we live." If that is true then what I know about where I live I've learned from books or from what other people have told me. I've added none of my own work to this history.

What do I know about where we live? I know what you would know if you opened an atlas, that we live on St. Raphael, the only inhabited island in the Green Islands, which lie at the southwest corner of Lake Superior off the coast of northern Wisconsin. St. Raphael is nine miles long and three miles wide at its widest point. We live there, my father and I, along with 413 other souls, stout, stoic island folk, some of whom you'll hear about from me, and some of whom you'd have to talk to yourself, if you are inclined.

In the summer the population triples, when the families who keep their summer homes here crowd onto the ferries, along with the tourists who come for the Indian shows. They bring with them most of the money that is made on St. Raphael and for that reason they are not liked. You have to agree that there's something dirty about tourist money, even if it's yours, or you have to agree at least that there's something sad about passing through a town that is not what it was, just to be shown by tour guides how it used to be.

Anyone who lives on the peninsula or on the island will tell you that this place isn't what it once was, though it hasn't been what it once was since before anyone who lives here was born. Just the same this awareness of decline lives in everyone, which may be why so many of the kids who grow up here leave. White people came here earlier and prospered quicker than anywhere else this far west on the continent, but it was a downhill slide from there.

As is true elsewhere, the history of our community began with a flood, with the myth of a great and sudden rising of the water that the Ojibwa have recalled for three hundred generations of their tribal memory, since before they came to

Wisconsin from the east, from Hudson Bay and from the Sault, where Lake Huron meets Superior. There are legends that say the people who lived here before were cannibals and performed human sacrifices in the vale overlooking the harbor where the church stands today, though when the French came they found the natives to be a likable people who were less likely to kill them than were the Huron to the east or the Fox to the south. The French and the Indians lived peacefully together for more than a hundred years and might have forever, if it hadn't been for the Seven Years War. After that, the British Navy took over with no earthly idea of what to do with the mission and the fur stations. Their warships patrolled the coast, but they rarely ventured inland. The missionaries died off and were not replaced. The Indians and the trappers meanwhile went on living pretty much as they always had.

Then came the lumbermen, Norwegians and Swedes most of them, and ore miners from Cornwall and Wales, until more people lived on the peninsula in 1845 than live here today. The country was getting civilized and everybody but the rich quit wearing furs. The timber dwindled, the lumbermen went off to fight in the Civil War, the railway that was supposed to run to Bayview was built farther south on a direct line to the deeper water ports at Duluth and Superior, and that pretty much scotched any dream of a metropolis.

Then came my father and I, sole members of the last wave of immigrants to come to the island. Like others, maybe Pop was looking for a place that looked like the place from where he'd come, a fishing village on the North Sea, but without the trouble he'd left behind. That trouble was his and not mine, but I say "we" just the same because as his son my future was tied to his. My father was an immigrant—leaving a country of exhausted possibilities for one in which possibilities exceeded the reach of the most optimistic imagination. But my father was also a fugitive—driven from his homeland by the scorn of his wife and her family, fleeing the scene of what some said was a capital crime—and so I became a fugitive too, though the crime I am talking about happened before I was born.

Our house looks pretty much the same after thirteen years as it did the day we moved in, between what used to be a Sinclair station and was now a cafe on the south and the corrugated metal boat hangar, deserted as long as we lived there, where Grey would be building his boats. More of the green paint had peeled and faded from our house. In the spring shingles fell like fish scales off the gambrel roof that stretched over the enclosed porch. The screen door, rusted and patched many times, sagged on its hinges underneath the old sign that Pop painted over in white with the words ZIMMERMANN CYCLES in red block letters. There was a smaller sign in the window in Pop's Magic Marker scrawl on a cardboard box bottom that said, "Flats fixed while you wait."

The bulb over the back door was out again. That made even more difficult the business of finding the lock with my key. Shoving open the rickety, particle wood door, I was hit with the smell of the shop, dust and grease and cigarettes, that has become part of the woodwork. I stumbled in the dark through the tangle of bikes awaiting repair that took up every available corner of the back shop this time of year, and up the narrow back stairs. I opened the kitchen door to more darkness and flipped the light switch. There were dishes in the sink. I was glad to see that Pop had gone ahead and had supper without me, because he didn't always. On the table was a small package, maybe four inches square, wrapped in red paper and tied with a black bow. I picked it up. I shook it. I was sure it was the watch. I set it back where it was so Pop could see me when I opened it. Looking into the darkened living room, I saw his head lolling over the side of his easy chair, mouth open, snoring. He'd pulled his coveralls down to his waist as he did in the evenings, a sweat-stained white sleeveless T-shirt hanging loose from his knotty shoulders.

Next to him was the quart of schnapps he'd bought for a graduation toast that he never made. Half of it was gone. Next to that was an open box of spokes, a wheel rim, a tube of chrome polish, and a can of Pabst. The light from the kitchen gave his skin a yellowish cast—as though he'd been cured in sulphur—except for the white crescent scar on his left shoulder, the reminder of an operation twenty years ago to repair one of the five broken collarbones he'd gotten in his career as a professional bicycle racer. Cradled in his right fist was a wheel hub. This time of year it was normal for him to bring the kind of menial work you don't need a lot of space for upstairs to finish, and no less normal for him to fall asleep in the middle of it.

My father wasn't a handsome man. I say that reluctantly because it was from him and not my mother that I got my broad nose, my narrow jaw, and my gaunt, wiry build. I'd been taller since I was sixteen, and the years of professional cycling had hobbled him permanently. His legs were bowed and his knees arthritic. He'd always reminded me of a tangled knot of sea rope you see coiled on the dock, clinging seaweed dried to the consistency of corn silk by the sun. You could only attribute the success he had with the divorced ladies of the island, which was considerable, to the law of supply and demand.

The light wasn't on and it'd been dark for three hours, which meant he must have been asleep at least that long. Trying not to make the floorboards squeak, I slid the hub out of his hand. He stopped snoring. I hesitated, but when he didn't wake up, I took up the rim and the box of spokes and went back to the kitchen. Sitting down at the table, I pushed the wrapped present to the far corner and slid a spoke through the eyelet on the hub and attached it to the rim with a screw, continuing the three-cross pattern that my father had taught me when I was eight. I'd just fixed the last spoke in place when I heard the scuff of Naugahyde and the sound of Pop's feet on the floor. He squinted as he stepped into the light and stood scratching the cropped brush of hair on his head with the pinky of his right hand.

We'd come to this island from Chicago, a city that I remember as a cartoon dream of shiny hubcaps, square lawns, and fat relatives, Uncle Karl, Aunt Berthe, my cousins Hilde and Silke, who dressed me in girl clothes and carried me around the house like a doll. For five years, my ma and pop slept on a sofa bed in Karl and Berthe's living room and I had a cot in the corner, which was like camping out every night. I liked the closeness of our lives when I was four, in spite of the whispered bickering I heard penetrating the blackness from my parents' side of the room every night. As I got old enough to understand the nature of the words they hurled at each other, I grew scared. Each threat of mayhem made my blood run cold beneath the covers. But as the years went by and still we hadn't found a house of our own, as my mother demanded my father do, I got used to the insults and even became comforted by their nightly certainty, until the one night that the whispers stopped.

She'd told no one that she was leaving: there was no one she could've told, no one who wouldn't have scorned her for even thinking of it. "There should have been a note," Berthe said. "She should have left word for Tomas." To her, this was the most unpardonable of offenses, though I thought at the time the fact she hadn't left word was a good sign, that it meant she would be back soon, that she might have gone down to the corner shop for cigarettes. The next day, I stood outside in the rain for an hour, partly waiting for her to come back and partly to see if anyone cared. When I finally gave up and came inside, Aunt Berthe put me in a hot bath and gave me dry clothes. I ate potato soup at the table. "So, Tomas," she said, "was it cold outside?" Like Pop, she pronounced her w's like f's—"fas it cold outside in the rain?"

"Yes," I said.

"Then," she said, "you fill know better than to ever do it again." And she was right about that. I never did.

"Thanks for the present," I told Pop.

He stared at the table not understanding what I was talking about until his eyes settled on the wrapped box on the table, and he smiled slightly and shrugged. "Open it."

I put the wheel on the floor and pulled the package toward me.

"Trudy did that," he said as I tugged at the cord.

"Nice," I said, tearing at the paper. It *was* a watch, a Timex, with a white face and a flimsy fake-leather band. Something less than I might have hoped for, but I needed a watch, and this one figured to do the job.

"I'll think of you every time I look at it," I said because that kind of stuff drove him nuts.

"It's all right?" he said. "Jack Reed said that was the thing to get."

"Yeah," I said, "it's a good one," but he wasn't listening. He'd walked to the stove where he poured himself a cup of coffee from the pot I'd made that morning and lit a Pall Mall with a kitchen match. Then he came back to the table, sat the cup down, put the cigarette into the ashtray, picked up the wheel, and studied the workmanship. "When are you going away to school?" he asked.

"I told you already."

He shaved the ash off the cigarette on the edge of the ashtray, plugged it in his mouth and laid the wheel down on the table. "Tell me again."

"August twenty-seventh."

"You save your money," he said. "I'm not paying you to go to school."

"I've got it," I said.

"You got it?" The smoke of his cigarette drifted toward the open screen, stopped, and blew back in on the wind off the lake.

"You got enough? Ray Dobbs peels twenty-dollar bills off a roll so fat that it does not fit in his trousers and gives to Callie. Forty, sixty, eighty—here is your books. Twenty, forty, one hundred, one hundred fifty—here is a coat. Three thousand, four thousand—here is a car to drive your books around."

"She's not going," I said.

"What?"

"Callie says she's staying."

He didn't know this, and it took him a moment to fit the news into his shouting.

"The money's covered," I said. "No sweat."

"No sweat?"

"No sweat."

He nodded in the direction of the hangar. "How is he getting on over there?"

"Grey? I haven't been over today. He's working hard."

Pop knew Grey as well as I did. There were a lot of good things you could call Grey, but a hard worker wasn't one of them.

He stared for a minute, his eyes soggy around the lids. I knew what the stare was supposed to mean and I ignored it, instead making a big production of setting my watch to the clock on the stove. "It glows in the dark," he said.

On the bed in my room was an oversized envelope with a red seal like the many others that had come from the university. And like the many other red-sealed and thick, white envelopes that had come from the university, Pop had opened it. This was something he didn't used to do—I suppose partially because outside of letters from Aunt Berthe I never had much mail to open before—but for some reason, he chose to see everything that came from the school as being for his eyes first. He didn't read English well, and I wondered what he could possibly have made of the sample syllabuses and course codes. This one was a list of expenses for my first semester. Residence fees $1,143.50, tuition 12-15 credits $432.00, recreation fee $25.00, material fee

$3.00 (I didn't know what a material fee was, but figured I could swing the three bucks). All of that would have been clear enough to him. Numbers he understood.

The total for the semester was $1,603.50. You didn't have to be good at math to figure that meant $3,207.00 for the entire year, not including summer school, which was probably out of the question anyway, and not including unexpected expenses, which I didn't include. My scholarship covered two thousand of that. Since it was spring, Pop likely had a few hundred dollars in the bank. In the winter, sometimes days would go by without us bringing in a cent. One day in May four years ago, we took in close to a thousand dollars in a single day. Let that stand as a full history of my father's prospects in business: one day four years ago we took in close to one thousand dollars.

I knew how much money came in, but I never knew how much went out. Pop was in charge of accounts payable. I'd say, "We're out of brake cable," or "If we're going to do this work we'll need a headset tool," and a box of brake cables or a forged chromium VAR headset tool would appear via UPS in the next couple of days—or one wouldn't. I don't remember how much that worried me or encouraged me about the state of our money affairs—except that I knew from an early age that the day I left his house was the day I was on my own. Pop had chosen a life for us safe from the support of what family he'd left, and in doing so, had more or less condemned me to the same fate.

Actually, we might have lived in Chicago forever, as bachelors under my uncle's roof, if we hadn't gone on vacation when I was six years old. On a Friday morning in April Uncle Karl came home in a new Ford station wagon, hung a closed sign in the window of the butcher shop, loaded the lot of us into the car, and we drove north through the farms and woods of Wisconsin. Hilde and Silke and I sat in the back with the luggage, our eyes following each new sight, a red barn or blue Harvestore silo, until each disappeared over the hill behind us.

And when Uncle Karl turned west along Highway 13, we crested a bluff, and I saw Lake Superior for the first time, glimmering like a candy wrapper in the afternoon sun.

Uncle Karl piloted the wagon through the curving, hilly streets of Bayview to where the road ended at the water.

"Why did we stop here?" said Hilde, who was seven and impatient.

"To wait for the ferryboat," Uncle Karl said, and because I didn't know what a ferry was, the images the word conjured in my head filled me with anticipation. And it was the first sight of the ferry that sets this day apart from the other days on the far horizon of my memory. Uncle Karl pointed, and I spotted the white rectangle of the bridge above the waves. I watched amazed as the bright vessel steamed into the harbor, pivoted smartly, and backed into the slip.

We rolled onto the car deck and were swallowed by the riveted steel of the superstructure. Once the ferry got underway, bullying through the swelling waves, we all got out of the car and stood along the rail and watched as the island grew larger. In spite of the signs of human life that were visible all along the shore, the piers, boat docks, and the occasional house, I felt like an explorer from a book. I had no idea at the time what would come of the discovering, but I was old enough to know that this was a significant crossing. The boat docked, the gates clanged down on the concrete dock, and we rolled into St. Raphael.

Once we set out on foot, the small town and the wind off the water brought out the Old Country in Aunt Berthe. She said hello to everyone we passed on the streets and led us to all of the souvenir shops. Inside she looked at every piece of bric-a-brac on every shelf, each time shaking her head and clicking her tongue at the price, then setting the item down carefully in its place.

We walked the town for two hours or more, until Aunt Berthe had run out of shops to go into. We were on the way to the beach when Pop yelled, "Wait." He motioned with his hand for us to stay put and walked into a green, shabby two-story house. The paint was peeling and as faded as the red and white sign above the door.

CHALMERS LAWN MOWER AND BICYCLE REPAIR

We all followed Pop inside and saw that the place was dark, except for the rays of the sunlight that seeped through the gaps in the shades and lit up millions of flecks of dust floating in the air. Everywhere there were mowers and parts of mowers, bicycles and parts of bicycles. The girls looked confused, as it was obvious that their mother was not going to pick up anything in here. Aunt Berthe looked back with an expression equal to theirs plus a little extra she added for herself. I wondered too.

The little man in the chair didn't get up as we came close. "Nothing to sell," he said in a cracked voice that scared me and Silke so much we took a step toward the door. Pop turned and motioned us outside, where Berthe sat on the one low front step, drumming her cheeks with her fingers, watching her daughters chase me around the For Sale sign in the yard.

It was the second time in my life where adults would make a big ceremony out of telling me something I already knew. They were back at the kitchen table, Uncle Karl and Pop, just in from work, Pop looking tired and Karl curious and a little nervous. Aunt Berthe sewed while she talked so she wouldn't have to look at me. "Your father is buying a store—with your uncle's money." She didn't say anything more and I realized I was supposed to speak. I didn't know what they wanted me to say. So I cried. I cried because I knew this meant the end of Aunt Berthe watching out for us and because I believed that once we moved my mother would never be able to find us.

Pop threw up his hands, "What is there for him to say?"

"It's an adjustment," Uncle Karl said. Again Pop made a gesture of frustration.

Sitting at my desk, I filled out the university form, faked a social security number for my father because he wasn't a citizen, stuffed and sealed the return envelope, and propped it against my door so I wouldn't forget to mail it.

I went over to my bed and unscrewed the brass cap on the right rear corner of my bedpost, snagged the protruding loop of string, and pulled. Out came five rolls of bills wrapped around the drawstring with rubber bands. I could have had Pop locked up for what he paid me, but it still adds up when you don't have to pay for food and where you live, and you don't squander your salary on useless things, and you keep an eye out for other chances to make extra.

There was no point in counting. I knew how much the rolls contained: five hundred in each, except the last, which had a little less. Which meant I was fourteen hundred in the black, money for books or clothes or bus tickets or anything else. Course I figured to get a job when I got to school, but I didn't know how much I could expect to get out of that. Ten years working for my father had taught me to guess low. I took the rubber bands off each of the rolls. I loved doing that, lining up the faces of the presidents and then putting them carefully back where I kept them.

Before turning out the lights, I lowered the bills back into the bedpost and replaced the cap. Then I lay on my bed in the dark, staring at the glowing dial on the watch face. It'd been a long day and it was still only five minutes to twelve. Matching my breathing to the ticking seconds, I watched the two green, glowing hands until they became a single arrow pointing toward the ceiling and the sky beyond it.

UP AND ABOUT

6:00 a.m. - pancakes and coffee
6:45 - a jaunt on bikes around the scenic roads
        skirting the shore of our island
9:00 - church
11:00 - work
8:30 - dinner: shell macaroni and sauce from a jar
9:15 - drop dead.

If we had a schedule for Sundays in the summer tacked up on the fridge—which we didn't—that's what it would look like.

That particular Sunday, though, was different because I was out of bed before Pop was. I had the coffee perking and the box mix and syrup out, when he came into the kitchen, his hair standing up in matted spikes after a hard sleep.

I tapped my watch. "The first day of my punctual life."

We took turns cooking. Not on purpose, it just worked out that way. Pop applied the same grim precision to cooking that he did to his work in the shop. Each pancake came out of the skillet a uniform ten centimeters. Any that were asymmetrical or browned beyond the golden shade were cast into the trash. We had maple syrup in a plastic squeeze bottle and orange juice. There was no conversation at breakfast. Even if we had anything to say to each other, we had the whole day together and both of us knew the value of pacing ourselves in the area of talk.

Once the dishes were in the sink I bounced down the stairs and made myself scarce. Pop had one daily chore he never liked me to watch. With his two bad knees and an arthritic hip, it hurt him to walk down the stairs. He gripped the handrail and lowered himself down the stairway in an even, rolling stride. At the bottom he used the hem of his T-shirt to wipe the tears of pain from his eyes. I dawdled behind as we wheeled our bicycles out onto Beach Street and coasted down the hill to Main. Then we rode past the marina and the park and under the canopy of trees that marked the town limit. This was how we did it since I was old enough to keep up.

Overnight a north wind had blown away the heat of graduation day, and a drizzle fell just hard enough to extinguish the mist that hung over the ground. We began slowly by custom, turning our lower gears quickly until the heat of our blood restored stiff muscles. By the putting green at the country club, he stood up on his pedals and bullied his way up the shallow rise. Beyond the clay tennis courts, the road jogs to the left and begins a lazy incline of about a half mile to where it meets Claremore Road at the westernmost point on the island. Pop slowed on this grade to make me come alongside.

At first sight he is not an imposing figure on a bicycle. In his torn T-shirt, moth-eaten cycling shorts, and cracked leather cleats, he rode hunched over the handlebars, churning fitfully like a crippled blacksmith. However, the more discerning eye would recognize the purpose and efficiency of an old sprinter in his form, his grip on the bars, and his short, powerful pedal strokes.

The men my father rode against back in his professional days came from the nations of Europe. They'd grown up in smoke and ruins and death. They'd survived the war and were tough and mean. All of them—the Belgians and Dutch and Italians— remembered the Nazis and none of them had any love for a German.

I closed on his right, as he had taught me to do. Pop said that all but the best riders will only glance over their left shoulder to see if anyone is catching them from behind. For as long as we'd ridden together Pop had treated these rides like a kind of on-the-job training, an apprenticeship in the profession of road racing. He never got tired of telling me what to do, as much for the pleasure of bossing me around as out of any hope that I'd amount to much. I caught him, looped my finger into his saddle stay and tugged, to let him know I was there. "Cinch your toe strap," he said.

We crested the next hill together, our pedal strokes matching identically. I was never sure whether he was preparing me for a life in the saddle—an occupation that had brought him little but hard times—or if it was just that he had nothing better to do with me. Agnes Reed always said that he wanted to turn me into a second version himself so that I could correct the mistakes he made, which makes sense, except Grey's mom is biased because she hates Pop for the way he treats me and has never understood him.

Pop's own father died when my father was five, sunk on a U-boat in the war. Aunt Berthe told me this. Most of what I know about my own father I know from her rather than from Pop, who wasn't likely to remember anything he didn't want to, and even less likely to tell you how he felt about it.

One thing he did talk about was a bike. This particular bicycle was new and yellow (a rare color in my imagining of my father's drab German childhood), left behind by his cousin Tomas—who I'm named after—when he went to join the paratroopers. The bike became Pop's when Tomas was killed at Rotterdam.

My father rode the yellow bicycle until the tires wore out and because there was no rubber, he made new tires himself by binding twisted rags with twine. "Was it hard to ride like that?" I asked.

"Yes," he said, "and that made me stronger," which was the sort of thing he always said, but I didn't believe him. It's the kind of thing parents tell their kids to justify their own lousy childhood. What boy would not have taken new rubber tires over a grueling lesson in calamity?

Sometimes I figured he'd used up all the sentimentality he could muster on that bike and had none left over for my mom or me. No other object held that much importance in his mind.

The bike he rode now he'd won in a trade show raffle. It was elegant, with a pearl finish that embarrassed him. I think he was relieved when a fall on a wet curve scuffed it up a bit. Mine, on the other hand, was a battered midnight blue of dubious pedigree that Pop cobbled together from old parts lying around the shop and then garnisheed my wages to pay for. I loved it like a dog.

You might think being in the business like we were that I would get the pick of the inventory, but if you knew Pop you'd know that's exactly why I didn't get. He was not going to have everyone on St. Raphael saying that just because he ran the one bike store on the island was no reason his son should have a new bicycle every time he wanted one. I had to be happy with the strays that found their way to the back door of our shop all summer long, or the ones that people left to get fixed and then forgot about.

We turned west at Claremore Road and rode in and out of the trees along the high bluffs. The clouds were giving way to the sun, which skipped off the water in the channel. It was the one sight along our route that could still turn my head after all the times we'd come this way. The road runs north by northeast along the leeward side of the island, descending from the bluffs and running along the beach to Sitwell Point. Beside the gravel shoulder, the scrub was suddenly alive with movement—a stir of russet and white and black feathers—and an eagle rose from the tall grass and crossed right in front of me, forcing me to brake suddenly. I shuddered, and as I did I felt Pop's hand on my hip. He was holding me up. "It almost got you," he laughed, shaking his head. That was Pop for you: there to keep me from falling and grateful to the eagle for making me look like a klutz.

At the far eastern tip of the island, the road ends at the water. We turned on a road called Cranberry Glen that winds through a cluster of summer houses, bigger and newer than most of the others on St. Raphael. This is a Sitwell development: sheetrock and aluminum siding and built-in gas grills that never seem to be lit on concrete decks and jungle gyms on the lawns that never have kids hanging off them. Like electrons, the owners bounce between the beach and the country club, never stopping anywhere in between.

Beyond the glen, traveling north, the asphalt gives way to dirt for a rugged climb and descent of a mile and a half. Here we had to busy ourselves with not going over the handlebars and going fast enough to make it to the crest. The downhill slope was just as treacherous, a ritual argument between speed and caution.

The wood gets thick there, and the temperature cools until the dirt drive meets Basswood Road, where the airport lies in a broad clearing. Just the one runway and the service sheds, it is the only sure way off the island in January. From there it's a two-kilometer dash into town. Nearly everything Pop taught me about strategy and tactics of road racing he taught me on the false flat from the airport to the ferry dock.

"Shift down," he'd yell at me, and side by side we'd tear down Basswood and back onto Main, our heads down, yanking the handlebars back and forth so hard I wondered how they didn't snap off.

Some nights, after a few schnapps and beer chasers, Pop would spread the clippings he'd saved about his career across the table, yellowed newsprint in a dozen languages from Flemish to Basque. This was always a solemn affair, with a lot of sorting and stacking, enough to convince me when I was much younger that he'd been an important man. I'd pick up an article from, say, a Spanish sports journal, studying the photo of a younger Pop gritting his teeth on a steep rise and ask him, "What does this one say?"

He would study the caption through bleary eyes, then shrug, and say, "It says, 'Ernst Zimmermann has done something remarkable.'" I don't remember how old I was when I figured out that he couldn't read a word of it, that he was making it up.

"I was—rabinous," he told me once.

"You mean ravenous?" I said, "like hungry."

He glowered at me.

This hunger was what drove him to several strong finishes in his first season and a stunning second place the following March in the Paris-Roubaix, the first major race of his second season. This hunger was what drove him to hoist his aching legs out of bed at five in the morning to train on the still-dark streets of Aurich. And it was what drove him—on a rain-slick cobblestone boulevard in Brittany, in the final meters of a field sprint that would have paid the winner a lousy thirty francs—to kill a man.

Under an arch of oak branches we reached the church mailbox, which had been our finish line for as long as we've been riding together. I had the line measured and could have beaten him easily, but I let him take it. Like I say, he taught me what I know. I let him win more in the days just before I left for school. It meant more to him than it did to me. There was a time when he would curse me for losing, back when he dreamed (if dreamed is a word you could ever associate with my father) that I would follow in his footsteps as a professional racer.

The island was waking up, and everyone was happy to see us. Ben Friendly was shaking a rug at the door to his tavern. He waved. So did the college girls who cleaned the rooms at the Marina Hotel and a family of tourists who must have thought we were a tourist attraction, which in a way I guess we were.

After our Sunday rides came church, where I was the only kid my age whose dad made him wear a suit. Aunt Berthe had drilled into his head the sanctity of the house of the Lord to the point where he was sure that if Jesus was to come back tomorrow you'd better be wearing a tie. I didn't mind it so much when I was ten.

The First Lutheran Church suffered the distinction of being the oldest landmark on the island and was mobbed every Sunday of tourist season. It was built a hundred and fifty years ago on the stone foundation of a French Catholic church that had been built by missionaries two hundred years before that, though there were no stones in the weed-ratted cemetery to mark their presence on the island. Nor were there any for the Ojibwa. Their burial ground on the inland hills had been turned over by plows and torn up by the first Norwegians, who had found out the hard way that this land wasn't good for growing much of anything.

Reverend Vogel was up with his family on Isle Royale on a fishing trip and Brad, the youth pastor, gave the sermon, which was about Jonah and the whale. He stood before the congregation in short sleeves and raised his arms for quiet. "I want you to think about the reverend up there on his bass boat," he said, in a loud voice, "and then think of old Jonah and the whale—which was probably only a perch until he got home and told his buddies in Nineveh." That pissed Pop off, I'm sure, because he didn't like our lives being compared to the lives of the Holy Immortals. "This big," Pastor Brad said, holding his palms a couple of feet apart and slowly spreading his hands. The laughter among the pews grew until everyone was laughing, except Pop.

My father thought he was pandering. He had a point. Even Vogel, who took his preaching seriously, had two kinds of sermons: off-season and tourist. The summer sermons were never his best. They were the general kind, of scripture and fable, a little like sitting through the same movie more than once. On the way out, Pastor Brad shook my father's hand and said "Ernst" in such a way as to show that he knew Pop didn't like what he was doing up there and could not have cared less. Pastor Brad started asking me if I was going with the church softball team to

Washburn when a hand locked on my shoulder. I knew by the grip that it was Sgt. Spires of the Wisconsin Highway Patrol.

"Staying out of trouble?" he said.

"You know I am," I said.

"Yeah, I know," he said. Spires had to be six and a half feet, with oversize forearms, the left of which was deeply tanned from driving the cruiser around all day. Outside of the park rangers, Spires was the only law we ever saw on the island. Since he lived out here he made a point of driving the circuit at the end of his shifts, and probably had a pretty good idea of the kind of trouble Grey and I got into. He socked me hard on the arm and said, "See you next week." I rubbed the charley horse all the way home.

The shirt and shorts I'd worn the night before still smelled of wood smoke from the bonfire. I pulled them on anyway, and we headed down to the shop, the footfalls of my rubber sneakers drowned out by the thunk of Pop's work boots. On hot days he didn't zip up his coveralls, and his collar was twisted in on itself. In one hand, he carried a can of Pabst and a pack of cigarettes and from the other, he trailed the rest of the six-pack, the plastic ring looped around his finger. When we got downstairs, there were so many bikes waiting to get fixed that we had to inch our way sideways to the benches. Pop set the beer down on the corner of the bench, lit a cigarette, glanced at the repair tag on the first bike in line, lifted it to the work stand and clamped it in place with a smack on the spring-hinged lever.

The day's work had begun.

In the spring and early summer we worked like cobblers attached to a retreating infantry. The unending stream of repairs from the tourists was swollen by the arrival of bikes from the locals, who dragged them out of the garage for a first spin of the season to find that their tires were flat, or that their wheels had been crushed under the Arctic Cat all winter. No matter what condition they came in, they had to be fixed in twenty-four hours, or else—according to our shop policy—we wouldn't charge for the work. This sometimes meant that we had to work until well after midnight, in spite of the fact that my father, while never appearing to draw any pride or pleasure from his work, was the fastest repairman I'd ever seen. On a typical day we might clear twenty repairs before noon, not counting the flats and minor repairs we did for the walk-in clientele.

Sweeping up was always my first chore of the day, though the floors never really got clean. The wood was scarred and oil and grime had worked its way into the cracks. They still smelled of gasoline from the days when Chalmers owned the place and all this was lawn mowers. In a town where wealth is measured by how many internal combustion engines you owned my father's first act when we bought the place had been to clear out anything with a motor on it and leave us at the mercy of the tourist trade. I don't think Pop, who'd never as far as I knew ever sat behind the wheel of a car in his life, had any specific objection to the internal combustion engine. It was just that he was against anything that was beyond his range of knowledge— which, given the size of the world in which he lived, was a whole universe of things.

A SHORT LIST OF THINGS MY FATHER KNEW NOTHING ABOUT

1. *Science.* Uncle Karl tells a story about the headmaster at their school who got arrested by the Nazis because he refused to keep his school open during bombing raids. Consequently, the education of Ernst and Karl Zimmermann consisted of not getting blown up. Since they lived through the war, you'd have to say they passed. When it was over they knew they'd survived, but they didn't know much else. As far as Pop understood, water was made of water, air was made of air. Which doesn't mean he thought the world is flat. It was more like he never had to know what shape it was since he'd traveled as far as he was going to and had no plans to ever reach the end.

2. *English.* My father talked a kind of ape English that he'd picked up on his own, learning only words that could be observed through action, mostly nouns and verbs. If someone said, "Hand me that wrench," he had *hand* and *wrench* down and he got the general idea, but if one of his ladies was to ask him, "How do I look in this dress?" as they sometimes did, he could only shake his head, which they took for the kind of indifference that made them throw themselves at him.

3. *Books.* Pop never read a book that I saw. He had two in his possession, both of them the Bible, one in English that Berthe gave him when we were learning English, and one in German after she gave up on teaching him. He never went to the movies. He hardly ever watched anything outside of *Bowling for Dollars* on television. Though once we stayed up late watching this movie called *Zulu*, about these English soldiers who fight off every screaming native on the continent of Africa. Amazingly, Pop remained awake through the entire film and when it was over and the British had won, he said, "Very good."

4. *Children.* Pop didn't see the difference between children and adults. He'd never had a childhood in the way we would understand. Which probably explained why he treated me the way he did. When she left, my mother didn't ask him to look after me. She may have expected that Aunt Berthe would do the job. The point was he didn't have a choice. It's hard for me not to wonder what choice he would have made if he had.

A SHORTER LIST OF THINGS MY FATHER DID KNOW ABOUT

1. *Loss.* His cousin Tomas died early in the war. Later came the disease and starvation and the firebombs. Pop was an orphan at six and had lost all four of his grandparents by the time he was eight. No matter how much you might love somebody I don't imagine you let the last death get to you like the first.

2. *Betrayal.* The way my father tells the story, Gilles LaSalle was a fat, fading French star. "Washed up," Pop said.

"A hundred meters to go, I was in front—the worst place to be," he said, adding a lesson in tactics to the story for my benefit. "I went left. 'If he wants to pass,' I said to myself, 'let him come around.' He tried—of course, and of course, I couldn't allow that," he said, "and I put an elbow in his way." Pop reenacted just how he had done this—a sharp, violent jab—and clapped his hands like cymbals. Crash.

Hundreds of racers signed a petition demanding my father's expulsion from the European Cycling Federation. Among the signatures on the petition were those of the three other German racers on the circuit.

Pop said, "My brothers turned on me."

3. *Disappointment.* In the shop, above the bench, in a dusty, wood frame, behind clouded glass, stands a photograph. The frame is mounted on a steel bracket and angled toward where my father stands. The picture is of Pop's only victory as a professional. He is standing, barely twenty, on a wooden dais, his fine fair hair, shaved on the sides and cropped short, is dirty but neatly parted. He looks like a raccoon in negative: his face blackened with road grime, except for the white circles over his eyes where his goggles had been. An inverted triangle of sweat stains his wool jersey. He is waving an enormous bouquet over his head and is flanked by two women in traditional costumes of the region. The woman on his right is broad in the hips and shoulders. Her chest strains at the bodice. Her hair is blond, braided, and curled around her ears like ram's horns. She is smiling at Pop as though she thinks he won the race for her. The woman on his left is small, dark, and though she wears the same style of dress as the other, looks like a girl playing dress-up with her mother's clothes. She is holding a bottle of mineral water with the label carefully turned toward the camera to please the sponsors. She has a worried look on her face, as though she is afraid she is doing something wrong.

Pop told me that the one on the right, the blonde, became something of a celebrity in the region, posing for pictures for tourist brochures and magazine advertisements for beer. The one on the left became my mother.

"Won the gold and married the silver," Pop always said about the picture. I don't look at it much anymore. I don't have to. Sometimes I saw it when I closed my eyes at night. I knew that she wouldn't be there when I opened my eyes again in the morning.

There were times, riding alone on cloudy days on an empty stretch of road, that I would pretend to be my father, winning his remarkable debut victory at Ghent, following the sweep of the road, the finish line coming into view, and him a half mile ahead of the next closest man. The unknown rookie, the lonely, mistrusted German in the pack. Near the end the narrow Belgian road opened into a wide boulevard, where a crowd of thousands lined the police barricades. "They cheered as I got close," Pop said, his eyes glowing with the remembered image, "and then"—a chuckle here and a lowering of his voice—"they went quiet. They saw me. But they didn't know who I was." I'd look over my shoulder to see no one coming up from behind, zip up my jersey, pantomime lifting my goggles onto my forehead. I'd blow a kiss with both hands and roll across an imaginary finish line with my arms raised high in the air.

PERILS OF CHESS CAMP

We finished the day's repairs early. The walk-in trade was slow. I thought if he'd let me, I'd go over to Grey's and see what he was up to.

"Pop?"

"Go," he said.

The hangar was a Quonset hut with a U-shaped roof of corrugated steel. It was built by the Coast Guard during wartime. In the thirteen years we had lived next door, I had never really known who owned the building.

"It belongs to the town," Grey said, the day we pried open the sliding door, inlaid with an anchor of chipped red paint, and crawled in on our hands and knees. "Jack looked it up for me. It belonged to someone else for a while. He leased the berths but wasn't making any money so he talked the town into buying to tear it down and turn into a parking lot. Nobody pays to keep their boat here anymore. What do you think?" he asked, as we stood in the dark, breathing in years of dust and neglect.

"I think it's a rusty pile of shit."

"Needs a little work," he conceded, but then that's what he'd said about Ray's canoe.

Crawling out, Grey tore his shirt. A circle of blood seeped through the white cloth. "You're going to need a tetanus shot," I said.

"Forget it," he said. "People would like me better if my jaw was locked up."

Within a week, a maintenance man from out at the airport came by and took off the old lock, installed a new one, and gave Grey the key. Then Grey took a claw hammer to the warped boards that covered the windows and opened the shutters. He tore out all the warped and decayed fixtures. And in the weeks since then the lights had been on even after we left the shop for the night. Outside, a pile of rotting wood had grown, and the Reeds' white Ford pickup had scooted back and forth to the ferry, returning each time with a bed full of lumber and supplies. Then a flatbed truck had arrived from the mainland carrying sheets of drywall. The front door had been stripped and painted a nautical white, the anchor inlay a fire-engine red, and on a piece of scrap wood in Callie's hand was written "Reed Shipworks."

I heard a radio inside tuned to the news and pushed the door open to an interior lit by hanging work lamps that were blinding in comparison to the gloom of our shop. The air smelled of fresh sawdust and chemical sealant, a big change from the first time Grey and I'd crawled through the busted slats. Then it smelled of rotted wood and something else, maybe piss or mold. Now it was all unfinished lumber and virgin sheetrock. The massive worktable that occupied much of the center of the building had been refinished. It was covered with the remnants of a picnic dinner, paper plates, wadded napkins.

Agnes and Jack Reed were at opposite ends of the table. She was playing solitaire. Jack was sorting through a box of screws and hinges. Grey was perched at the cable spool laid sideways on which he set his plans. Only Callie, at the far end of the hangar on a ladder with a paintbrush, looked like she was doing any work.

Agnes looked up when she heard the door slam. Her eyes were going. She held her glasses above the bridge of her nose, as though she was trying them on for the first time and studied the rows of overlapping cards in front of her.

"Hey," I said.

"Tom," she said, in her way, which always sounded like a question. "There's pie left."

There was a play on a black queen she was missing. I tapped the table to show it to her. She leaned closer and closer until she saw it. "No thanks," I said.

"What's it like to be a high school grad?"

"It's funny you should say that," I said, "because I was just thinking it didn't feel any different."

"Well," she said, "I guess that's to be expected."

"I guess," I said. I didn't know what she meant.

"Grey said the same thing, but then he doesn't technically qualify."

"Hey," Grey said, "I heard that." He was wiping ink from a broken ballpoint onto his skin. In the summer Grey never wore a shirt. You couldn't make him. He had on the red corduroy cutoffs that Agnes threw out at least once every summer since freshman year and, on a silver chain around his neck, an Ojibwa arrowhead, a relic of the Battle of Otter Island. Sometime since I'd last seen him he'd braided his hair into pigtails. Grey fixed his hair all kinds of ways when he was bored. If he had been anyone else he would've gotten the crap kicked out of him, because this was still northern Wisconsin, after all. But on St. Raphael, like in school, Grey Reed set the standard for fashion, hair and otherwise.

Jack looked up from his hardware and squinted. He wore glasses too. So did Grey's little brother. Everybody in the Reed household had wrecked their eyes on books, except Grey.

Callie jumped off of the ladder. In her oversized work shirt and red bandanna she looked like one of those heroic women factory workers of World War II. "Well," she said. She placed one hand on her hip, the other sweeping the room like she was a game show model, "what do you say?"

When she asked me this, Grey, Jack, and Agnes looked up from what they were doing and waited. I didn't expect my opinion to mean so much. Looking around at the clean-planed surfaces, the new wooden gangway leading up to the sail loft, and the varnished windowsills, I had to admit that they'd done something very good in no time at all. "It looks terrific," I said. "It really does."

They all smiled and I felt happy for them and sad for myself at the same time, because I knew that this had nothing to do with me.

"Where's the Toad?" I asked, meaning his little brother Todd, who we called the Toad because of the similarity in the sounds and because he frankly looked like one.

"Chess camp."

"You're kidding."

"He told you he was going."

"I know he did," I said. "I thought he was kidding."

"He wasn't."

"All they do is play chess all day?"

"Yeah, he said there was a riot once when one of the counselors tried to get them to go outside for archery. And they had to stop sending them out in canoes because they'd take their little portable boards with them and kept crashing into each other because they were looking at the board instead of watching where they were going. You have to know that none of them can swim worth a crap."

"Boys," Jack said. "Enough." He was as mild-mannered as a superhero's alter ego but he was no pushover. Jack had traveled the world in the Army and for the Associated Press. Now he edited the *Star*, the island weekly, and, Grey said, read seven other papers a day, just to keep up with the events of the world. In that regard he was as informed as anybody I knew.

"We are happy when our children take an interest in anything," Jack said.

"When you're parents, you'll understand," Agnes said. This is the sort of thing she said a lot. I'm sure she believed she did the best for her boys and as much as that should've been its own reward, she wanted them to know it too.

"Come here," Grey said. "Check this out." We all walked to the north end of the structure. Grey pushed a square red button and a new aluminum door slid upwards. The new door replaced a wooden one made of broken slats and smashed windows, at least one of which I'd busted myself.

"Go ahead," he said. I pushed the button and the door slid back down.

"And look at this." He pulled on a hanging rope and a retractable ladder slid down, on silent rollers.

Grey made an "after-you" gesture with his hand and I climbed to the top of the ladder, poking my head through to an uninterrupted plane of sanded wood. "The sail loft," Grey called from the bottom rung.

All of this had come out of nowhere, like Grey had created it whole with a wave of his hand.

When I climbed back down, Jack and Agnes were gone.

Grey said, "I thought they'd never leave."

"Nice having them around, though," Callie said. "They're useful."

"They do what I tell them."

"And they gave you five thousand dollars," Callie said.

"They gave you five thousand dollars?" I said.

"They didn't give it. They loaned it. That's the agreement," Grey said.

"How are you going to make money?"

"I saw a notice down at the marina for this sloop some guy wants to sell. I figure there's got to be a lot of boats like that, boats their owners can't afford anymore or don't take out as much as they thought they were going to when they bought them. All they need is a little push. We'll be here to push them. They sell them to us, we fix them up, and sell them for twice what we paid."

"Don't you think there's someone at the marina who takes care of that?"

"No," Grey said. "I mean if a guy comes to them and says he wants to sell his boat, they probably ask around, but I bet that's as far as it goes. The way I'm thinking is we do the asking. We look around the marina to see what boats stay in their slips all summer."

"It could work," I said.

Grey said, "It will work. I've got every angle covered. This is going to be the biggest thing to hit the island since steam navigation."

Callie laughed. "That's what he told me, anyway. I told him I don't care if he makes me rich as long as he doesn't make me starve."

Her face and hair glittered with stray flecks from the electric paint sprayer. She looked tired from work, two days of worry and no sleep, since her dad went missing. Callie looked a hundred percent different from the first time we'd seen her, six years earlier, waiting by the docks, in her white knee socks and patent leather buckle shoes, a plaid jumper, white blouse, and pigtails.

Grey and I were dawdling down to the ferry for the first day of seventh grade, going to school on the mainland after seven years at Cabot Elementary, and he'd shaded his eyes from the sun with his notebook and asked, "Who might that be?"

"Terri Gustafson," I said.

"Nah, the one sitting down."

"Some Fib," I said, FIB being an acronym which technically stood for Fucking Illinois Bastard but which we applied democratically to anyone who visited our shores. Up here you had us and then you had your Fibs and your Jibs, your tourists and your Indians, with your Jibs commanding somewhat higher esteem since they were at least from here. That was the feeling among us kids anyway. Among the grown-ups I guess it was the same only maybe more so, despite the fact that with the Fibs you had the tourist dollars and with the Jibs you had problems: the Spear-fishing Problem and the Bingo Problem and the Basically Acting Like They Owned the Place Problem.

Terri Gustafson twirled the new girl's binder on her fingertip. When Terri came close the girl would grab for the binder as Terri snatched it out of reach. Then, remembering herself, the girl would settle back on the bench, fold her arms, and blow air through her teeth in exasperation.

Grey walked up behind Terri and caught her by the wrist. He twisted her arm behind her, pushing her elbow up her back as high as he could without hurting her and then, smiling, jerking it higher. Terri yelped like a dog, dropped the binder on the ground, and backed away clutching at her shoulder. She glared at Grey and then at the new girl, like she was trying to figure out what alliance this dark, kinky-haired stranger had formed with the most popular boy on the island before school had even started. Grey picked up the binder, brushed the dust off Bobby Sherman's pretty-boy mug, and handed it back to the girl, who took it without thanking him.

When the ferry came, the girl climbed the stairs and sat behind the pilot house. Terri trailed us at a safe distance, choosing to mope on the starboard side of the boat, while Grey and I staked out our usual spots on the rail to port.

We were hanging over the side like always, spitting into the waves, when Grey said, "Go up there and ask her what her name is."

"Why don't you?"

"Because you want to know," he said.

I scaled the metal stairway and found the girl sitting on the wooden bench, not looking at the water or anything but the closed door to the bridge where Pete drove the boat.

"Grey—that's Grey down there—he wants to know your name," I said.

"Then why did you come?"

"I guess I was closest."

"Callie," she said.

"Callie?"

"Uh-huh."

"Thanks," I said and slid down the handrail to the car deck.

"Callie," I told Grey.

"Where's she from?" he said.

"How should I know?" I said.

"Didn't you ask?"

"Nope."

"Tell him to ask me himself," she said, once I had hauled myself up the stairs for a second time. I turned to go get him but then there he was standing behind me.

"He wants to know—" I started to say, when Grey blurted, "So are you like black or what?"

She made a face like the kind Pop made when he leaned on his bad hip.

"I'm only asking because they'll be asking," Grey said.

Something about that made her laugh. "Who?"

"The kids."

"They'll ask you?"

"They will when they find out I know."

"How will they know you know?" she asked, trying to sound mad but not.

"Somebody's going to ask," Grey said. "So—"

"So what?"

"What should I tell them?"

"My father was born on the island of Jamaica," she said, with the trace of an accent that proved that at least she was from somewhere else.

And from that day on, where it had been Grey and me, it would be Grey and Callie and me. Grey granted her membership into our exclusive society before he ever knew that Callie was a name she had spoken just then for the first time, that it was a blending of Catherine Leila, the name given to her by her mother.

Grey reached under the table and pulled out the battered White Owl cigar tin he kept his weed in, opened the tin, and flicked a paper off the pack of Zig Zags.

"I should clean the brushes," Callie said.

Grey watched her go but didn't say anything. She was trying to tell him there was work he could be doing and any argument he raised would only end with him having to admit she was right.

"She talk to her dad?" I asked.

"She said she won't call him."

"Why does she think he didn't show up?"

"She doesn't know what to think. Hell, maybe he just up and headed back to Jamaica?"

"Why would he do that?"

Grey beamed and put his thumb and first finger together. "For the *ganja,* mon."

"She pretty mad?"

"Wouldn't you be?"

I thought about that. "No. But I see enough of Ernst."

"Heard that," Grey said. "Can you make it to the docks by six tomorrow?"

"Why?"

"We're going out to Cowards Island."

"Who?"

"You are. Me, Cal?—You said you'd go."

"When?"

"When we talked about it."

"I got to work. I didn't much yesterday and I promised Pop."

Grey twisted the paper taut, licked the gummed edge and drew the whole joint through his moistened lips. He conjured a Bic lighter out of his pocket, fired the end, and handed it to me after holding the smoke in his lungs for close to a minute. "So blow him off," he said.

"You know what would happen if I did."

"What would happen? Look, sooner or later you're going to have to stand up to him. Shit, you're moving out in a couple of months. Just tell him, 'Pop, Grey and Callie and I are going to be taking a little boat trip tomorrow. Now you can pound the holy hell out of me, but this is the way it's going to be.'"

"Like it's that easy."

"It could be," he said. He looked at me as if he knew what he was saying might not be true and didn't really care.

"No, it couldn't."

"Grey," Callie yelled from the other end of the hangar.

"In a minute," he yelled back.

"Grey," she yelled again.

He rolled his eyes, licked his fingertips and squeezed the end of the joint. "She's killing me," he said.

"I should split," I said.

Grey said, "Cool about tomorrow?"

I waved over my shoulder, a wave that could have meant anything, though I already knew I would go. Once I got outside I looked for light in the window of our place, which all of a sudden looked pretty shabby.

Trudy Schmidt's car was out in front of the house. They weren't in the kitchen or living room. Heading for the can I heard splashing in the bathroom. I had to go bad and was about to knock. Then I heard Trudy laugh and thought better of it.

I went to the kitchen and pissed in the sink.

TALES OF THE NORTHLANDS

Grey jerked the starter cord. The Briggs & Stratton shook itself awake after its winter hibernation. He guided the tiller back and forth in easy, fluid arcs as he steered us out of the slip, the marina, and the harbor, at which point he turned west. From there he rounded the long tip of St. Raphael and made due north for Cowards Island. Callie and Ashley sat on the forward bench, Ashley with her legs twisted sideways and her feet up in a calendar pose so her new sneakers didn't get wet, while I squatted amidships with a Folgers can, bailing for all I was worth. Waves pounded the hull with the hollow clang of a steel drum. Before long, it was only water in every direction. At twelve feet and sixty-five horses, the boat was too small and the motor too underpowered for the open lake, but Jack never refused us the use of it because we always came back and because he believed— we liked to think—that we had a natural right to these waters.

I'd remembered during the night when we had talked about making this trip. Now things had changed. I was starting to resent Grey for talking me into missing a second day of work. It was easy for him to tell me to blow Pop off. When the day was over he'd have Callie and he'd have Jack and Agnes and the Toad. All I had was Ernst, which might not have been much in comparison, but he was all I had just the same, and it didn't do any good for me to go out of my way to make him mad. Before

I went down to the water, I'd written him a note that said, "Gone to Washburn to get kerosene, back aft." That was plausible. We used kerosene to clean grease and oil and dirt off of bike parts and he'd talked the day before about needing more. As for what I would say when I came home, I had no idea.

Callie got seasick. She sat with her head down and a St. Cloud State U sweatshirt wrapped around her shoulders. "Focus on a spot on the horizon," Grey said, "you'll feel better."

Callie shook her head. "I don't care if I puke."

Cowards Island, the smallest of the Green Islands, lies five miles due north of St. Raphael beyond a narrow channel between Long Cape and Federal Island. The guides on the tour boats tell the story of how it was once a lush wood until a disgraced Ojibwa warrior was exiled here, his tribesmen hoping that, with the abundance of food and shelter, he might live many years of shame and contemplation. But the manitou of the water was angered by the cowardice of this warrior and turned the rains and the winds and the fish away, leaving him to die a wretched death of starvation and exposure. And that is why, supposedly, to this day nothing grows on the island, little more than a quarter-mile long stretch of sand and limestone with a crown of scrub brush and a single ragged elm, which they say is the soul of the deserter.

They tell the same story in school, though it is strictly crap. The truth is the island was named for Alfred J. Cowards, a majority stockholder on the Soo Line Railroad.

We beached the boat in a shallow cove on the windward side of the island. A Budweiser can near the water line, footprints in the sand, and the charred remains of a fire among a circle of rocks, Cowards Island was known to all who sailed these waters, but we had always thought of it as ours. Callie spread the blanket and we dropped the jug of water and carton of cigarettes onto the sand beside it. Grey started a fire. He and I took off our shirts and lay on our backs on the blanket while Callie sat on the bottom edge, between our ankles, with her arms around her knees and watched the water. From where we sat we could see eight of the other islands of the chain, all of them uninhabited, looking as they must have looked when the French trappers paddled this coastline.

This was the last day we would spend together and, the way I saw it, the reason for this was Austin Jacobs, AP English teacher at Ashton High. Jacobs came from New York City by way of Madison where, he told us, he'd been a big shot in something called the Socialist Student League. We liked him at first because he rode a motorcycle, and he seemed to like us, particularly me and Grey for what he called our working-class paradigm. The first half of the year he cut us all kind of breaks. But as the weeks went by, as we found new ways to take advantage of him, he was forced to recognize that we had no political consciousness. By the time we got to *Hamlet* he was pretty much through with us.

The funny thing was Grey really liked Shakespeare, particularly *Hamlet*, much more than he liked all the other classics that Jacobs had tried to get us to appreciate. Grey said the play was about how the old want to destroy the young.

He wrote an essay called "Old People Screw You," in which he proved that the evil of the characters was proportional to their ages, which we would have all thought was what Jacobs was looking for, but Jacobs returned the paper drowned under a river of red ink, with a note attached saying the grammar skills were so poor he couldn't grade it. Grey flipped out. He stopped coming to class altogether and Jacobs failed him—failed him in more ways than one, I guess you could say, though Grey thought Jacobs did him a favor.

We'd planned this day as a chance for us to get away by ourselves before we split up. Now we didn't know what to do or say. Mostly we smoked and talked about dopey things, things we used to do but didn't anymore. Callie told a story about when she and her sisters were young and they all got stuck in the mud in Winona, Minnesota, and her father had come and pulled each of them out of their boots. The story took a long time to tell because she was laughing so much, and there didn't seem to be a point to it, but we laughed too, hoping, I think, to make her laugh some more.

Ashley was restless. She hadn't been our friend, and a lot of the stories we told were at the expense of kids she hung around, the Gustafsons, the Rossmeiers, the Talbotts, and the others whose parents hobnob with the FIBs who keep houses up here in the summer. I wanted to feel sorry for her, but I couldn't somehow.

Callie got up, stripped, and walked naked to the water. Wading up to her ankles, she stumbled on something beneath the water, raised her arms from her sides to steady herself and, standing on one foot lifted the other out of the water, catching it in her hands and turning up the sole to look for damage. She looked like a crane, like a creature not born in the water but native to it.

Grey jerked off his shorts and sprinted down the beach. He splashed past Callie as he dove in and thrashed around, wildly cartwheeling his arms and kicking up flumes of white water, saying, "Come on in, the water's divine."

Ashley said, "Up for a swim?"

"It's fucking freezing," I said.

"You won't even notice it."

I didn't believe her but I didn't want to look chicken. We got up and pushed our shorts down to our ankles.

"Hold my hand," she said. I did and together we ran to the waves and dove. The force of the dive carried me a long way before I had to kick my legs. She was wrong about the water. I did notice and came up shivering and gasping for air. I saw that Ashley was ahead of me and I kicked hard to catch up. I'm not a great swimmer, but I'm better than most, and didn't want to be beat by a girl, especially not this girl. I speared the water, driving through my shoulders with each stroke, but when I looked again she was still ahead, gliding on her back. Like Callie, Ashley was at home in the water, like all of us, a manifestation of the geography of our childhood. She swam just fast enough to stay ahead of me. I rolled over on my back trying to hide how bad I wanted to catch up to her and was surprised at how far we'd swum from shore. Grey and Callie, now sitting at the water's edge with their legs intertwined, looked small against the Soul of the Coward towering behind them.

"I'm going back," I yelled to Ashley, hating this game of tag, and hating being It.

"Okay," she said, not winded at all.

"You coming?"

"No."

Ashley said, "We should let them alone, don't you think? Let's go up here a ways." And we swam parallel to shore for a couple of hundred yards before turning toward the beach. Again we raced. This time I kept even, though I couldn't tell if she was tired or if she just felt she had made her point. When we reached the shallow water, she scrambled to her feet and churned through the breaking waves onto the sand.

I watched her run, her skin pink from the cold water. I charged out of the water and chased after her, figuring even if I was a slower swimmer, I could at least outrun her. Which I did: grabbing her by the hips from behind, I tried to pull her toward me. "Quit it," she said, slapped my hands away, wriggled free, and ran ahead over the rise at the center of the island and down the other side. There I caught her again. "Here," she said swiping at the sea grass and dropping to the sand.

I lay beside her. She grabbed the back of my neck with her palm, pulled me toward her, and stuck her tongue down my throat. As a rule we didn't kiss on the mouth, but I felt how much she wanted to by how hard she held my skull.

She sat up cross-legged and slouching, her pale nipples pointing tiredly toward the sand.

"I wasn't sure if I should ask Callie about her dad."

"I wouldn't. It's a sore subject."

"Did you?"

"We've talked about it. She called down to his house. Her stepmother says he left when he told Callie he was going to. She called the State Patrol. Dolores thinks he just took off, said he talked about it all the time."

"Do you think he would?"

"Search me."

"If you could go anywhere in the world where would you go?"

"I don't know," I said, "Australia."

"Let's go."

"You mean like now?"

"Why not? See the world and be back in time for school."

"Can't afford it."

"I'd pay."

"Yeah, you would."

"I'm serious."

"It's not going to happen."

Ashley pouted. "You want to stay here with them."

"For as long as I can," I said.

"Come on, I don't want to talk about this," she said and to prove her point slid her hand up my thigh to my crotch. "I don't want to talk about this now."

She opened her legs and took me inside her. She slid up and down, coming down slow and then going up fast. When I came it felt like a flood pushing outward from my spine. Then I lay with my head on her belly, the sounds of her stomach rushing like the waves. We both fell asleep, tangled up like that, or we fell into something like sleep, the heat of the summer sun and the exhaustion of the day and the sex. When I opened my eyes again, it felt like late afternoon. The wind rustled the trees along the shore. I lay with my eyes half shut, squinting into the setting sun, as Ashley sat up, looking dazed and sleepy, rubbing her eyes—her skin blotched red all over—and becoming suddenly modest when she caught me looking at her, as though she had awakened from a dream that she was naked outdoors to discover that she really was naked outdoors. And suddenly it was like we were both a little shy and embarrassed. Without talking much we went looking for Callie and Grey.

"We were going to send a search party," Grey said when he saw us.

We smoked and drank warm water from the plastic jug. Callie raked her hands through the sand, gathering twigs, smooth-worn pebbles and bits of sea glass. These she shook in her cupped hand like she was rolling dice and scattered them on the blanket. Grey asked her what she was doing.

"I'm going to see what's ahead for us." She spread the treasures around with the palm of her hand and pointed to a green triangle of glass. "Tom, this is you," she said. "See how you're alone?"

"Where are we?" Grey asked.

"Here and here," she said, pointing to a red granite pebble and a bleached birch twig.

"Are we together?" he asked, trying to see over her shoulder. I saw that they weren't, but Callie said, "Yes."

"Does it say if I'll come back?" I asked her.

She looked at the configuration for a long time before she said, "Yes, it says you will—but we won't be here when you do."

"Where are we going to go?" Grey asked.

"I can't tell," she said. "Only that we won't be here."

"What about me?" Ashley asked. "Tell me what's going to happen to me."

"This is you," and she nodded to a flat, almost perfectly round stone, far away from the others. "In California."

"She's making this up," Grey said.

Callie looked like she wanted to sock him. "It's true," she said. "I'm making up our future."

Grey shrugged then, not knowing the future was closer than we ever could've guessed. By six o'clock the sun was in our eyes, and the shadow of the Forsaken Warrior of Cowards Island stretched away from us across the sand. "We have to go, if we want to get back before dark," Callie said. Instead, we talked about spending the night. There was enough water and the fire and the blanket. For a few minutes we sat quiet, all picturing, I imagine, the night ahead. Then, without any other conversation that I can remember, we were packing to leave. We made it halfway to the harbor before sunset and then it was dark— nothing but the sound of the motor and the waves on the hull— the four of us alone on an immense, black, shimmering sea, steaming south without running lights toward the beacon on the breakwater.

As we idled into the slip, Grey saw them first. "Hey, Cal," he said, "is that your mom's car?"

Callie looked where he was looking and said, "Shit."

Under the floodlights, Dolores sat on the hood of her LeBaron convertible, her legs crossed and her feet perched on the front bumper, smoking a cigarette. Mr. Reed stood next to her, with his hands in the pockets of his beige windbreaker, leaning against the bumper, scanning the bay.

"Did you tell them where we were going?" Ashley asked.

"I told Jack," Grey said. "Cal?"

Callie nodded, but I don't think she was listening.

"I hope they didn't call the sheriff," Ashley said. "My folks will kill me."

Grey said, "Do you see the sheriff?"

Dolores was so lost in whatever she was thinking about that she didn't notice the boat approaching. She had her hair tied up in a green scarf that matched her blouse and tight white slacks that stopped halfway up her calf. Grey jumped onto the dock, knotted the line on the davit, and shouted, "Hey," as casual as anything. And still Dolores looked for another second before she recognized who it was. When she did, her face got serious. She threw her cigarette into the water, slid off the hood, tapped Jack on the shoulder, stomped down to the dock, wagging her finger, and said to Callie, "Out, now."

Jack waited until he saw that Dolores had a bewildered Callie out of the boat and halfway up the dock before he said to the rest of us, "Go home."

"What's going on?" Grey asked.

"Just do it," he said.

Grey cocked his head as though he was about to object when we heard a wail from shore, a girl's voice, Callie's voice. She was standing with her head on her mother's shoulder, gripping her mother's arms, her whole body shaking.

We looked at Jack. He flattened his hair to his head with the palm of his hand. "Her father is dead."

The kitchen was dark but the radio was on. There would be rain tomorrow with winds southeast, gusting to twenty miles per hour, a small craft advisory likely. I stuck my head in the front room. The lamp was on but Pop wasn't in his chair. Then I heard him breathing. I turned around to see him asleep at the kitchen table in the dark. His head was on his Bible—the German one, which was always a bad sign—and he was clenching his walking cane in his right fist. A voice in my head screamed: "Run." The Reeds would let me stay at their house. But if Pop came looking for me, that would be the first place he'd go. Which meant if I was going to run, I'd have to run farther than that. This was the first time I'd ever disobeyed him on anything that mattered.

Untying my laces without moving my feet, I slipped out of my sneakers, and bent to pick them up when I heard a crash behind me. Schnapps splashed my feet, the thick peppermint smell suddenly everywhere as though I'd stepped into a tub of it, and he was standing over me. I said, "Hi," and the cane came down on my neck, sending heat rushing down my spine.

"Wait," I said, and he hit me again. This time I made a run for my room, but he shoved me into a wall, and I fell. He hit me again, on the arm, as I fought off the blow. The cane went up again and came down on my collarbone. My right arm went numb. When I tried to stand up, pushing myself up with the one arm that was still good, he swept the shaft of the cane along the floor and took my legs out from under me.

He was smaller than I was, past forty, and blind drunk. I could have jumped him in the dark, taken the cane and beaten him to death with it if I wanted to. But I didn't. I didn't I guess because I figured I had it coming. And so I curled up in a corner and let him hit me until his arm got tired and he cussed me in German and dropped the cane at my feet.

DOLORES

The next morning the sun came up across the lake, like it did every day, but nothing was the same. Callie's dad was dead. I stood at the kitchen window, leaning on the cane Pop had used on me the night before and watched a procession of two vehicles, a white pickup and a green LeBaron, roll through the morning haze to the ferry dock. In the murky light, I could pick out Callie in the passenger seat of the Chrysler, and Grey riding shotgun in the Ford. I watched as the ferry arrived and lowered its gates.

Pop had come into the kitchen and was pouring a cup of coffee. Sometime during the night he'd picked up the bottles and cans and had taken a dishcloth to the liquor on the floor, which was still sticky. The smell of peppermint lingered.

"They're leaving," I said.

He sipped at his coffee and made a sharp face as it burned his tongue. He looked at my leg, then at the cup in his hand, and said, "Who was he to you?"

That made me nuts because he was right. I'd only met Professor Darling once in my life. Grey and I were fishing and Callie brought him down to the dock. He'd come up from his college to retrieve Callie's little sisters because Ray didn't want them around anymore. Callie's father wore a gray wool jacket and blue slacks, even though the temperature was over ninety.

He was very tall and thin, like Callie, with the same narrow chin, and darker than Callie but not as dark as I might have expected. He stood, looking over our shoulders at our red and white bobbers rocking on the swells, not one drop of sweat on his face. We fished, and he watched silently, until Grey pulled in a perch, at which point Professor Darling clapped his hands together and said, "There, so," as though the catching of one, puny fish signaled the end of the show.

"Catherine," he said, and Callie said goodbye to us and they walked up the hill. I felt sad as I watched them go, the only time I'd ever seen them together.

Grey said, "We're almost out of grubs."

"He was Callie's father," I said, sounding melodramatic, even to myself. Pop shrugged as though the point had been made.

I looked out the window again in time to see the ferry disappear in the fog. When I turned again he'd disappeared too, as quietly as he had come, and I thought, if he's going to keep that up, he's going to give me the creeps.

I called Grey's house. His mother answered.

"It was a car accident," she said.

"When are they coming back?" I asked.

"Jack wasn't sure," Agnes said. "Two days, I think. He went off a bridge."

When I got down to the shop, Pop had split and would be gone the whole day. There were about thirty-five bikes waiting to get fixed. I snared the first in line, a kid's banana bike, set it in the repair stand, and read the complaint on the manila repair tag tied to the handlebar, which said in Pop's scratchings "*Nchts vrnd, 2nd*," meaning in his Anglo-Germanic shorthand, "Won't shift into second gear."

I went to work.

The problem was easily fixed by cleaning some dirt out of

the indicator chain and oiling the transmission cables. It took only ten minutes.

By noon I'd finished eight. It hurt to stand on my leg, and I only managed to stay on my feet by shifting from one foot to another. I clipped the cable on a brake job, capped it with an aluminum ferrule, and slammed open the handle on the workbench, letting the bike bounce on the floor. By the time the sun hit the front window, I'd finished twenty repairs. There was still no sign of him.

It was after dark when I finished the last of the repairs, a little girl's one-speed with baseball cards clipped to the frame with clothespins and a fatally dented back fender. I wheeled it to its spot in line and went to the phone.

Ashley answered on the first ring. I said, "What are you doing?"

"Sitting here, wondering when you were going to call."

"Well, I'm calling."

"Want to come see me?"

"You mean at your house?"

"Don't be dumb."

"Where?"

"The statue?"

"Okay."

She said, "Poor Callie, huh?"

As I was hanging up, I heard the back door slam and turned to see Pop and Trudy coming into the shop, each of them carrying a bag of groceries.

"There he is," Trudy called out and started my way, but Pop handed her the bag he'd been carrying and steered her toward the stairway. Pop looked at me, and then at the row of finished repairs. "Clean this mess up and take out the trash before you come upstairs," he said.

"I was going to," I said.

He glared at me like he thought I was lying to him and walked away. When I heard his footsteps on the stairway, I said,

"Fuck you." The footsteps stopped for a second. I guess he was deciding whether to come back down and let me have it. Then they started again, heading upward.

I sat on the front porch, my feet dangling over the end, looking down toward the statue of the Founder ringed by begonias in the middle of the drive leading up from the ferry dock. The last tourists of the day idled in line, their taillights glowing red. I lit a cigarette and listened to the crickets and the occasional splash from the harbor that might have been an anchor or a jumping fish. The ferry arrived and no one got off. The lines of cars went down in orderly rows, the gates went up, the ferry rumbled out of the harbor. Then it was quiet.

A second later a car rounded the bend. I thought, Sorry, buddy, you just missed it. The Marina Hotel made half its money off these jokers who stay just a minute too long at the beach. But then the car went under a streetlight, and I saw that it was Sitwell's black Dodge Dart. It amused almost everyone in town to the point of hatred that a man of such means would drive so hideous a car as the Dart, though among the kids it had acquired a kind of retro cool.

Reaching the driver's door, I glimpsed an old woman's flowered scarf and dark glasses. I climbed in the passenger seat. "What's with the getup?" The car smelled queer, like an old woman's perfume mixed with rubbing alcohol.

"I'm incognito," Ashley Sitwell said and laughed.

The cracked vinyl rustled underneath me like paper. "Smoke?"

"Uh-uh, not in here," she said. "My dad'd piss a kidney."

I put the pack back in my pocket.

"No—give me one. I come back home and pick up all sorts of bad habits."

"You're blaming me?"

"I'm blaming you for a lot of my problems."

The car's lighter wasn't working. She stared at the coil like she was trying to heat it with her eyes. "Have you thought any more about us going away?"

"No, 'cause I can't."

"Why not?"

"How would that go? You dragging me around and paying for everything."

"You make it sound bad. There's lots of stories about people who started out that way."

"And where do they end up?"

"They get what they want," she said and pulled off the scarf, pushed her shorts down to her ankles. She lay back, sliding a shoulder beneath the steering wheel, glasses still propped on the bridge of her nose.

I didn't move.

She sat back up. "What's the matter?"

"You can't just make me," I said.

"If I was Callie, I wouldn't have to make you."

"What the hell's that supposed to mean?"

"You should have seen yourselves the other night, holding her like she was a piece of glass that would smash into pieces if anyone let go. A glass vase—brown glass."

"Jeez," I said, "her dad just died."

"So what? I mean really. Do you think everyone would be crowding around me if mine did?"

"No and maybe that's the point."

She socked me hard on the shoulder. "Shut up."

"Because you hate him," I yelped, massaging the spot.

"Who says?"

"You do."

"Who doesn't talk like that about their folks sometimes?"

"Grey doesn't."

"I know he doesn't. That's because Jack and Agnes are so fucking special." I put my hand on the door handle. "Where are you going?"

"Home."

"Great, so I've fucked everything up." She was crying. The glasses fell on the floor and Ora Sitwell's scarf was tangled in her hair. I tried to touch her and she went hysterical, shaking and crying until her nose was dripping. "Forget it," she said.

In the dark hall at the bathroom door, I nearly ran into a body in the doorway.

"Excuse me," Trudy said, holding my father's robe closed at the neck with one hand and a cigarette a couple of inches from her mouth with the other.

"You scared the shit out of me," I said.

"Sorry," she said. "Need to get in here?"

"No."

"Yeah, you do." She turned and flicked the butt into the toilet. An impressive shot considering the seat was down. I decided I liked her and I would be sorry to see her go. "My daughter's your age."

"I know," I said. Dianne Schmidt was a sophomore and well on her way to getting a rep as a serious slut.

"You know my DiDi?"

"By sight," I said.

She eased past toward my father's room. Too much mascara made her eyes into black hollows in the poor light of the hall. "There's chicken salad in the fridge," she said.

"Thanks," I said and yawned.

"Tired?" she asked, as she pushed the door to Pop's room.

"A little," I said. "He keeps me busy."

"Tell me about it," she said and pushed the door shut behind her until it latched.

It had been more than a day since I'd eaten. I felt like throwing up, but I had a rule against that, so I crawled into bed and lay still in the dark until the feeling of nausea went away.

The next day Pop wouldn't even look at me, going so far as pretending to look for some phantom fallen screw, when I walked by his bench. There were enough repairs to keep the two of us busy until well after supper and on past dark, when he crushed the last cigarette of a four-pack day into the ashtray, swilled the dregs of the last can of the day's six-pack, and went upstairs.

The day after that, I woke up to an empty house. Pop was up and out riding without me. There weren't many repairs to be done and fewer customers on an overcast day, so I thought up whatever I could do to look like I was working. I swept the floors and took the few bicycles we had for sale out on the front porch to be dusted and waxed. I was patching a tear in the screen door when I saw Callie and Grey coming up the street.

Callie I saw first and had to look twice because I didn't recognize her. The clothes were right—the sleeveless T-shirt and cutoff shorts—but her hair was cut short.

"Hi," she said, stepping under my arm at the screen door.

Grey followed behind. "How'd it go?" I said, and he shook his head and blew air through his teeth.

The trash cans were almost empty but the chore gave us an excuse to get outside.

"It was a horror show," Grey said. "Callie and her mother fought all the way to Rice Lake. We stopped to get gas and Dolores called Callie 'an ungrateful little pill,' and Callie says, 'Well, you won't have to worry about that anymore,' and Dolores says, 'What's that supposed to mean?' And Callie says, 'Buy a giant clue.' And it's like that until Jack suggests that we switch around and Callie gets in the pickup with me, and Jack agreed to ride with Dolores, which pretty much means he doesn't have to get me anything for Christmas, as far as I'm concerned. Then we get to the funeral home where you had rows of chairs over here, and rows of chairs over there, and the coffin in the middle. We come in. His other kids are over there with the new wife and all this family of hers that actually flew up from Jamaica. They don't talk to Dolores, they don't know who we are, and they're all black, and so you got this black-white thing going on, which is the last thing we want, but what can we do? And Callie doesn't want to leave her mom alone because she feels crappy about what they said on the trip down."

"I guess people do stuff for different reasons."

"I guess," Grey said. "Then when we were leaving Callie does this weird thing. She went over to the casket. There was a picture of her dad next to this candle, and Callie picked up the picture and set it down on a table across the room."

"Why?"

"Don't know. I didn't ask."

"What's going to happen now?"

"Beats me. Callie sure doesn't know. She doesn't want to stay with Ray and Dolores. We'd like to get some money and get our own place. Jack and Agnes said she can move in with us until then." Grey sees the bruise on my arm. "What'd ya do, crash?"

"Pop hit me," I said.

"Aw man," Grey said, "you really can't stay."

"No choice," I said, as I pushed the door open. "Anyway it's just a few more weeks. How bad could it get?"

Back inside, Callie was sitting on the counter and Pop was showing her how he could pick up a stool from the bottom with only one hand. A feat that never failed to kill down at the tavern, I'd never seen him try it in the shop. "All from here," he said, standing and massaging his forearm. She obliged him by closing her thumb and index finger like a caliper around his biceps. "Ooh, strong, Ernst," she said, looking confused and amused. "How do you like this guy?"

"It's pretty tough," I said. And Pop stared like I was making a crack, but he didn't say anything. In fact, Pop didn't talk to me the rest of the day or the next day or—no harm in jumping ahead here—for the rest of the summer.

JACK REED

It was creepy at first, sharing a house with somebody who wouldn't even talk to you. But after a few days of trying to trick him into talking to me, I got used to the silence, and after a few days more, I got to like it. Pop never had much to say on good days so the silent treatment wasn't that much of an adjustment. Days went by and then weeks, and then the entire month of July. Neither of us cracked.

Then one day in August, when we were closing up, Jack stuck his head in the front door. "Callie and Agnes went over to buy contact paper in Washburn. Who's up for a beer?"

Pop and I looked each other in the eye for the first time in days, both of us knowing that if one of us said yes, the other would have to say no. So I said yes because I wasn't enjoying sulking around the house as much as he was.

When I caught up with Jack in the bar, he was alone.

"Where's Grey?" I asked him.

"Home," he said. "He's beat."

"You must be, too," I said.

"Not me," he said, smiling, "just getting my second wind," which was funny if you knew Jack.

Friendly's Tavern was a popular place, owing to the fact that Ben Friendly had a monopoly on drinking outside of the country club and the bar at the marina. It was just past five by the Hamm's beer clock above the bar and the regulars were already two deep at the rail.

Most everyone was on their first of the day and so the bar was quiet. Even the jukebox, which played mostly the kind of country songs that people like to hear after they're drunk and feeling sorry for themselves, hadn't been turned on yet. There was a considerable commotion going on in the back room. It was Monday, which was euchre night. I ducked into a booth along the wall. Jack got Greta Friendly's attention with a wave and she brought over two bottles of Pabst. Greta never asked, "What'll you have?" You always drank at Friendly's what you drank the first time you came in, beer or brandy old-fashioneds, it didn't much matter.

"How's the town scholar?" she said, as she set the bottles down on the Formica in front of us.

"Oh, not feeling too smart, today, Greta," I said.

And she said, "Well, then you've come to the right place. Jack—"

Greta told him she wanted to run an ad for their Labor Day pig roast and they talked about that a little and when she left Jack said, "Actually, I'm glad it worked out this way. The two of us. Who knows how many more chances we'll get to talk before you go."

"Sure, you can talk to Grey any time."

"True," he said, laughing a little. He smoothed the zipper on his windbreaker and pushed his glasses back on his nose.

"So the funeral was kind of tough?"

He sipped his beer and thought. "What did Grey say?" Jack was always doing that. If Grey or I asked him what he thought of something he would turn the question around on us. I used to think this was because he held no strong opinions, but I'd come to see that it was because he wanted us to form opinions of our own, without having to worry that he might know more than us and disagree.

"He said it was kind of sad."

"It was kind of sad."

"He also said that Callie and her mom had this huge fight and Callie was moving in with you guys."

He cocked his head, "Well," he said, "if loving Callie like she was our own daughter was all we had to do to make everyone happy, then our job would be easy."

"How come it isn't."

"Callie lost her father, but she's not an orphan. And until she turns eighteen, we have to respect Dolores's right to raise her child as she sees fit."

"Do you really believe that?" I said, a little too loud, and I thought I caught a rare flash of anger in Jack's eye.

"It doesn't matter what I believe," he said. "Dolores is a proud and independent woman from a proud and independent family."

What he meant was Dolores Kraus had grown up doing whatever she wanted and getting away with it because she was pretty in the way rich girls can be: well-looked-after without being beautiful—and because she was a Kraus, and everyone on the island believed that the Krauses did as they pleased. When she was young she'd turned down a scholarship to a women's conservatory in Oshkosh to go to college in Boston and study art history, and no one said anything because it was the privilege of the rich to educate their children in the East. Even when she got knocked up by a professor and dropped out to marry him the worst anyone said was, "Figures." But when she came home the next summer with a baby girl the color of an oak leaf at Halloween, well, then they had something to talk about.

I liked to hear Jack talk about the old days and he liked talking to me about them because I was the only person who cared.

"Our fathers made this place what it is, such as it is. Not much to boast about but, it's their legacy—and our history," he said. And it was true. Ashley's grandfather built this town on lumber money. Jack's dad had run the paper before Jack did.

Dolores's father Millar Kraus came to this island in the Depression, a forestry agent for the government.

I looked over to the bar and saw that Sgt. Spires had come in. He was in uniform so I figured he hadn't come in for a drink. There was an unwritten rule that the Friendlys were free to serve minors as long as we were with a parent, and it didn't have to be our own parent, so I didn't worry about getting busted.

"Of course," Jack said, "none of that has anything to do with you in the end."

I watched Spires on his way to the door. "What do you mean in the end?"

"When it comes time to reckon."

"You mean when I'm dead."

He smiled. "There's a lot of reckoning you do before you die. You're going to face a lot of choices, and you should know that each choice you make is the only one you were ever going to make. See?"

"Nope."

"Grey thinks it's the fault of his teacher that he's not going to college."

"It is," I said. That seemed clear enough.

"And where did the man get this power?" Jack said, and from the way he looked, I could tell he wasn't kidding around. "Would you describe Jacobs as a powerful man?"

"No."

"In the worst view of things all Jacobs did was treat Grey less fairly than he treated his other students, right?"

"I guess."

"Has anything like that ever happened to you?"

I laughed. "Daily."

"And what do you do about it?"

"Cuss and keep going."

"Exactly," Jack said. "Grey is the reason Grey is not going to college. If going to school was something he really wanted to do he'd stop at nothing to do it." As I was listening to him I peeled the label off the bottle and laid it on the tabletop. "Look, you and Grey each made a choice. Whether it was a good choice or not doesn't really matter. You may or may not be happy about that choice. Right now I'm betting, no—" he paused and waited for me to confirm his guess. I nodded my head. "Then you realize that by having made that choice you are limited to a certain set of choices the next time around and ultimately these choices that you make add up to the only life you were ever going to lead."

"By the way you make it sound, it doesn't matter which way I go because all of those decisions are already decided."

"I'm saying only your first choice is determined. After that you have to be more careful. It's up to you."

"Pop—"

"He's got nothing to do with this—except you'd do well to make your father understand why it's important for you to leave."

"Yeah," I said. "It's kind of funny, isn't it? Me going off to school when Pop wants me to stay and Grey staying here when you'd just as soon he leave."

"Yes, it is funny." He slid out of the booth. "Come on," he said, "I can see that I'm—what's it you say?—freaking you out."

The air had gotten warmer with the night. It smelled of rain as we stepped outside. "We'll have to do this again before you leave," Jack was saying, but I didn't say anything back because I was half listening to him and half watching a passing car that looked in the glare of the streetlight off the black hood like it might be Sitwell's Dodge. It disappeared into the dark before I could be sure.

I went home, found the phone without turning on the light and dialed Ashley's number in the dark. Her line rang about twenty times, and I was about to hang up when her mother answered.

"Is Ashley there, please," I said.

"No," Mrs. Sitwell said. She sounded confused at the question.

"Will you tell her Tom called?"

A couple seconds went by where I guess she must have been thinking about it. "No," she said again and hung up.

"Jack says hey," I told Pop as I passed him where he sat on the couch on my way to the bedroom. He grunted.

Next morning, he was sulking again and even went so far as to—swear to God—throw a wrench at my head when a customer brought a bike back that he said I had fixed wrong.

"Jeez," I shouted.

He stared, the rage building inside of him forcing his lips to mouth words that he didn't speak out loud. On my way out, I slammed the door for the effect of it and didn't much care if I ever walked back through it again.

Out on the porch, I stamped around and smoked a cigarette and tried to figure out what to do. Not coming up with anything permanent, I decided to go over to the hangar to see how the Reeds were getting on. I hoped they'd all be over there, but it was just Grey and his brother Todd and some man I didn't know. He looked like he could have come up from the country club, Fib probably, rich maybe, but frayed enough around the edges to fit in. The white blazer, sweat along the hairline, he could've been an old thirty or a youngish forty. Grey saw me come in and turned the man away from me so all I saw was their backs. I figured this was some guy from the marina and thought I'd bug the Toad while they finished talking about whatever it was.

The work on the hangar was done. There were walls and a false ceiling over the office where there had only been the corrugated metal arching from the ground uninterrupted overhead. The floors were clean, except for drifts of sawdust in the corners, and the walls had been painted white. The place smelled of planed wood and varnish, the smells of a new enterprise. Grey's little brother was hunched over the long workbench that dominated the center of the space.

"Hey, Tom, look," Todd said, "our first boat." Somehow he'd managed to come back from three weeks of chess camp paler than when he left. His hair was stringy with sweat. The boat he was talking about was a couple of feet long, constructed of painted-over milk cartons. "It runs on a solar cell, here," he said and tilted it so I could get a look. Actually, it was kind of cool, but I didn't say so. I don't know why not. Habit, I guess.

He flicked a toggle. The propeller purred and then died. The guy talking to Grey turned. "Take it outside," Grey hollered. "Tom, take him down by the lake."

I would've told him to get lost if he was alone, but this was business so I shoved Todd outside.

"The sun charges the batteries," he said.

"No kidding," I said. The Toad thought everyone was dumber than him. It helped us feel better about picking on him.

"I'm not going to the lake," I said. "Charge it up here."

He set the boat on the sidewalk in the sun and we stood looking at it a couple of minutes.

"When do you know it's done?"

"The longer it charges the longer it runs," he said and waited like he expected me to mock him again. Then he said, "I'm taking it to the beach."

"Be my guest."

Seeing the man talking to Grey up close, I chose old-looking young, out of the age options.

"You a friend of his?" he asked me.

"Yes, sir."

"Sir?" he said, with a kind of laugh. "Sir's the police." He held out a hand for me to shake. "Natch," he said.

"Huh?"

"Howard Natchell. Natch." He reached into the inside pocket of his jacket and produced what looked like a ticket stub. I looked at it and saw it was a business card.

Nowadays the guy who changes your oil's got a business card. Back then I had only seen them handed out by the salesmen from the wholesaling firms. They didn't come by our shop much because we rarely bought enough of anything to make the trip worthwhile. When they did come by it was most of the time with bad news, a man in a brown sports jacket, leather sample case splayed at the stitching, delivering the words: Owing to a failure of the purchaser to manage payments, all future orders will be shipped COD. After that it got more personal: "Sorry Ernst, but that's just the way it's got to be."

His name was written in raised silver letters almost invisible against the light blue or gray of the card, in the center of the card in machine-faked handwriting,

Howard J. "Natch" Natchell

and in the lower right-hand corner in small block print letters, in parentheses, the single word:

(PHARMACEUTICALS)

"Sail any?" he asked me.

"Some."

"I'm looking for crew sometimes. Interested?" He nodded as though he knew the answer.

"Aren't you selling your boat?"

"Why would you say that?"

"Figured that's what you're talking to Grey about."

"Yeah," he said. "I'm always looking to deal." Then he cocked his thumb and shot me with his forefinger and moseyed on down Main in the direction of the harbor.

"Going to buy a boat from him?" I asked Grey when he stepped out on the porch.

"From Natch? I might," he said. "He's got a couple, that sloop at the marina and another over in Michigan. He's a drug dealer."

"Really, you think?" I said.

Grey thought he owned the monopoly on sarcasm on the island. "Didn't I say go with Todd?"

"You did, but I didn't. He's a big fella now."

"Natch is looking to unload the sloop."

"Yeah? How's that going to work?"

"He wants four grand. It's worth twice that as is. I buy it, fix it up, and ask for ten."

"Man, it's that easy?"

"What've I been telling you? Except."

"What?"

"I haven't got four grand."

"What have you got?"

"See there's start-up costs."

"How much is that?"

"What I'm into Jack for. He lent me the five thousand. Out of that I've spent about three to get the place in shape."

"Three hundred?"

"Three thousand. What are you, an idiot?"

"How should I know? Three thousand bucks is a lot of money."

"Sheetrock and tools and it adds up."

"So you've got two grand left?"

"Around there."

"What are you going to do?"

He didn't answer, instead he glanced down toward the beach standing on his toes to catch sight of Todd safe on the sand.

I said, "Have you seen Ashley?"

"Since when?"

"I don't know."

"Look," he said, "all I've got to do is get that boat in this hangar. From there on out everything else takes care of itself. The money's out there waiting."

RAB AND THE SONS OF LIBERTY

The morning before I was supposed to leave, I was struck with an inspiration. After almost two months of not talking, my father and I settled the question in a manner that suited us both: on the road. He was sitting at the breakfast table, ignoring me, and I said, "Pop, got an idea. I'll race you for it. If you win, I stay," I said. "If I win, I'm gone and that's the last you have to say about it."

He blinked and studied his cup, like he was trying to foretell the outcome in the steam. He set the coffee down, looked toward the window, and—for the first time in eight weeks—talked. Or sort of talked, he said, "Uh." And, just in case it wasn't clear what he meant by that, he reached his right hand across the table for me to shake.

We rode the first couple of miles slowly, as had always been our custom. It was a muggy late-August morning, the kind that makes the heat and the damp lawns and overgrown greenery seemed permanent. At first I felt glad to be out riding, the two of us together. I'd missed this those last weeks. I would miss this when I went away. The fact that we weren't talking seemed stupid and pointless. Then I remembered that it'd been his idea and that nothing I'd tried could get him off it. "Nice out, huh," I said. He sprinted away from me.

I caught up easy enough and made him pay for his surliness, kicking up the tempo until my lungs burned. Now it was Pop fighting to keep up. I pushed harder until I had reached the top of the hill. The landmarks of our route passed faster than they ever had. We reached the far end of the island before Pop caught up and was riding next to me. I offered him a drink from my water bottle. He shook it off. We turned east and flew past the dump and the airport. In seconds the white cross on the church mailbox came into view.

By the church some tourists, gray-haired and stooped, wandered the cemetery, clearing grass and dirt away from the inscriptions on the headstones. Old people are nuts for cemeteries. I looked that way as we went by, and Pop sprinted past with his head down. That maneuver guaranteed that I would trail him as we rode past the turned heads of our neighbors and out of town again.

On our second time up the rise to the bluffs, his face was red. Over the next ten miles we changed leads a dozen times— one of us pushing ahead and the other ducking into the slipstream of his rear wheel to catch a breath. Neither of us let up until we reached the airport for the second time when my father sat up in the saddle and coasted. I slowed up, detecting a smile on his lips. He accelerated and slowed again, trying to dupe me into passing him, but what I knew I'd learned from him, and I didn't fall for it.

Two hundred yards from the church, he stood up on his pedals trying to open some distance. I caught him easily. Seventy-five and then fifty yards and I swung past. Forty yards to go, I heard him coming on up my left. I swerved across the yellow line to cut him off, but he kept coming and I kept moving left on a diagonal. Less than ten yards to the line and I felt his elbow against my hip, heard his raspy breathing and smelled the thirty years of cigarettes. I left less than a shoulder's width of the road to get by and still he tried. In one motion I leaned into him and thrust out my arms to push my wheel across the line ahead of his.

The next second, I heard an explosion of splintering wood and the sound of his bike hitting the pavement. Pop groaned as the impact knocked the air out of his lungs. I squeezed my brakes and the bike skidded sideways. Turning around I saw him crumpled next to the mailbox, which was broken in half, with only the back left on the post and the cross hanging upside down by a single nail. I thought I had killed him. Then he rolled over, and I saw the pain on his face. I got to him as he was trying to stand and told him not to move.

There was a gash on his forehead and his shoulder was pushed toward his neck at a sickening angle.

He spat blood and said, "Tie."

"What?"

"Tie," he said again. "You didn't get past me."

Reverend Vogel was culling dead petals from the geraniums in the church window boxes when he heard the crash and came running. Pop was lying alive but very much in pain by the road on his left side and rocking one way and then the other in an effort to drive the hurt from his body. Reverend Vogel looked at him and then at me. "What happened?"

"He hit that," I said, pointing at the shattered replica of the church.

He went back to the church to call the state police and Ben Friendly who was the only person we knew on the island licensed in the practice of emergency medicine. Pop kept trying to stand. I wouldn't let him. At some point when I was watching down the road for the sheriff or the state patrol or at least the Friendly car, Pop got to his feet and wandered across the road. I got a start when I saw he'd moved then looked toward the church and saw him standing, his right shoulder monstrously raised higher than the left, like a bloody scarecrow in the thick grass of the cemetery.

We got him into the church and laid him on a pew, Reverend Vogel taking off my father's shoes and using them to prop his head. I looked at his white feet, his toes clenched like hoofs. Pop kept saying, "Okay. Okay," over and over, his face twisting in pain each time we tried to move him. Ben came with his medical tackle box, sat Pop up, and gave him a shot.

"What'd you give him?" I asked.

Ben said, "Shut up."

He said Pop had at least one broken bone and maybe a dislocated shoulder. He said we should go to the clinic in Ashton.

Pop said, "No, no, no."

Ben settled on a cheap-looking blue sling and said if Pop was permanently crippled he better not try to sue over it— unless he was prepared to pay out the same amount for a beer next time he walked into his tavern.

"Deal," Pop said. He stood up to go and fell like a leaf, cracking his head on the way to the floor. Then it was just a matter of loading him into Ben's car and getting him to the mainland before he came to.

I sat on a hard bench in the hall of the Ashton clinic as the nurses came and went carrying one x-ray after another. When Pop found out where we had taken him he clammed up and refused to answer any of the doctor's questions.

When they let us take him home, Jack and Agnes came over and helped Pop, loopy from painkillers, to bed.

"You packed?" Jack asked me.

I'd forgotten. "I can't go now," I said.

He held up a hand to shut me up. "Ernst'll be fine. Any one of us could look after him as well as you could," he said.

Until I was back in my room, I didn't give any thought to what I would take, or how I would fit it all into the blue Bellwether backpack, which was all I was going to be carrying. Greyhound one way to Madison was twenty-two dollars, not including seven dollars they would have charged to ship my bike, and then another three on top of that to insure it. So I decided to ride my bike down to college.

On the back of a brochure from the university I scrawled a list of the essential items and checked them off as I piled them on the bed.

TO PACK

1 pair jeans	1 toothbrush
2 T-shirts (black)	1 tube Crest
1 sweatshirt	1 razor (w/ 5 blades)
3 pairs underwear (white)	1 can deodorant
4 pairs socks (3 white, 1 wool)	1 bar soap

(1) 6" Crescent wrench
1 pair pliers (needle-nose)
(1) 5 mm Allen key
(1) 6 mm Allen key
1 convertible screwdriver (w/ Phillips and flathead bits)
4 tire levers (2 aluminum, 2 plastic)
1 spare inner tube (700c)
1 spare tire (collapsible)
3 spare brake/derailleur cables
1 roll handlebar tape (white cotton)
1 flashlight
1 lighter (Zippo)
1 road map (Wisconsin)
1 compass

1 Bible (King James, paperback)	1 film can marijuana
1 copy *Johnny Tremain*	1 pack Zig-Zags (gummed)
1 copy *Lou Gehrig, Captain of the Yankees*	2 packs Marlboros

My first impression when I saw all this stuff was that I'd need a trunk. Then I set about the task of making it all fit. I used the Gehrig book, which was a tall picture book that I got from Aunt Berthe for my seventh birthday and the Bible (given to me by Brad, the Youth Pastor when I graduated from Sunday School) to construct a frame, pressing the baseball book against the back of the pack and laying the Bible, which had a hard spine, on the bottom.

On top of the Bible, I set the other books, jeans, t-shirts, and my sweatshirt. The weed I stashed beneath a false bottom in my shaving kit, piled the toiletries on top and zipped it shut. I packed the tools in a soft leather case that I bound with a bungee cord. That left just enough room to snake the flashlight and cigarettes into the puckers that opened between round and square edges. When everything was in, I pulled the strap tight. Fully loaded, the bag weighed a ton. It hit the floor with a thud when I dropped it, and Pop shouted a groggy, "Hey" from his room.

I set my alarm for 5:30 and lay on my bed thinking about what I wanted to take that there was no room for: the red flannel shirt I wore every day of my Junior year, my Farm and Fleet parka with the chainsaw gash on the left sleeve from where Grey was playing Freddie Krueger on a birch that fell in their yard in a storm, and all my cassette tapes that took me days to dub.

All I knew about the future came out of the brochures that had arrived in our mailbox at the rate of a half-dozen a week all summer. There was a picture of Rosewalter Hall, my dorm. There were schedules and course descriptions. There were letters from fraternities, which looked like a blast, live-in clubs where guys dressed in tuxedos for charity, until I told Callie, who set me straight. ("They're dicks.")

I fell into a sleep without dreams and woke the next morning with the ringing of my alarm. In twenty minutes, I'd showered, dressed, eaten breakfast, and was ready to leave. But Pop wasn't up yet and I heard nothing from his room. I drank more coffee and stuffed an orange and a couple of bananas into my bag. The doctor had said we were supposed to wake him up in the middle of the night and take his temperature to make sure he didn't have a brain hemorrhage.

Just when I thought he'd expired, I heard the creaking of bedsprings, and he appeared in the hallway, walking close to the wall to steady himself. He looked a little like Marlon Brando in *On the Waterfront*, the way he walked, favoring the right side of his body, that likely having to do with the broken collarbone, the separated shoulder, and the three broken ribs. Every movement required ingenuity. He had to tilt his whole body to pour a cup of coffee and then squat until his arm was level with the table to set the cup down. Every move of his arms or legs knotted his forehead with pain. He lit a cigarette, striking a match one-handed, and picked up the paper from the night before.

I watched him pretend to read for a long few minutes, then said, "I guess I'll get going."

He folded the paper and swatted my hand away when I tried to help him up. We must've looked pathetic, Pop and his injuries and me bracing myself against the sink, as I swung the heavy pack onto my shoulder. We *were* pathetic: Pop not able to talk to me even when I was going to be gone for months, and me not able to tell him I'd miss him. I snagged my bike and together we walked out the door and down to the street. It was cool and foggy. You couldn't see as far as the ferry dock. I slid my arms through the straps of my pack and straddled the bar.

"Well," I said.

He squinted in the morning sun, the lines on his face fanning out from the sockets of his eyes like spokes from a hub. "Got everything?" he asked,

"I think so." Then I noticed his boots weren't tied and had to climb off the bike, set down the bag, and get down on a knee to tie them. He kept moving his feet away from my hands so I couldn't get a grip on the laces. "Come on, Pop," I said. "You're going to have to get somebody in every day to do this."

He made a face and I knew he'd sooner break his neck than ask anybody to get down on their knees on his account.

When I stood up, he pulled his right hand out of his pocket, and when I shook it, I felt a wad of bills in his palm.

"I got enough," I said, but he wouldn't take the money back.

"Take it," he said. "If you need help later, go to somebody else."

I told him, "Thanks." I meant thanks for the money, not thanks for making me feel like a shit for leaving him by himself in traction.

The Reeds' pickup came rattling down the road. From the way it weaved I guessed Agnes was driving. That was something Jack liked to let her do, he said, because it was his duty as a newsman to keep the citizenry on its toes.

"We're on our way down to Washburn and figured we could take you that far," Mr. Reed said from his window.

"That's okay," I said.

"Come here, then," Jack said. When I walked to his side of the truck, he handed me a small, black, plastic box. "This was supposed to be Grey's, but he won't have much use for it." I opened it and saw that it was a black pen with a clip that looked like real gold.

"It's a fountain pen," Mrs. Reed said.

"Do you know how to use one?" Mr. Reed asked.

"No idea," I said, and they laughed.

"When you're on the ferry I want you to look under the cardboard," Jack said, "Not until."

I said, "Gotcha," and waited for them to pull away before I climbed onto the saddle.

I said, "See you, Pop."

Arms folded, he said, "Don't waste time."

"I won't," I said, though I didn't know whether he meant on the way to college or during the rest of my life.

I coasted onto the ferry ahead of the Reeds, climbed the stairs to the bridge, and rapped on the glass. Pete waved me in.

"There's the man," he said. Pete was short and wide around the middle, but hard, and thickly tanned. He'd run the ferry for as long as I'd lived on the island, and for just as long people had said that he'd lived another life before he had come to the island. What that life had been we didn't know, though we guessed it had something to do with the tattoo of Jesus on his right forearm. "You're the only one this year. You're the only one going as far as Madison."

"That can't be right," I said.

"No? Think about it."

"Stu Hansen."

Pete shook his head. "St. Olaf's," he said.

As he eased the boat out of its slip, I named a few others from my class who I thought were going, and each time he told me why they weren't. Every year the *Star* publishes the pictures of the island kids who will be attending the University of Wisconsin. It's an honor Jack doesn't extend to the ones attending more famous schools out east. Every year I'd see the pictures and admire the kids without exactly knowing why, except that they were supposed to be admired. Having just learned that my picture would appear alone on the front page this year, I didn't know what to feel, except someone must have made a mistake.

We scanned the water of the channel, as the mainland drew closer in front of us. "When you coming back?"

"Never."

He laughed. "You'll be back," he said. "It's only a matter of when."

"When do people usually come back?" I asked.

"Thanksgiving. Some of them. Almost all of them at Christmas. A college town is no place to be at Christmas," he said. "You'll find that out."

"How come?"

"How the hell should I know," he said, keeping a hand on the brass wheel. "Christ, you're a hard one."

I was quiet, and he must have thought that he'd spooked me because he reached in his pocket and pulled out his wallet. "You'll want money," he said.

"No," I said. "I'm all right there."

"Really?" he said and thought about this. "Well, I got to give it to you," he said, "so don't argue with me." He pushed a bill into my shirt pocket. "Take over for a minute," he said, stepping sideways away from the wheel. I stepped in. "There's your course," he said. "Keep your fucking hand off the throttle."

I steered the ferry through the placid water of the channel until it was time to change course. Pete put his hand on my shoulder. "Keep your nose clean," he said.

The Reeds were standing in the bow at the rail. Agnes had raised her glasses from her eyes and was craning over the side.

"What are you looking at?" I asked.

Jack said, "Mrs. Reed thought she saw an eagle."

"There," she said, "by the water line."

"That's a buoy," Jack said.

"Well it looks majestic, just the same."

While their backs were turned, I opened the pen case they had given me. I lifted the cardboard base, and found five hundred-dollar bills, new and stiff as hacksaw blades.

"Man," I said. The way people were throwing money at me was starting to freak me out. "You know I can't take this."

"We knew you were going to say that," Jack said, "which is the only reason it's not more. We would have done better than that for Grey, so quit while we're all ahead."

"I'll think of it as a loan."

"If you have to."

We heard the engine go in reverse and turned to see the slip approaching. I shoved the money into the pocket of my shorts. Holding onto the rail, I mounted my bike and cinched the toe straps. Out of the corner of my eye I caught a last glimpse of the Reeds. He looked nervous and little tired around the eyes; she smiled, but her mind was somewhere else. The gate hit the asphalt with a clang. Mr. Reed said, "Go get 'em," and I rolled off the deck onto solid ground, pedaled up the hill, turned left onto Highway 13 and spun out of Bayview, heading south.

10

THE CARHOP'S TALE

It was 310 miles from our porch to the Rosewalter dormitory. I figured to make the ride in two days. I planned on covering two hundred before dark but I missed the turnoff from 63 onto Bayview County G and reached the town of Cable before I realized my mistake. This detour took me only five miles off course, but by the time I found County M, which cut through the southern tip of the Chequamegon Forest from the west, I had lost an hour that I wouldn't be able to make up.

In Clam Lake, I stopped at a gas station. The old man behind the counter stared at me as I wheeled my bike through the door.

"On some kind of bike trip?" he asked as he rang up the quart of orange juice and dozen donuts I bought.

"I'm riding down to college."

He slapped his palms on the counter. "Oh, heh, isn't that a stunt," he said and offered me a bag, which I refused. "Think we'll have Ogilvy back?"

"I don't see why not," I said, though I didn't know what he was talking about.

"Still there's no guarantee that he'll ever be the same. Ankles are troublesome."

"Yes," I said, recognizing that even if I had known then—as I learned in time—that Ogilvy was the best flanker the Badgers had had in twenty years, I couldn't have given the man the assurance he was looking for.

County GG ran due south through the forest. It was lowland, mostly pine, dotted with small, algae-green ponds, and patches of birch rising white out of a ground fog. I thought about the man's question, about the injured football player and wondered if I would be expected to know more than I did about the game. Maybe, I thought, you just pick those things up after you've been on campus a while.

When the forest gave way to farmland a few miles north of Loretta, I'd ridden eighty miles. My watch was in my pocket where I'd put it to keep myself from looking at it every few seconds. Consequently, I had only a vague idea of what time it was. My guess was that I wasn't far off schedule, but it was a cool morning, my pack was heavy, the roads were unfamiliar, the land more hilly than I'd remembered, and I was tired. The sense of adventure I'd felt when I left gave way to doubt.

What had been wooded marshland was now rolling pastures. I fought my way up each hill, coasted down the other side, rolling to the base of the next. And so it went for several miles. I rode, hearing sounds of civilization around me but not seeing another soul, until I rounded a corner and saw a battered pickup parked on the shoulder. The roof was half caved in and its blue paint was faded almost white by the sun. As I got close I saw that the bed was filled with watermelons and on the rear gate sat a man in a white cowboy hat and a girl in a pink-and-white-checked dress. They were dark skinned, and I assumed they were Ojibwa until I got closer and saw that they weren't. The truck had Arizona plates. The girl's hair was long and snarled but her dress was clean. The man's mustache, which stopped at the edges of his mouth, was flecked with gray hair. He looked old to have a daughter that young. It being just the three of us on that particular stretch of road, I thought it would be rude to pass without talking.

"Hello," I said.

The man lifted his finger to his hat. The girl disappeared behind his arm.

I pointed at the watermelons and said, "Do you have anything smaller?"

"Smaller? Si," the man said and dragged a basket of peaches onto the tailgate, tossed me one, and waved me off when I tried to pay him for it. The two of them watched as I ate it. The girl asked the man a question I didn't understand, and he shook his head. The peach wasn't ripe, but I told them it was good and tossed the pit into the high grass.

"You're not likely to get much business on this road," I said.

"Truck broke," he said, nodding at a snapped fan belt that lay on the asphalt like a dead bull snake.

I asked where they were from. "Monterrey," the man said, "Mexico."

"What are you doing up this way?"

"Apples."

The girl had climbed off the truck and was poking my front tire and pushing at the brake levers. I said, "I think she wants a ride." I hoisted her up by the arms onto the saddle.

"Too little, I think," the man said, but he saw that she was enjoying herself and he didn't stop me. Her arms weren't long enough to reach the handlebars, so she grabbed my arms with both hands.

The girl shouted something to the man, and he answered her in a whisper.

When he gave me a bag filled with plums and pears, I handed him a wad of bills from my pocket, and, as I did, saw one of the C-notes that Mr. Reed gave me sandwiched between the ones. I started to take it back, thought better of it, and pushed the top bill over with my thumb so that he could not see the one beneath.

He refused.

"Buy a new belt," I said, pressing the money into his palm. I waved bye-bye to the girl and rode away before he could count it.

I rode the next several miles no-handed, eating fruit out of the bag and trying to make up my mind about what I'd just done. The day might come when I would need the money. I also worried that I might have hurt the man's pride, that he might tear up the bill and come looking for me. Then I remembered the broken fan belt. Maybe he would use the money to fix the truck, then come looking for me. I saw a Western like that once.

About an hour before sunset, a wind picked up from the southeast. I was prepared to sleep on the ground, but not in the rain, and I turned south toward a town actually called Little Chicago, thinking I could find a motel. There were none and I rolled south, getting only a couple of miles before the skies opened.

Riding a bike in a rainstorm is like driving a convertible through a car wash. Your tires kick water and mud up in your face. The setting sun against the thunderclouds glowed a jaundiced yellow. I pedaled blind for miles, telling myself over and over that it couldn't rain this hard for long. And yet it did. For miles, I pushed on against sheets of water, seeing nothing but the wet asphalt as it passed beneath my front wheel.

I was concentrating so hard on not riding off the road that I nearly missed a drive-in root beer stand, hidden from view by a row of trees.

All the stalls were deserted except for a black Chevy pickup with monster tires parked on the opposite side of the service island. The rain beat a patter on the canopy. I pressed the button on a dented, orange intercom. When the waitress came out to take my order, the guy in the truck honked his horn. She gave him the finger. He threw the truck in reverse and hit the gas, kicking gravel everywhere. The girl ignored him, writing on a pad she held to a plastic tray with her thumb. She was sixteen, I guessed, and pretty, with brown hair tied in a ponytail sticking out of an orange visor, which was part of a uniform that didn't flatter her. The shirt was too tight across her chest and the shorts made her ass look big. "Wo jeez," she said when she saw me, "looks like someone got a little wet."

"You noticed," I said.

"Not much gets by me."

"Want to get me a hamburger and a float?"

"Please."   .

"Please."

She pretended to think about it. "Where you going to put it?" she said. "Trays go on the window."

"That your boyfriend?"

"Who?"

"Guy in the Chevy."

"I'm so sure," she said, and when she was gone I laid my bike on the narrow strip of pavement beneath the canopy, then took off my pack and T-shirt, which made a sucking sound. The girl returned propping a tray on her shoulder. "The manager says you got to put your shirt on. It's all the same to me but he says you got to put it on."

"It's wet," I said.

"Sorry," she said and made a face as I pulled it over my head. She said her name was Lois. She said she got off in fifteen minutes. She said, "I know a place where you can dry off."

I ate the hamburger and float as fast as I could swallow. The clouds were gone, and it had turned into a lush summer evening. I watched the traffic ease by on the highway. The pickup that had been at the stand when I pulled up soon returned. The driver leaned across the passenger seat to stare at me—I saw mirrored shades and a mustache—then sped off.

"Asshole," Lois said. She was standing over me, looking a lot better with her hair loose, her apron and visor in one hand and two cans of Pabst dangling from a plastic six pack holder in the other. "Come on," she said and led me through a stand of pine behind the drive-in to an old shed that listed so far on its foundation that I thought it would fall over when she pulled the door open.

Inside there was a trailer with an insecticide drum on back and a generator on wheels. The air smelled of turpentine and varnish. I left my bike just inside the door and followed Lois through a forest of empty fruit baskets. Lois lit a candle and dropped the beer and her work clothes onto an old mattress that was bare except for a ratty hunting blanket.

"You wouldn't have a cigarette in there?" she said, flopping on the mattress and pointing to the spot beside her where she wanted me to sit.

"Fact I do," I said. "If they're not soaked." I unzipped the pocket and saw that the waterproofing had held up pretty well. She sucked hard enough to put the match out and I had to strike another to light mine. "Here," she said, "ashtray," and handed me an empty sardine tin.

"You live here?"

"Sometimes," she said. "Where you from?"

"Up by Superior," I said. "I'm on my way to school in Madison."

"Prove it," she said.

"You'll have to take my word for it."

She looked at me out of the corner of her eye, trying to think up a question that would trip me up. "What's your wager?"

"Huh?"

"What are you wagering? My stepsister Sherlisse—she don't live with us—wagered in business down in Madison."

"Major," I said. "What's my major."

She didn't know what I was talking about. "Whatever," she said.

"History," I said.

"Get out of here. You know all that?"

"Not yet."

As she thought up her next question, I thought I heard the big-tired truck slowing on the highway and waited to hear it turn onto the gravel. Then it was gone.

"Who's the guy in the pickup?" I asked.

"Just some guy," she said. She took a sip of her beer and then set it down so she could pull her shirt over her head. Her breasts swelled in a sweat-stained bra that was a size too small as she reached behind her and undid the fastener. It snapped free with the sound of a rubber band breaking. "I used to go with his brother when this guy was away in the Coast Guard."

"So?"

"So I got a little girl. After I broke it off with Wayne's—that's this guy—brother, I got pregnant with this other guy, C.C.—who's not very nice."

"What's the C.C. for?"

"Nothing, I don't think," she said.

She leaned back against the wall and propped the beer on the bare skin of her belly. She waited before finishing her story to see if I was going to kiss her and when I didn't she continued. "Anyway Randy—that's Wayne's brother—Wayne tells Randy or I guess Randy tells Wayne that he wanted to have a kid with me and then Wayne comes to me and says if I was going to be so stupid, how come I couldn't be stupid with Randy."

"How come you couldn't?"

She thought about it. "He never asked," she said. "And now Wayne keeps coming around and saying he's going to get C.C. only he doesn't know what he looks like because C.C. lives over in Marathon City and don't come around here." She ground her cigarette into the tin, though there was more than half of it left. "Probably shouldn't be smoking if I'm pregnant, but I don't smoke 'em all the way down."

"I thought you said you had the kid."

She took my hand and poked the index finger into her belly. "C.C. wants a boy," she said. "Someone who'll look up to him since there's no one on earth who would." Then she lifted my hand to her tit and held it there. Her skin was cool, and I didn't pull away. "Not bad for having a kid and one on the way," she said and lay on her back to slide out of her shorts.

"Nope."

She rolled onto her hands and knees, her breasts hanging down to her elbows and soft, brown fur peeking from between her thighs, and she said, "Don't you want to get out of those wet clothes?"

I undressed and lay on my back because I didn't want her that way. She curled into my arms and her breathing got heavier as I moved my hand down her stomach, until I realized that I didn't want her at all. I didn't know if it was Wayne or C.C. or the thought of making it with somebody's mother, but I was sure. "Is it okay if we just sleep together?"

"Sure silly," she said and slid her hand between my legs.

"No, I mean *sleep* together."

She must have understood because I felt her breath and heart slow almost as the words were out of my mouth. We fell asleep under the blanket, her with her back turned, me with my arms around her. When I woke up once in the night at the sound of a car on the highway she was still there. When I woke again in the morning, she wasn't. On the table was a quart of root beer in a plastic jug and a note written in pencil on the back of a guest check that said, "See ya, Lois," with eyes and a smile drawn in the *o,* in the dot above the *i,* and in the lower arch of the *s.* Like three witnesses to a crime.

Considering how far I had ridden the day before, I felt awfully good as I snaked the strap on my bag through the handle of the jug and got ready to ride out. It wasn't long past dawn. The shutters of the stand were closed. For Lois's sake, I hurried to the highway before I was seen, though I doubt she would have cared if the whole town knew. At that hour of the morning there was nothing on the road but farm traffic and eighteen-wheelers. I hated the idea of sharing the road with them on a hazy morning, but I had a good ten miles before I could pick up a quieter road. Just south of Little Chicago was a sign that said, Marathon City 9 and I figured to get that far before stopping for breakfast.

I accelerated to pass a tractor, gave the farmer a wave, and veered back to the shoulder before a tanker rumbled past, throwing dust in my eyes. As it disappeared over the rise ahead of me I saw a second truck heading toward me and saw that it was the truck I'd seen at the stand the night before. As he passed, the driver stared through his shades, though the sun was not out yet. He hit the brakes when he recognized me and I heard him squealing through a U-turn. Pointlessly I sped up, sprinting to the top of the hill. The pickup sped by and skidded to a stop in front of me.

The first thing I saw of the man was a black cowboy boot stepping from the cab. Then he was standing in front of me and I saw he was a good half-foot taller than me. I stopped, straddling my bike, and said, "What's up, Wayne?"

He stepped forward and tagged me with a fist to the chest that knocked me on my ass. Then he stood over me, his shades reflecting the stunned look on my face. He raised his fist when I tried to get up to show me what I'd get if I did. He said, "Hear this, C.C., you shit, anyone can have sex, but it takes a man to be a father." Then he got back in his truck and drove away, leaving me lying in the road in a pool of root beer.

Aching in my chest and in the tailbone where I hit the ground, I dragged myself to the side of the road where I sat in the grass until the tractor I passed earlier rattled up the road and stopped a few feet short of the cracked jug.

"Have a spill?" the man asked and then the humor of his question struck him and he laughed. "What'd you hit?"

"Not sure," I said.

"Where you heading?"

"Down to the Dells."

He looked up the road as if he was trying to see my destination on the horizon.

"I'm going as far as Marathon," he said. "Throw your bike on back."

"That's okay," I said, testing the shoulder on the side I got hit. "I'm okay."

He stared for a minute, then climbed down from the cab. "Get on," he said. He lifted my bike off the road, straightened the handlebars, and wheeled it back to his trailer where he tossed it onto a hay bale. "You're not okay."

Because there was something in the way he said it that made me believe him, I climbed up and sat on the fender.

"Kind of late in the season for the Dells, isn't it?" he said, shouting to be heard over the engine.

"Soonest I could get away," I said. "Only been once. My dad, my uncle and aunt, and my cousins and I stopped on our way up from Chicago. Truth is, I'm on my way down to the university." The whole while I talked, the farmer nodded his head, or at least I thought he was until I saw my own head bobbing in the rearview mirror from the vibration of the engine and I realized he hadn't heard a word I said.

He stopped at a crossroads north of Marathon and cut the engine. "You'll want to head down that way," he said, still shouting, though I could hear him well enough. "The highway just gets busier from here on south. You can take that road as far as Junction City."

"Thanks," I said and tried to give him a couple of bucks from my pocket but he wouldn't look at it.

"Try to keep your behind on the seat," he said as he rattled off.

Around two o'clock in the afternoon, I reached Wisconsin Rapids, where I bought a hot dog from a vendor at a softball tournament and leaned against the outfield fence to eat it. I picked a team to root for, Ed's Fiberglass, only to see them fall behind by fourteen runs in a sloppily played fifth inning.

West of Port Edwards I picked up Wood County Highway G and followed that south along the river. It was pretty country and flat in relation to the hills that rose on both sides of the valley. Late in the afternoon I reached Mauston where G met highways 12, 58, and 82. After thinking it over I took 12, which turned out to be a mistake because of the traffic. I backtracked to 82 and followed that due east until I picked up the county roads again. The detour cost me an hour and meant I would sleep another night on the road.

It was getting late when I rolled into the Dells. I looked for the attractions that I remembered from when we had come through thirteen years earlier.

Twelve years and a summer later, King Cole's Castle was closed down for the season. And the robots from Robot World, which I had remembered as space-aged, were galvanized tin and PVC tubing, and looked, slumped powerless on their stands in the dark, kind of ghastly—dormant but not benign, like a race of zombies waiting for the signal to wake.

Neon vacancy signs were lit all along Highway 16, but the sky was clear, so I coasted out of town and found a good place to camp in a dense patch of wood overlooking an amusement park. It was closed like everything else and the lights were turned off, except for a single bulb on the ticket booth beneath the Ferris wheel.

I set up camp beneath an oak tree, where I could see the amusement park and the road to the south. Using my bike, my air pump, and my jacket, I fashioned a tent, then sat down to smoke a cigarette and wait for dark, which came fast.

Hoping to find a pear from the Mexican's truck, I rummaged through my bag. There were none left. I came out instead with my worn copy of *Johnny Tremain*, dug around some more until I found the flashlight, opened the book to the first page, and heard my Aunt Berthe's voice, "'On rocky islands gulls voke. Time to be about der biss-ness.' Like so," she'd say and point to the pencil drawing of the gulls.

Uncle Karl and Aunt Berthe, but especially Aunt Berthe, took the job of turning us into Americans very seriously, too seriously to suit my mother, who didn't like having to sleep on a cot and didn't like it that my Pop was allowed to work with Uncle Karl at the butcher shop while she had to stay home. Berthe spoke to us in English, except for the many words she didn't know, for which she lapsed into her native Frisian dialect. And every evening she kept us at the table after dinner for our lessons in practical conversation.

"Mr. Butcher," she would say, with a nod at my uncle on the couch, in case we didn't get it, "I fould like four sausages." She would wave four fingers, "four, fo-were." Once we had learned to shop, she taught us useful weather conversation. "Today fas dry, but tomorrow fill rain."

After a half-hour of these drills, we read. She gave my father an English version of the Bible, which he was to read. It was an assignment that would occupy the next twenty years of his life and one that did him no good at all.

Berthe made my mother copy recipes from the food ads in her women's magazines. She sat at the table, legs crossed in the blue jeans that my aunt let her wear only in the house, a pencil in her teeth, her foot bouncing up and down, and her lip turned upward to blow her bangs out of her eyes. My mother never could take much of this without getting exasperated. She didn't like the way Aunt Berthe bossed her around or the way Pop always took sides with his sister-in-law.

While my parents got on the best they could in the dining room, Aunt Berthe read to me on the sofa, her arm around me, squeezing my head into her breast each time she turned a page. She read me many books, all meant to teach a lesson to a boy beginning life in America, but *Johnny Tremain* was the book out of all these that I liked the best. It was about a silversmith in the American Revolution. He is apprenticed to the Lapham family, who all like him because he is good-looking and talented at silversmithing for a boy of fourteen. His problem is that he is vain, so vain that he picks on the other boys and doesn't see the payback coming until it is too late. Johnny burns his hand on a cracked mold that Dove (the dumbest and laziest of the Lapham apprentices) gave him on purpose. The Laphams, who liked him so well before, throw him out, and he has to find his own way in the world.

I'm sure Berthe picked this book to show me that there was a lot about Johnny's life that was like mine. Like him, I lived in a house that wasn't my own, like him, I lived with girls who bugged me, and like him, Aunt Berthe hoped, I'd be a working man of good character because she believed it was the duty of Germans who came to this country to be good workers, not soldiers or policemen.

Setting the book face down on the grass, I retrieved the weed and papers from my shaving kit. The pot was the last of an ounce we got from Alvin Deere at the beginning of the summer. He said it was Columbian, but we suspected it came from farther north. It's funny how much importance we attached to such things, especially since we had no idea what we were talking about. I lit the end with the Zippo, and held the smoke in until I coughed. For the first time since I'd been on the road, I felt a sense of confidence and purpose. I felt as if I had mastered a difficult undertaking and proved myself worthy.

Once the last of the joint had burned down to a roach, I trained the flashlight on the book again. Since the first time my Aunt read it to me, I had always skipped the last chapter "A Man Can Stand Up," in which Johnny's best friend Rab is killed. I skipped it because I didn't like books that ended that way and because I liked Rab better than I liked Johnny. I liked Rab for seeing things clearly and I hated it that he died.

But I read the chapter again that night and saw it wasn't that bad. Rab dies, shot by the Redcoats, but not before he gives his musket to Johnny, who figures out for the first time what Rab knew all along. As I was reading, I thought about Aunt Berthe and then about my father and Grey, and I wondered about what everyone was doing back home—Pop asleep in his chair, the Reeds watching TV, and Grey and Callie out riding around.

There was the sound of a breaking twig in the woods. I switched off the flashlight and lay flat. All night long the woods had been alive with noises. Branches and twigs had fallen from the trees with the regularity of a light rain, but this had been a footstep. As I lay still, I heard a second and then a third, each closer than the last. There had been a lot of murders in this county (every one of which made its way onto page three of the

Star), and that's what I was thinking about as I clenched the flashlight in my fist and shouted, "Who's there?"

No one answered. The footsteps stopped. "Who's there?" I yelled again, and again no one answered, but the footsteps resumed, only a few yards away, and I felt a chill as I realized that whatever it was was not afraid of me. Knowing I was cornered and hoping for the element of surprise, I charged forward, switched on the light, and saw first the yellow eyes, then the white tail as the skunk turned its rear end toward me.

Luckily, it was not as scared as I was. It waddled away, annoyed, but not enough to waste any of his stink on me. Feeling the need for some kind of atonement for my cowardice, I opened *Johnny Tremain* to its back cover and with a ballpoint pen wrote the following principles:

1. I will be loyal to my father.
2. I will be a worthy representative of Zimmermann Cycles.
3. I will not do anything to prove Jack wrong in his trust of me or otherwise embarrass him.
4. I will be loyal to Grey and Callie.
5. I will not be afraid.

When I finished I read what I'd written and felt wise and still a little high and didn't remember falling asleep. I woke at dawn sore in the legs and tired. With nothing to eat for breakfast, I broke camp and began the last day's ride. There was not much farther to go, sixty miles, seventy tops. Still I felt like I'd never make it. I rolled onto Highway 18 convinced that I was making a serious mistake, that I was destined to be the failure Pop thought I was.

The sun had just cleared the hills to the east when I reached the Wisconsin River and the ferry at Merrimac. It was a whole lot smaller than the boats back home and connected to the far bank by a cable. The ride was dull and yet by the time we reached the terminal, and I saw for the first time the roads I would get to know very well, I felt much better about things. The air was cool and the sun came and went behind a screen of fast-floating clouds.

At Waunakee—"The Only Waunakee in the World" if you believe the sign—I picked up County Q and followed that south toward the windward side of Lake Mendota. At the junction of County M there was a long, steady grade. Cresting that hill, I saw on the horizon the mirage of a city. It lay beyond a blue lake. In the center, the dome of the capitol, colored ivory in a shaft of sunlight that split the clouds, stood on a hill above a squat skyline. Nothing about the vision looked real, but I rode toward it anyway, trusting the map.

PART II
ROBOT WORLD

ROSEWALTER

The courtyard bustled with human traffic: kids wrestling suit-cases through doorways, mothers cradling electronics. There were rows of bike racks filled with rows of bikes, locked at odd angles, a comforting sight, but the obvious carelessness and neglect with which they were arranged convinced me that I wouldn't leave mine there. The door beneath the stone arch bearing the name Rosewalter was a glossy brown and tacky to the touch, as I found out when I planted my hand on it, just below the Wet Paint sign.

The door opened on a second set of doors, which in turn opened onto a lobby of black-and-white-tiled floors. Bulletin boards hung on two walls, bare except for the odd thumbtack and the silhouettes of flyers faded on the cork by the sun. The maritime smell of fresh varnish, and the walls with a fresh coat of crisp white, obscured the traces of the last class, I supposed, and left a blank canvas for the new one.

Two guys came jogging down the stairs carrying tennis rackets. "How's it going?" one of them asked me with such familiarity that I thought I must've known him from somewhere.

"*Great,*" I said, but not until after they were out the door, the word echoing up the stairwell.

At the third floor, I popped through another set of doors, with the word *Neough* above them on a wooden placard, and followed the numbers on down the hallway to 304, the ratcheting sound of the bike's freewheel clucking assurance.

The room looked more cramped and bare than it did in the picture in the brochure. It was half the size of my room at home. The mattresses were stained and sagged. The desks were small. There were two closets and two short, pine dressers just inside the door. I opened the desk drawer. It was empty except for a concert ticket, torn in half. Some memento the previous resident had wanted to save but didn't think enough of to take with him. I threw it in the gray metal trash can on my way to the window. The fire escape was tagged with a red hexagonal sign that said "Stop! Alarm Will Sound."

I tried the mattress on the east wall. The springs shrieked so I dropped my bag on the other one. From the halls I heard shouting and a collision and thought about how different all this would've been if Grey had been there. Probably we would have dropped all our junk on the floor and gone to find Callie and then all gone out to have a look around, see this new place and get some idea of what it was going to ask of us. Then I thought about how if Grey and Callie were here I would always be hanging out with them and not meeting new kids. I thought about Mr. Reed. If I had asked him if it was for the best that I was down here by myself, I had no doubt he'd have said yes.

I got antsy just sitting there, waiting for something to happen, thinking about everything I didn't have and feeling like a refugee or a war orphan or something, so I struck out into the hall, down the stairs past guys and their parents hauling stuff in and out of the elevators in rolling canvas bins. It seemed like everyone had both a mom and a dad with them. I tried to picture Pop trailing behind me with a lamp in his hand.

Outside I walked along the drive and down the first street I came to, which curved eastward and up a hill that wasn't high but was steep and I felt in my legs the exhaustion of three days on the road. At the top of the hill, shaded on three sides by maples was a brick building with a domed roof that I recognized as the observatory from the brochures, though it looked better in person. Turning north, I could see the entire lake, which was strange to me. I felt that a lake that you could see all of at once was—as nice as this one might have looked in the sun—was, well, inferior to Superior. But there were more sails than you'd see in a similar stretch of Superior, and the green water and white caps against the red bluffs on the far shore were a pretty sight.

I turned the tarnished knob to the door of the observatory, expecting that it would be locked. But it wasn't. I opened it, stepping into the most amazing room I had ever been in. The curved walls were covered with bookshelves from the polished wood floors to a brass rail that ran the circumference of the room below the iron railing of a walkway that circled around at the height of the domed metal roof. The functionality of the space reminded me of Grey's sail loft, a structure devoted to its purpose, and I thrilled at the thought that the whole university could be made up of such buildings.

I didn't see anyone inside and thought about calling out so nobody would think I was busting in or anything, but it was as quiet as a library and I didn't want to disturb the silence. Walking along the shelves, I scanned the spines of the books, mostly reference works, guides and charts, with Roman numerals as titles. I followed the circle of the room to a rolling ladder that was anchored to the brass rail above my head. I climbed the ladder and found myself on the walkway around the dome, and followed it until I got to the narrow rectangular opening through which the telescope looked. The telescope itself was a remarkable thing, at least twenty feet long. It was rotated by an elaborate mechanism of cogs and pulleys that looked very old but impeccably maintained. I stood on my toes and looked backward down the lens into blackness, gray black concentrating into a center of pure black. I turned and poked my head out of the opening and saw pretty much the same view I had from outside only higher, and then somebody from below yelled out, "Hey."

Looking down, I saw a lady standing in the center of the room, shading her eyes to look up at me. She lowered her hand from her face and I saw that she was wearing glasses on a chain. "You'd better come down from there," she said.

I did and could tell from the change in her attitude that I'd scared her, but she wasn't scared anymore. "You're really not supposed to be in here," she said, and as I got closer I saw that she was younger than I had thought at first, quite a bit younger.

"Sorry," I said. Up close, she was cute in the kind of way that people who don't try to make themselves cute can be.

"Are you a student?" she asked, pushing her glasses back onto her nose to put me in focus.

"Going to be," I said, one of those times when you kick yourself, because I could've just said yes.

"Do you need something signed?"

"Signed?"

"Your registration form? You're an Astronomy major?"

"No ma'am," I said.

"Physics?"

"History."

For some reason she laughed at that. "Well that's good, too, isn't it?"

"I hope so." I looked around. "Do you run this place?"

Again she laughed. "No," she said, "I'm a graduate student." Her laugh was getting on my nerves, but then I didn't know what a graduate student was so maybe I wasn't as smart as I thought I was. I think she could tell she'd hurt my feelings because she said, "Do you want to see it move?"

The truth was I was feeling kind of dumb and wanted to leave, but she'd been nice not to call the cops or throw me out so I said, "Sure."

We climbed a narrow stairway that actually spiraled up through the mechanism to a platform with what looked like a tractor seat bolted right in front of the eyepiece. "Sit there," she said. I did. She turned a key that unlocked a lever which she pulled. The entire room seemed to move. She gave me a look like you would to a kid going on a fair ride for the first time, half "isn't this great?" and half "don't be afraid," which annoyed me because I was neither scared nor particularly excited to be on the thing. She kept her eye on a pointer at the base of the assembly that tracked a series of numbers and dashes. "We use the coordinates on the floor to orient the lens in the direction of the object we want to look at. After that we adjust the azimuth of the cylinder using this lever here. Nowadays," she said, "this is usually done by computer, but this is more fun, don't you think?" She pushed the lever forward and the platform stopped. "Now look through there and tell me what you see." I put my eye to the eyepiece and saw nothing but empty sky, shimmering and bobbing in magnification.

"Nothing," I said.

"You're looking in the direction of the Crab Nebula and yet you can't see anything. Do you know why that is?"

"Because it's not dark out?"

"Exactly. Come in any Wednesday night when it's not cloudy and you can look at anything you want."

She told me her name was Elise.

When I got back to the room the door was open, and I heard voices coming from inside. I stopped at the doorway and saw my future roommate, Dennis Shipman, for the first time: sitting on the bare bunk between his parents, learning how to write a check. He was a small, pale kid, as short as Pop and skinnier, with skin like onion paper and vanilla-yellow hair combed in a part as straight as any line segment.

"No, no," Ship's father said. "Don't write 'dollars.' It says dollars on the check over here so you don't have to do that. Cross it out."

They didn't notice me, so I leaned against the doorjamb and waited for them to finish.

"He can't cross it out," said his mom. "He has to write another one."

"He can't write another," his father said. "They cost money."

"He's got to write another," she said. "We can't cash that one after he's scribbled it all up."

The father looked at the check and said, "Write another one."

I knocked then. Three raps with the back of my hand. Ship jumped to his feet like I'd caught him abusing himself, and his parents watched him in case he tripped and busted something before they turned to see who was at the door.

"304?" I asked.

"Excuse me," the mother said, probably thinking, the way I must have looked, that I'm a deliveryman.

"Room 304?" I asked again, more unsure than the first time, because now they had me wondering too. His mother took a blue piece of paper out of her purse and scanned the page.

"Zimmermann," I said, "Tom," before she could get to my name.

"Yes," the father said. "Dennis. It's Tom," and made a gesture that told us we were supposed to meet in the middle of the room. They watched him walk toward me and shake my hand as though they had practiced this before, too, like with the checkbook.

"There you go, you two," the father said.

"Yes, that's right," said the mother.

"Where you from, Tom?" asked Mr. Shipman.

"Here in the state, sir. Up by Superior."

"Cranberry country," he said, so loud I swear to God I jumped.

"Yes, sir, I think you can get them up there," I said.

"In the store," his mother said, standing and sorting her keys between her fingers.

The father was not in the same hurry. "Bet you're a beer drinker," he said. "I know a place."

"You can't drink up here, Dad," Dennis said, though that wasn't true.

"In my day, the RAs would turn a blind eye," Mr. Shipman said. The mother looked at me. "Some other time," she said.

I would find out later that Mr. Shipman had done pretty well for himself in bowling equipment and Mrs. S. was the trophy that comes along with that kind of success. "We remember our years in college a little too well," she said, as she steered Mr. Shipman toward the door. I caught a whiff of her perfume on the way by. It smelled sweet and European.

"What was the rush?" I asked him after they were gone.

"She doesn't like to fuss," Ship said. "You know they got racks for your bike downstairs."

"Not for this one," I said. "It's invaluable. I practically sleep with it."

He sat on the bed that didn't squeak and asked, "Which one do you want?"

"The one you're on is fine with me."

He stared at me, then got up and moved to the other bunk without saying anything about it. The springs moaned when he sat down.

Opening the top drawer of one of the dressers I found Ship's boxers folded and arranged according to color, light to dark. I dumped the contents of my bag in the other drawer.

"Is that all you brought?" he asked.

"It's all I have." I lit a cigarette.

"Can't smoke in here," he said.

"Who says?"

"It's in here," he said, holding up his copy of the residence manual. When I reached for it he pulled it away with a smile on his face and I figured out he made it up.

"Liar," I said and blew smoke in his face.

He threw the book at me. It fluttered and fell at my feet. I knocked him over a chair and then we were rolling on the floor, him clawing at my face, until I got his shirt up over his head and pinned his arms behind his back.

"Quit it," he said.

"Give," I said.

And he seemed just about to, when there was someone yelling, "Hey, hey, hey," and tugging at my collar, pulling me backward into the air and away from Shipman's throat. Thinking I was getting ganged up on I spun around ready to slug whoever it was and saw a round, fleshy head sticking out of an enormous white T-shirt. "Get him off me, Howie," Dennis said. The fat guy looked at the paper he was holding and said, "Zimmermann?"

"Yeah," I said. "Why?"

"Howie Klug, your resident assistant," he said. "What are you doing to Shipman?"

"Nothing," I said.

"Not much," Dennis said.

Howie glared at him. "Let me give you two a quick heads-up," he said. "You know what's sure to get an RA written up around here, surer than if some guy from his floor jumps out a window? That's having to switch guys out of their room 'cause they can't get along. You know what happens to me if I have to switch two residents?"

"What?" Dennis asked. He'd gotten his shirt off his face and was clawing at the furniture to get to his feet.

"I don't know," Howie said. "This has been my floor for three years and I never had to switch anybody. Whatever's up with you two, work it out, and if you can't work it out, seek professional help. Get unpacked, make your beds, and turn in."

"I haven't got any sheets," I said.

"What? Why haven't you got sheets?"

"I kind of had to travel light," I said.

Howie cussed under his breath and left but came back about an hour later with a folded stack of bed linens of different colors and tossed them on a chair while Dennis was dropping socks into drawers and slamming them shut. "I asked around the upperclassmen," Howie said. "You'll have to give them back when you get your own. The sheets go to Johnson in twelve, the pillowcases to Larsen in nine, and the blanket's Anderson's over in Frautzer."

Dennis didn't talk much for the rest of the night, though he didn't have the will to ignore me altogether. Over the next weeks, me and Ship—as I and eventually everyone on the floor came to call him—worked out a truce. I agreed to smoke in the room only when he was gone and then only by an open window. In exchange, I reserved the right to never talk to him again unless I felt like it. Of course, I didn't tell him about that part of it. He believed he had won total victory, when the truth was I violated my end of the bargain whenever I felt like it and at the same time never let him forget the power of the silences I imposed upon us. As I did that first night, lying awake in the dark in our new room, listening to Dennis Shipman cry himself to sleep.

REPUBLIC

The day you pay your tuition is the day you're on your own. No one to tell you where you're supposed to be or when you're supposed to be there. You can major in Modern Dance or Molecular Biology, make dean's list or flunk out, as far as anyone knows or cares. That kind of freedom can be welcome, if you grew up with one person in your life who is always telling you what to do. It can also be intimidating—if you're used to one person always telling you what to do. Especially when you're walking west toward the edge of campus for course registration with no clue of what to do when you get there.

Shipper, red-eyed from the night before but also anxious for me to forget the fight ever happened, wore a canary-yellow Lacoste tennis shirt and yellow plaid Bermudas, with matching watchband. He had, by my count, three of them, the watchbands, in patterns of blue, red, and yellow, and two pairs of shorts in each color. If that had been the worst I could've said about him we might have become friends. But it was not. And what was worse was enough to make me despise him. Ship was a man who understood that he could get what he wanted provided he was careful not to want more than he could get. In my case, all he wanted was for me to like him, which was reason enough to not like him.

The Stock Pavilion to which we were to report was just that, a stock pavilion, a low structure of stone and wood with the interior shaped like a rodeo ring and a floor of dirt and sawdust. A network of ropes directed us toward a row of tables with letters of the alphabet above them. When the clock struck 9:00, the line surged forward. Some kid let out a loud "Moo," and there was laughter and then another moo from somewhere down the row, and then everyone was mooing.

By virtue of being in the relatively empty Zs I moved faster than the Shipper's Ss and didn't see him for the rest of the day. At the first table I gave my name and was given in return a large form on heavy paper stock and sent to a second table. At the second table a guy stamped the corner of my form with a red seal and sent me to a third table. At the third table the woman removed the stamped corner of my form along a perforation and placed that card in an indexed file in front of her. She sent me to a fourth table where the guy stamped a different part of the form with a stamp that looked a lot like the first and said, "Now go to your assignment committees."

"Where are they?" I asked.

"Which one?"

"All of them."

He said, "They're listed in your timetable," like it was something I should have known.

"Oh," I said, because it probably was.

These days you just call a computer and you're registered for classes, but it was not all that long ago that registration resembled a scavenger hunt. Once you got your form you had to go to the assignment committee for each class. Each assignment committee was in the department for that class. In the landscape of the university, each of those departments was in its own building, each building like a sovereign country.

The first class I signed up for was trigonometry. Math was in Van Vleck Hall, a modern high-rise at the end of Charter Street. This Indian guy—Georg, by his name tag, without an *e*—sat at a table in front of a blackboard with the words "Freshman Math Assignments" on it. He glanced at my form and said, "Do you have the prerequisites?"

"The what?"

"Have you completed the classes you needed to complete and received at minimum the lowest grade you are permitted to receive in order to register for Trigonometry?"

I looked him in the face and said, "Yes, I have." It turned out that I had, but at the time I thought I was lying, which was a kick. He stamped my form and turned back to the equations on the page in front of him. "Are you my teacher?" I asked.

Again he looked up from his book, stared for a moment, and said—with obvious relief—"I will not be your teacher."

I left Georg thinking that I wasn't going to like math much.

While I waited for the elevator I had something of an inspiration. Reasoning that my schoolwork at high school was going to pale in comparison with what I had to put in now, it occurred to me that there was nothing wrong with hedging at least one bet. So I registered for first-year German, figuring I'd keep how much of the language I knew secret until I had to use it for the test.

Having worked that out in my head, I was feeling pretty proud of myself as I walked from the modern Van Vleck to the relic Bascom Hall to sign up for my history course.

When I told the girl at the table of the History Department assignment committee that I needed History 105, Survey of History for Majors, she pointed at the blackboard behind her. "Closed," she said.

"What does that mean?"

"It's full. No more room."

"I think I have to take it," I said.

"Let me see." She crinkled her nose and scanned the page I handed her, shrugged, and handed it back to me. "You're right, you do."

"So I can sign up?"

"Next semester."

"You're telling me I'm a history major but I can't take a history class?" She stared at me as if to show there was nothing she could do, and then I guess she must have taken pity on me because she said, "You know, I think the professor might actually be in his office. You might ask him for a waiver."

I walked down a corridor of checked tile until I found the door with his name on it, ducked my head in and saw a man in a sleeveless white T-shirt, large shorts, and sandals with black socks. He had his feet on the desk and held the string to the window shade to his nose.

"What am I doing?" he asked in English-accented English.

"Sir?"

"Bring your powers of inductive reasoning to bear."

"It looks like you're trying to yank the shade off the window."

He considered the shade as though what I'd said had made him think about what he was doing for the first time. "Indeed it does. However, what sense would that make? Why would a sane man pull the shade off a window of a public building with the sun as blinding as it can be at this time of year? He would not. Therefore, although your observation is keen, your hypothesis is flawed. Would you care to try again?"

"You're trying to pull the shade up."

"Good, yes, and?"

"And you want the light to come in."

"What? Oh yes of course, but no. Perhaps the question was not clear. What I hoped to be able to do was to raise or lower the shade from my chair here. I got up to lower the shade and noticed the cord was rather long and wondered if it would be possible to operate the shade without getting up. I have determined empirically that it is not. Why are you here?"

"I need my thing signed."

"Which thing is that?"

"My form. See I need 105 for Majors and they said it was full and they told me I couldn't get in unless you signed my form saying I could."

"*They* did?"

"Yes."

"And who would these sinister forces be?"

"The assignment committee."

"What, would you say, makes you worthy of such a dispensation?"

"I got a scholarship."

"Ah, did you now?"

"Yes sir, the Ida Singer. It's a—"

"I was the judge this year."

"Then maybe you read my paper—"

"It was an honorary position. In an historical sense, what are your interests?"

"Like do you mean what history do I like best?"

"Exactly."

"I don't know. I like the old stuff more than the newer stuff. I come from up north. I like that, the trappers and the Indians."

"That's grand," he said. "It's a fine thing for a student of history to take an interest in where he's from, provided."

"Provided?"

"Provided you understand the difference between history and folklore."

"So does that mean you'll sign my form?"

"What's one more student more or less, eh?" I slid the form across the desk. He signed it, like a ballplayer signing an autograph, scrawling quickly and smiling as he slid the form back across the desk. Then he motioned me closer and took my right hand in his and looked through narrowed eyes at my fingernails. "Did you know that during the French Revolution the Jacobins went around looking at people's hands to see how dirty they were?"

"No, I didn't, sir. Why?"

"To determine whether or not they would be guillotined."

"Which was good, dirty or clean?"

"Dirty," he said and winked.

"Thanks," I said.

He pointed to the window. "Pull that shade down on your way out, would you?"

The next afternoon Howie got the guys from the floor and the girls from downstairs in Kleine. We tossed caps and shirts on the grass to mark the boundaries and we chose up teams for touch football and had a great time of it. There had to be at least twenty on each side, way too many for a proper game. Play got rough among the boys, with everyone smacking into each other. As the afternoon went into the evening, the game took a more definite form. People left, the teams reformed, and the personalities and skills of the players revealed themselves. I caught a couple of passes, once getting knocked hard to the ground and came up with grass stains and a split lip, feeling like I'd passed a test. Shipper took a beating. Some of the guys took it as their personal duty to flatten him whenever he got close. Ship took his beating like a man, though it was clear he wasn't having any fun. Finally some of the girls took pity on him— "Come on, guys, quit it."—helping him up, brushing the grass off his shirt, which would have brought humiliation on your average young man of eighteen, but Ship was not your average young man of eighteen.

The game broke up when it was too dark to see. Somebody got a broken nose and had to be taken up to the health center with a T-shirt pressed to his face. The rest of us limped back to our rooms smelling of sweat and dirt.

On the way up to the room, I saw Ship sitting in the TV lounge with a baggie of ice on his eye. "Hey," I said.

"Hey," he said.

"You did good out there," I told him.

"Did I?"

"Sure."

He made a face like he didn't believe me. "Howie shouldn't let them just hit people whenever they feel like it."

"I guess nobody meant anything. You coming up?"

"I'm staying down here."

"Good thinking," I said, "maybe some of those Kleine girls'll come through. They love a man with a black eye."

He lifted the ice off his face to look at me through a half-closed lid. "You think?"

"I know it."

With Ship downstairs, I called Pop as soon as I got into the room. The phone rang a couple of dozen times before someone picked it up. It was Trudy. "Hello?" she said.

"Hello? Is Ernst Zimmermann there, please?" I said, like that, because I didn't recognize her voice right off and I thought maybe I had a wrong number.

"Tom? Honey," the voice said, "it's Trudy Schmidt. How are you doing?"

I flopped on Ship's bed and twirled the phone cord with my finger. "Good, I guess. Can I speak to Pop?"

"Let me see if he's around—" There's a long silence and I'm thinking where does she think he's going to be if he invited her over. "He's not, honey, can I have him call you?" she said, and I knew she was lying for him.

"That's okay," I said. "I'll try again."

Well, if that wasn't a kick in the teeth. In fact, I thought I'd trade places right now with Ship sitting down there with the ice on his face. I couldn't tell what made me madder, that I had to talk to Trudy or that Pop wouldn't talk to me. Maybe, I figured, he was finding out how hard it was to keep the shop going on his own and that had him pissed off. One thing was sure, I wasn't going to call him again. I called Grey's house and got to talk to everybody.

Agnes answered. "What are the students like?"

"Kind of all different."

Jack said, "Make us proud, son."

Grey said, "Hey, fuckface."

Callie said, "Bring me a sweatshirt."

Dewar Dooley's class met in a three-hundred-seat lecture hall of flaking white walls and high windows that on cold days were fogged by the steam that leaked from the corroded radiators. Knowing it was going to be full, I showed up a good fifteen minutes early to an empty room, took a seat up front figuring the better to hear, and sat pretending to read until it was time for class to start. When the hour struck, the seats around me were still empty and I thought maybe I had the wrong room, until I looked over my shoulder and saw every seat from two rows behind me on back filled. I was going to get up and move but then Dooley came in and crossed the dais to the lectern, and I was left sitting stupidly alone. Even from the front row, he looked small, standing in front of the map of the world that stretched from one wall to the other. He tapped the microphone and two speakers hanging on each end of the front wall squelched.

"Can you hear me in the back?" he asked, his breath rumbling through the woofers.

"We can hear you in Milwaukee," some kid shouted and the floor rumbled with laughter.

"Growing up in Galway," he began, "there was a sign scrawled in a drunken hand on the wall of the pub in my town that said, 'Will the last man off for America please turn out the lights.' One by one they left, the men of our town. I had no desire to go, until I came to realize I had even less desire to stay. That was twenty years ago—stowed away on a hay barge at the age of seventeen, to tell the truth of it, just to see what all the fuss was. As you might imagine, I held the States in low regard. You seemed an unnecessarily hard country to an immigrant boy. Well, here I am still."

Dooley never read or looked at a note card and ignored the chapters assigned in the syllabus altogether. His lectures (like that first one on the Rise of European Puritanism) jerked from one event to another. This country's history, which in the hands of Mrs. Furst, my fifth-grade teacher, was a storybook that stretched heroically from the day the first Furst set foot on the New World, was transformed by Dooley into a bloodied quilt of bad ideas and great delusions, all leading to vast catastrophes, which themselves changed absolutely nothing.

It was like being in church, listening to a man tell stories that had no clear point.

After class, as the hall emptied, I passed Dooley at the stair leading down from the dais. He stood listening to some student who wanted him to read a paper he'd written. "The part about the hay barge wasn't true, was it?" I asked him.

He looked up from the paper like I'd reminded him of something he had to do. "Zimmer?" he said.

"Zimmermann."

"What was your question?"

"I said the part about the hay barge, you made that up."

"Why would you presume that?"

"Well, I was thinking who's going to pay to haul hay from Ireland when you've got so much of it here."

He raised an eyebrow, as though he was trying to decide how to answer.

"I didn't mean anything by it. I just thought you might be putting us on."

"Right you are," he paused. "Zimmermann."

"Sir," I said.

"What do you do for money?"

I didn't know what he was getting at. "I have a nest egg."

"Then never mind."

"What?"

"I have an opening for work-study. But if you're fixed."

"I'm not," I said, "fixed. I mean who couldn't stand to make a little money?"

That night, I called Callie and Grey when I got home to tell them about Dooley's class and the job and everything. We talked for hours on the phone that night and the next and almost every night for weeks. That was until the school sent a $300 phone bill to my home address. Pop opened it, hit the ceiling, and told Jack, who, Callie said, was similarly steamed because the Reeds' bill was just as big. Jack got Grey and me on the line, made us promise to quit, and talked to us for a long time on The Lost Art of Letter Writing, this being back when people wrote letters.

While that advice was lost on Grey, I became a prodigious letter writer—"prodigious," (meaning here something closer to "voluminous" than "colossal") being the sort of word I used a lot in my letters of that era, since I took Ship's advice and bought a thesaurus. "I read somewhere that word power means people power," he said. It was the sort of thing he said a lot. "A thesaurus, that's the thing to use if you have to write a letter."

I wrote Pop twice a week, then less after a couple of months went by and he hadn't written back even once. I wrote Aunt Berthe every Tuesday and could always expect a reply by the following Monday. Callie and Grey I wrote three or four times a month, though only Callie wrote back. She always wrote in purple ink, with big curling girl letters, circles over the i's, and doodles in the margins. They were mostly the local news, the same stuff we talked about on the phone: Who was going out with who ("Dianne Ellis and Alvin Deere, can you believe it?") and who was grounded and who was driving on a ticket, who thought I was cute now that I was out of town and they were free to confess, and later there was more and more about Grey and what she called "his whole boat thing."

He hadn't bought the sloop from the guy called Natch, but landed a wooden sailing dinghy, clearing two hundred on the deal, after more than a hundred hours of work. "His whole boat thing is keeping him busy as you might have expected. He told me to say that business is likely to pick up. And he said to tell you that you sounded like a fag in your last letter. I know that's his way of saying he misses you."

It was hard work, writing letters home. I wrote to Pastor Brad and the Reverend. I sent postcards of the capitol dome at night to Hilde and Uncle Karl, and even sent a note to Todd with a brochure for an engineering exhibition they were having. I sent a letter to Ashley, too, trying to sound neutral, folksy—collegial. The letters to Mr. Reed were the hardest, and I wrote him more often than anybody else, mostly because he wrote to me the most and sent me back-issues of the *Star* every week. Looking at the paper from far away, it seemed thin and unimportant. Usually I just skimmed the pages for names I knew and tossed them in the bin next to the mailboxes. The letters I kept. And a lot of what he said I hung onto, as well, and called it wisdom.

My mental clock stayed set on island time. I woke up before six every morning and rolled my bike out of the courtyard and struck out across the soccer fields, the grass, turned brittle with frost, crackling under my tires. Usually I rode south or west, out of town into rolling pasture land, corn fields, and dairy farms, getting lost and finding my way again. On these rides I thought about the future or nothing at all pretty much equally, never about the present or past, and came home after Ship and everyone else on the floor had gone down to breakfast. I'd skip the cafeteria for coffee at the student union, where the walls were covered with murals of Paul Bunyan and his blue ox Babe. Painted in oils, the plaque said, back in the thirties by an artist of the WPA, they are all muscles and heavy boots and rolled shirtsleeves. And I liked them—particularly the one that showed the great fistfight between Paul and Big Swede, so rugged a brawl that it is said to have gouged out the Great Lakes. Here was a creation myth I could relate to, more local than the Bible and the flood and born out of the kind of struggle I understood.

Before I knew it I was living two lives, a solitary morning life and a school life: my classes and my job with Dooley and everything that came after, dinner in the clattering dining hall, the library at night with its hum of muffled conversation between carrels, and the beer parties in neighboring rooms, where I came to know my floor mates through a spreading web of acquaintances.

THE RED AND THE BLACK

The work I did for Dooley was easy, photocopying handouts for class, mailing letters, ordering textbooks from the bookstore, so I found other things to do, dusting and sweeping (and more than once fixing a broken window shade), all of which he hated watching me do because he said it offended his senses to see manual labor done in his presence. But I liked going there and I liked having a job to do for money. It was quiet in the office. After years of working with Pop I'd learned to keep my mouth shut and to keep out of the hair of grown-ups, which Dooley seemed to appreciate.

One morning when I came to work I heard a voice that wasn't Dooley's in his office. I didn't open the door because I thought he might be holding a tutorial or something. The voice was loud and deep and was shouting, "What do we want from you? What do we want from you?" and a large form moved back and forth casting a shadow on the opaque glass of the door. Then I did go in because it sounded like somebody was shaking the professor down.

The speaker was tall and fat, balding and bearded, and as such easily taken for older than he would turn out to be. My opening the door distracted him only slightly from the next sentence directed at Dooley behind his desk. "What we want from you is a letter."

"What sort of letter?" Dooley asked and, seeing me come in, nodded.

"A letter of recommendation." That from a second voice hidden behind the open door, this one higher than the fat man's and asthmatic.

Dooley laughed. "What could I say from experience to recommend you?"

"That we're cute," a third voice, a girl's, also hidden behind the door.

One of the owners of the two unseen voices pushed the door shut, so that I now saw a skinny man with small round glasses and an uncombed tangle of blond hair on a head disappearing into a heavy trench coat, sitting on the edge of Dooley's wide leather couch. Next to him, lying on her side on the remaining expanse of cushions, with her head propped on her palm, a girl.

"Hi," they said at once.

Roy and Harold I'd seen before. Even on a campus of forty thousand there were faces you saw more than others and these were two of them. For one thing, they were always together, a mismatched pair. Roy wore old clothes: a fedora for his prematurely balding head and baggy trousers and suspenders to conceal his hemispheric belly—while Harold circled him like an electron, smoking and chattering constantly. For another, they were showmen. Wherever they went, they carried a lacquer suitcase and folding table, which they set up on the library mall, and sold various products they had invented.

The girl I hadn't seen before. She wore a black turtleneck, black pants, and the black canvas shoes that all the girls were wearing that year, the clothes and the dark shine of her hair making the skin of her face seem that much paler. She was, as she suggested to Dooley as a point of recommendation, cute.

"What am I recommending you for?"

I went to sit on the radiator. The heat burned through my jeans like an iron and the metal seared my palms. "Shit," I yelled.

Drucilla looked in my direction as though she'd heard a noise from far away. She spoke. "The Stovepipe Bequest." Her voice was the voice of an actress, no doubt, as surely as Roy's was the voice of a pitchman, and Harold's was the voice of a killer.

Dooley raised his eyebrows to show surprise. "Do you mean the Ebersol grant?"

"Don't sound so shocked," Roy said.

"Did you know Ebersol?" the girl, Drucilla, asked.

"In passing. I replaced him. Of course, I should say 'succeeded.' He could never be replaced, an institution at this university for forty years. There is a story about him at the Alumni Ball"—he looked at them and then at me—"which is best told at another time. He belonged to a school of historical study of which he was the founder and sole adherent. He held that a man's life could be reconstructed by documenting every scrap of paper he ever touched. His *Lincoln,* his key to all histories, occupies twelve volumes. It's less a history than a compendium of litter."

"Yeah?" Roy said—he couldn't have cared less—"well, he donated an annuity for which a student director is chosen every year to produce a play on the condition that whatever play gets produced must be about Lincoln. Which constrains things, as you might imagine."

"Because it has to be about Lincoln," I said.

He paused to look at me. "What did I just say?"

"Doesn't sound like the sort of thing you'd be interested in, Harold," Dooley said.

"Exactly right," Roy answered for him. "The trick is to turn the idea on its ear. Is it ear or head?"

"How do you do that?" I asked. I had no idea what they were talking about but I wanted to sound like I was keeping up.

"I'm not sure how *you* do that. If you're Harold you write a play about John Wilkes Booth. Harold says he's been influenced by the French Romanticist school of play writing."

"What is that?" Dooley asked. "George Sand, Alfred de Musset?"

"Exactly," Harold said.

"—founded in the belief," Roy continued, "that plays are better read than acted. Harold chose a one-act because he says it's the most odious theatrical form, which he believes is perfect for Booth, an odious figure in his own right, as well as a thespian of the nineteenth century—and all that that entails. If you ask me, I'm not sure he's worked out the distinction between being bad for the sake of form and just being, well, bad."

Harold raised his hand to be heard. "I'm making progress there," he said. "It's not hopeless material; he wasn't a bad actor, Booth—bit full of himself."

"That'll be a stretch for you, Harold," Dooley said.

"This is the closest we've been to getting our hands on the means of production," Roy said.

"We don't have to tell you how important that could be," Drucilla said.

Dooley studied a stack of papers on his desk. "And I don't have to tell you that you can expect a certain amount of attention from the administration."

Roy said, "That's half the point. We view this as an opportunity for redemption."

Dooley raised his cup to his lips.

"You know what we're capable of," Roy said. and Dooley choked, spitting tea across the blotter on his desk.

"Oh yes, I do know that," Dooley said. I guessed he was referring to their peddling of what they called the infamous "Endtime Elixir," a performance I'd witnessed the first week of the semester. I'd run into them outside the library where they'd attracted a crowd.

"Friends," said Harold, wearing a straw hat and swinging a bamboo cane, "are you going to wake up in your shelters on the day after the Big One drops with bad morning breath and a bottomless sense of remorse for the annihilation of humanity? Well now you don't have to."

"Will it sterilize radiation burns?" a man—obviously a plant—asked from the front row.

"I'm glad you ask. Of course, it will. Why, sir, if ingested in sufficient doses, it will sterilize you."

The man handed over a buck. "That's right. One dollar. Who's next?" As he was speaking Roy appeared, wearing a dirty bed sheet. His face smeared with ashes, he carried a sign that said, "The End Is *Near.*" There were giggles from the crowd as he hobbled up to the table.

"Here you are, my good man," his partner said, handing over a bottle. The prophet Roy emptied the contents in one swallow, smacked his lips, and continued on his way.

"There you are, ladies and gentlemen, you're not going to get a truer testimonial than that. Step on up. Plenty for everyone. That's right, a dollar—"

The people surged forward, waving dollar bills above their heads. I joined them, made my way to the front of the line, handed over my money and the short one slapped a bottle into my hand. The words "Endtime Elixir" were written on a hand-glued label in an Old West script. Below them was a photograph, cut and pasted from two fifties-vintage snapshots: one a family picnic in which a mother reclines on a plaid blanket, the children toss a ball, and the father lifts a glass, while a super-imposed mushroom cloud swells on the horizon. I unscrewed the cap and took a swig. It tasted like mouthwash and had a kick to it that took my breath away.

When Crowder and Sing, charged with violating academic rules against bootlegging, had defended themselves to the dean of students, they insisted that they had made no false claims about the contents of the elixir. In fact, they had made none at all. The dean, according to the article in the *Daily Cardinal*, had reminded them that selling bottled alcohol without a tax seal was a federal offense. They were put on probation and warned "not to do anything like that again." Of course, by then they'd become celebrities and the bottles of elixir (most of which were swallowed by their owners once the contents were published) became collector's items.

"I'm not sure how producing a deliberately tedious play about a loathed historical figure presents an opportunity for redemption," Dooley said.

"That's our challenge," Drucilla said.

"What assurances do I have that you'll behave yourselves?" Dooley asked.

Crowder lifted his fedora from the chair where it sat. He spun it on his finger and lowered it onto his massive head. "None whatsoever."

"Fair enough," Dooley said.

"Well," Harold said, slapping his knees with his palms and standing, "we'll wait to hear from you."

Drucilla uncoiled from the couch and put her black shoes on the floor. "But we won't wait too long," she said.

"You shall hear when it is time for you to hear."

I watched them walk to the door. I wanted the girl to look at me and, as the door was shutting on her, she did, bending her head back through the doorway, just long enough to say, "See ya."

Elise Winters sat at her desk in a narrow corner of the observatory surrounded by a horseshoe of scattered paper. The window was open a crack and cold air blew in with the early dark of a fall afternoon. She pulled her sweater tighter around her neck.

"You cold?" I asked.

She shrugged. "A little but it keeps me awake. I need to finish this."

I picked up one of the papers. "What is it?"

"Radio contour images."

"What are you looking for?"

"This." She pointed to a fried egg configuration of concentric lines on a page of graph paper.

"What for?"

"I'm comparing this point to its previous plot to see if it moved in relation to this object."

"Why would it move?"

"First we see if it moved, then we ask why."

"How come you want to know?"

"It's something to know."

"I mean what good will it do to know?"

She tilted her head back and tapped her pencil on her chin. "None maybe. We can't choose what we're curious about."

This was how our conversations usually went. I'd come back to the observatory when it was dark out and stood in line with a bunch of kids to look at Mars and the rings of Saturn through the telescope. On that visit, I'd seen where her office was. Sometimes I would stop by on my way home from campus when I saw her light on. I liked her because she had a chain on her glasses to keep her from losing them and because she was smart in the way Dooley was smart without being stuck up about what she knew. I'd tell her about school and ask her about what she did when she was new at school and she told me about the all-girls college she went to in California and what they did for fun, which was basically nothing that I thought of as fun. I didn't tell her about meeting Drucilla. I told her instead about how Fräulein Menendez, my German instructor from Buenos Aires, had gone ahead and given us a quiz even though she had forgotten to warn us that it was coming.

"Yes," she said. "You have to expect that from your professors. It's not like high school. Here, the professors have their own work to think about, and anything you ask of them is asking too much."

"Do you have a boyfriend?" I asked.

She lifted her glasses to her mouth and chewed on the end, smiling, kind of. "Why would you ask me that just then?"

"I don't know," I said, feeling I had made a big mistake. "Just popped into my head."

"Well," she said, smiling more now, "I guess it's a fair question among friends. No," she said, "no boyfriend."

I pointed at the diagram in front of her again. "What is this we're watching move?"

"It's a quasar in the constellation Lyra."

"Why not look at it in the telescope?"

"It's too far away."

"But this doesn't look like anything."

She put her glasses back on and arranged the papers before her, which I took as a sign that I should go. "Never underestimate the importance of looking at an old thing in a new way."

Ship made a face. "Who'd you say it was?"

"Drucilla."

"Drucilla what?"

"I don't know. That's why I'm asking you."

He was sitting on his desk with his feet on a chair, paring his fingernails with a chrome clipper from a leather manicure case his parents gave him when he moved in. "How come you want to know?"

I didn't answer him.

"You want to get in her pants."

"Jesus, Ship. No one says that anymore."

He slid the clipper into the case and zipped it. "Turn your back," he said. Ship kept the key to his desk hidden in a coffee mug on his bookshelf. I knew where it was and he knew I knew, but we both pretended. After I heard the drawer slide shut I turned to see him pulling a pencil out of the spiral binding of a small, black notebook. He flipped to a blank page and licked the pencil tip.

"She's a theater major?"

"As far as I know."

"You're not sure?"

"No, I'm not sure. Could be theater, could be history."

"What's she look like?"

"About five feet."

"Wow, short. Hair color?"

"Brown," I said. "Dark brown, maybe black."

"Long or short?"

"Short."

He made a face.

"What?"

"Nothing."

"What?"

"Well, did you ever think about it? Short girl, short hair, theater major?"

"What are you talking about?"

He put up a hand to shut me up and asked, "What about boobs?"

"What about them?"

"Does she have any?"

"What do you think?"

"Big or little?"

"I didn't notice," I said.

"You didn't notice?"

"No, I didn't notice. How's that going to help, anyway?"

He mumbled something like, "If you didn't notice . . ." and wrote in the book. Then he held it at arm's length and studied the page. "Not much to go on, but I'll see what I can do."

Ship had to act like I was putting him out to obscure the truth, which was that he lived to do favors for me—for me or for anyone who asked. It is how the Ships of the world get by. In exchange, we tell them things. I told him things. I told him things I never would have told anyone else because I felt like I owed it to him. He called anyone he even vaguely knew "a good friend" and never worried about how many would have said the same about him. A friend in Ship's mind was a friend, indeed. He counted me as his friend, as his best friend on campus, and he paid for the privilege.

When I turned my back again so he could hide his drawer key, I noticed a slip of paper on the edge of my desk. I picked it up and read, "Dear Dennis Shipman—"

"Here, this is yours," I said.

"What is it?"

"How should I know?"

He looked. "Oh, did I leave that over there?"

"I guess," I said and tried to hand it to him.

"You didn't read it, did you?"

"No, why should I?"

He smiled broadly. "Well, I guess there's no harm in you knowing, although the announcement won't be made for another week. I've been chosen one of the Faces of the Future."

"What's that?"

"Well," he said, studying my expression as though he was going to give me bad news, "there's a calendar."

I laughed. "Oh my God, are you naked?"

"Come on, it's not like that. I'm February."

"That's the shortest month."

Ship snatched the letter from me. "You shouldn't make fun. It's for charity."

In the days that followed, I watched for Drucilla wherever I went. I was obsessed. I scanned the faces I passed between classes, in the lecture halls, and at the free movies on the commons. It was ten days before I saw her again. I was climbing the broad concrete stairway that led from Van Hise to Van Vleck Hall and picked her out of the crowd coming down. She sported a leather motorcycle jacket with silver studs and had a green army satchel slung over her shoulder. Somehow she managed to read from the paperback book in her hand as she descended the steep flight of stairs. For a second I wondered if this was actually her (there'd been a lot of false alarms), until her bangs fell into her eyes and I knew for certain. As I watched her walk by, I tripped and landed hard on the concrete.

"Walk much?" a voice behind me asked.

Dooley was taking the teakettle off his hot plate by the window when I went to his office. He glanced up from his tea bag as I slouched into the armchair beside his desk. He stuffed his shirttail back into his corduroy trousers. He was always stuffing his shirttail into his corduroy trousers. In five minutes it would be hanging loose again. "What?"

"I'm in love, I think."

Running his fingers through his hair, he set the steaming cup down on the blotter on his desk. "Oh, Heaven pity us."

"You know her."

"Do I?"

"The girl who was in here a while back."

An eyebrow raised. "There've been so many."

"No, you know her. She was here with Crowder and Sing."

Now both eyebrows. "Drucilla Gordon? Sweet mother of Christ."

"Don't worry. She's out of my league," I said, hoping he'd argue.

"Well, you should be happy for that," he said.

"You're saying she is, out of my league, I mean?"

"What? Oh, league, I'm not sure it's that, although she is a few years older and a far cry wiser than you."

"You mean experienced?"

"I'm sure I have no idea what I mean. I've known that girl since her first day of school and I don't know that I could tell you the first thing about her, except that she drank grape soda pop and had an instinct for trouble, which at an institution as permissive as this, requires a fair deal of creativity."

"I don't think it would matter to me what you said."

"Tea?" I shook my head. "It would be conventional for a man in my position, a man older and—I hope I don't flatter myself here—of some influence upon you—" I nodded my head—"to counsel you to follow your heart, to learn what lessons you can through the heartbreak that will inevitably follow."

"But you're not going to."

"As you ascertained from the construction of my sentence and my inflection, I'm not going to do that. What you're experiencing is not love. When people your age say, 'I'm in love,' what they mean is 'I am infatuated.'"

"And I could say that's what people your age always say to people my age."

"Just as I cautioned you not to confuse history with folklore. The one is real, the other a sentimental interpolation. You have a promising future and the rare opportunity not to be sidetracked by distractions."

"Sounds like you speak from experience."

"Mine is a familiar story: A young man comes to this country with only the shirt on his back and falls in love—falls in love, mind you—with a lovely young entertainer he spies first on stage. The young man receives a fellowship to study at a prestigious southern university. The object of his love may not follow because the local laws prevent her from plying her trade."

The day I left to go home for Thanksgiving, I saw Drucilla a third time. I was walking through the Union on my way to catch the bus north. The beer hall was already crowded and loud with students who'd finished their classes. I was passing a bank of tall windows and, because there was a storm coming, I happened to look out at the lake. The weather was vicious, there was a north wind blowing off Mendota, and the patio chairs of the terrace, which were filled in the summer months, were deserted except for three figures huddled at a green table beneath a naked maple. Because it was an unusual sight, I stopped and looked. It was Crowder, Sing, and, pushing back from the table with the toes of her boots, Drucilla Gordon.

Crowder stood up from the table and, waving his arm at the lake, shouted. Harold and Drucilla watched and then laughed and clapped, oblivious to the cold, leaning forward now and then to refill their beer glasses from a pitcher that sat in a tuft of snow on the table.

Sing looked my way. I ducked out of the window and ran for the bus.

HOLIDAY

The bus dropped me at the ferry ramp and dieseled off into the night. I stood at the water's edge in a light snow. The coach had been refreshingly plush, with reclining seats and a toilet and ashtrays on the armrests, this being back in the day when you could smoke. And smoke we did, and drink from goatskin wine sacks and smuggled flasks. Some guys in back from Waupun, where the prison is, got up a game of cards. After dark, a sense of enclosure and fatigue took over. The darkness outside turned the window into a mirror and I tried not to stare at my reflection.

At Hurley, the last passenger other than me—a girl in a white parka and boots to match—climbed off, and then it was just me and the driver riding the last miles to where the state ended at the lake. Bayview was decorated with all the schizophrenia of a tourist town off season, a lighted wreath on a lamppost in the square, lights along the eaves of the North Woods Motel, and a Santa clutching a Coke in the window of the Kroger.

Across the channel I made out the lights of the ferry moving against the black form of the island. This weekend would be the last of the runs for the season. Coast Guard cutters patrolled daily for ice. As the wind rattled the brittle rope against the flagpole, I stepped into the shelter of the doorway to the ticket kiosk and watched the lights grow larger, oscillating with the sweep of the radar gear.

The ferry arrived empty and I waited alone to board. I didn't know the roper (they called him that because he handled the lines and herded the cars on), but he wouldn't take my two dollars when I tried to give it to him. "You it?" he asked.

"I'm it."

It was nuclear winter, utter cold, utter dark, moonless and overcast. Snowflakes rushed into the boat's lanterns. Then the blacker presence of the island against the black of the water, as a covering of snow became visible on the ground and bare trees, then the harbor lights and, closer in, house lights came into view. Two figures sat huddled beneath the statue of the founder. The gate dropped and I stepped onto the island. Grey and Callie brushed the snow from their jeans and trudged down the hill, inking footprints behind them as they came.

Grey's face was invisible in the fur-lined tunnel of his parka hood. Callie's blaze-orange snowmobile hat sat cockeyed on her head. She wiped her nose with one of the wool socks she'd pulled on over her mittens.

"Hey," they said.

The grimy smell of the shop hit me as I wrenched the screen door against the weight of the snow. I navigated in the dark to the stairs and called, "Hello?" I opened the kitchen door. Pop didn't answer. I switched on the light and dropped my bag with a thud loud enough to be heard throughout the house. Still nothing. That's when I noticed the curtains on the window over the sink, light blue, with ruffles on the bottom and pulled back with ties of matching fabric. On the table, a butter dish with a spotted ceramic cow reclining on the lid. In the bathroom, I opened an orange plastic box on the ledge beside the sink to find rows of spiked hair curlers rising out of their base like a toy missile silo.

"Pop," I whispered at his door. Nothing. Walking into my room it was like I had been there only hours earlier. Nothing had changed. By that I mean nothing. The room was just as I had left it, drawers shut, the closet door ajar, even the dent on the blanket where my bag had last been before I lifted it to my shoulder remained.

On Thanksgiving morning, I woke to a racket in the kitchen and walked down the hall to find Trudy in an aqua housecoat, a Virginia Slim clamped in her teeth, crouched in front of the kitchen cabinets dragging pots out on the floor. She looked up not at all surprised to see me standing over her in my underwear.

"Hi, hon," she said. "Looking for the double boiler. You didn't run off with it, did you?"

"We don't have one."

"Shit—well, coffee's on."

"Where's Pop?"

"He'll be up shortly."

"Bit late."

"It's a holiday, hon. Your father's a hardworking man," she said, somehow making it sound like that was my fault. "Here, come on." She hoisted herself up and took a coffee cup off a wood rack we didn't have when I left. "I'm not cooking this morning, so you'll have to make do. I was going to make yam casserole, but without the double boiler, it'll have to be Rice-A-Roni stuffing. What do you think about that?"

"Pop and I are going to the Reeds'," I said.

"And we don't want to show up without a dish to pass. How would that look?"

Like every year, I was thinking, but didn't say so. I heard the toilet flush and Pop came down the hall, tugging at his pants. My first thought was that he looked like a cartoonist's drawing of the father I remembered. The effects of the crash remained in his posture, which listed to the right to favor the side that took the most punishment. Yet at the same time he was bigger, not fat but thicker in the legs and arms. When he saw me he grunted, kind of, and nodded. His shoulders stiffened as I went toward him, so I settled for a pat on his good shoulder. "Hey, Pop, *wie gehts?*"

"You got here," he said.

"Piece of cake," I said. "Long as you know where to get off. I'm doing good at school, if you're wondering. I mean not good, you wouldn't say, but all right, an A, a B, and two Cs at midterm, which don't count, so I can get them up by the end of term. I'm taking four classes. You can take four or five. Six, too, I think if you get a waiver, but who'd want to do that? I'm taking four because I got to work like you know and I figure there's no harm in getting the lay of the land before I jump in with both feet." I don't know how long I went on like this before I realized that I was talking very fast and Pop just sat there smoking and staring at the table and nodding in this spasm-y kind of way, like he was trying to get a bug away from his face. "So what I'm saying is I think I'm doing fine, all things considered."

"Well, that's all very nice, isn't it Ernst?" Trudy said.

He made a noncommittal gesture with his hand.

"You wouldn't believe how much he's worried," she said.

I wouldn't believe he worried, I wanted to say.

"We read they're raising the prices," he said.

We read? "They raise tuition pretty much every year. I was expecting it. Anyway, I got a job with Professor Dooley. I said so in my letter."

Then Trudy started talking about the "gals at work." She spends ten hours a day with the gals at work and as far as I can see can't stand any of them, but without them and Dianne and her ex she'd have nothing to talk about.

I got up and went downstairs without saying I was leaving.

Trudy's domestic impulses didn't extend to the shop. Bikes were clustered in corners or lying on the floor rather than the usual ordered rows. Empty Pabst cans cluttered Pop's workbench. His beanbag ashtray was full. There was a second ashtray I'd never seen before, a ceramic job with the name of a Vegas casino on it, also overflowing. The picture of him and my mother was gone from above his bench. Just the aluminum mount that held it remained, twisted at the end, as if someone had broken it off with a good amount of force.

I picked up the bikes lying on the floor and set them on their kickstands, emptied the ashtrays and beer cans into the trash, and before I knew it I had a broom in my hand. Rather than go back upstairs and watch Pop stare at Trudy as she droned on about the cost of a dye job in Duluth, I washed the counters and dusted the bikes, straightened the display racks and cleared the outdated paperwork from the order files. I noticed a stack of unopened mail, bills mostly from the looks of them. The money side of the business had never been my business and I would have caught hell if I opened them, so I left them propped against the metal file we kept our repair orders in.

When I was done straightening up I hauled the trash out. The temperature had dropped violently during the night. It was a brilliant and bitter sunny morning as I stood shivering next to the dumpster, staring across the water toward the mainland. On my way back to the door I noticed the light on in Grey's hangar and headed over to see what he was up to.

A gust of wind blew the door out of my hand. I saw Grey and someone else bent over the worktable.

"Shut the door, asshole," the other guy yelled. He raised his head and I recognized him as the man who'd given me his card before I left for school.

"It's okay, Natch," said Grey.

"What's up?" I said.

"That's for us to know and you never to find out," Natch said, laughing in a nervous way so that I couldn't tell if he was joking or not. He ran his thumb along the mirror that lay on the table leaving a smudge between a few grains of powder. "This the guy?"

"I'm the guy who what?"

"Nothing," Grey said.

Natch stood up from the table. He was wearing a sheepskin coat that made him look, with his leathery skin, like one of those nineteenth-century polar explorers. "Wait a minute here," he said. "I'm having a conversation with my friend and here you come in and I'm wondering just what exactly is your problem."

"I said it's okay," Grey said.

"I was talking to your friend here," Natch said, staring at me and pointing at Grey with his thumb, "about expanding his base. That's all."

"His base?"

"His capital base and I ask him doesn't he maybe know anybody else who could kick in some cash to finance an operation should the opportunity present itself and he says, 'I don't know. Maybe my friend—'"

"Tom," Grey said.

"So I say, 'Make sure your friend understands that you're offering an opportunity, because otherwise he'll think you're a deadbeat until he sees the money coming in.'" Then Natch zipped up his jacket, shook his hair free of the collar, and left.

"What the hell?" I said to Grey once he'd gone. Grey tossed the rag he was holding onto the table with the same fatigue in his shoulders that I saw from Pop at the end of a day. I looked around the shop. In just the three months I'd been gone the walls and surfaces were all battered and scuffed and there was a layer of sawdust on the floor as deep as a December flurry. Whatever he'd managed to scrape up in the way of work, he'd been hard at it.

"Forget it," he said.

"If you say so."

The hull of a sixteen-foot sailing scow sat perched on the davits in front of him. "I had to throw on a patch," Grey said, "Guess where it is."

I walked up one end of the shining white hull and down the other, craning my neck to see if the light could catch an imperfection. "Here," I said.

"Not even warm," he said and patted a spot farther aft.

"Who's this one for?"

"Thinking of keeping it myself."

"You got the canoe."

"A sail can take you farther than a paddle."

"Little small for the lake, isn't it? You could swamp it in a heavy chop."

"Then I guess I'll hope for fair weather," he said.

I watched him move along the gunwale of the boat. He'd painted the rail black and was stripping away any paint that bled through the masking tape with a razor blade. "Want to give me a hand?" he said. "There's another blade over there."

Picking up a clean blade, I set about scraping drips of black from the white of the hull. I'd only gone a few inches before I looked up and saw Grey gaining on me. In the time it'd taken me to go a half foot, he'd finished his side and started on mine. I watched for a minute, trying to pick up on the flicking motion that worked for him, but it was no use. Somewhere in just a few months, he'd become a craftsman, and I had nothing in the way of skills to match him. "I should get back," I said, "I didn't tell Pop where I was going."

As I washed my hands in the kitchen sink, Trudy came up behind me and said, "Let's wear our church clothes, hon. We're guests."

It was at Thanksgiving dinner that year that I got the idea that something happens to people when they turn forty that makes them go permanently nuts. There was no other explanation for the way that Jack seemed to be falling deeper into his newspapers, or the way that Agnes in her increasing blindness had begun to see a happier world that didn't exist or the way Ray grew more and more arrogant as his fortunes fell or the way Dolores's bitterness had become so hard that you couldn't have chipped it with an axe or the way that Trudy convinced Pop she was a sex symbol or the way that Pop had allowed his world be to be transformed by Trudy in my absence to an empire of his own virility. Or maybe it was the gløgg that stirred things up. Jack at the head of the table looked a mile away from down at our end, where Callie and Grey and Todd and I sat with our knees rammed under the card table, as he ladled the steaming liquid into cups to be passed around the table. We had to duck around the centerpiece that Todd built (a candle windmill) to talk to him. The centerpiece played "Turkey in the Straw" as it turned, which was pretty cool the first ten times.

"Oh, I had a little chicken and it wouldn't lay an egg," Agnes sang quietly.

The gløgg flowed freely into our cups except for Todd who couldn't have any and Callie who said she didn't want it. Dolores and Ray arrived late, after a detour through the marina bar. Ray wore a pumpkin-colored blazer over a black turtleneck. Dolores wore a brown dress with a corsage shaped like a cornucopia that was so big the spilling fruit reached her chin. Ray pulled her chair back and almost tripped over the rug in the process. She sank unsteadily into the seat, not even noticing her husband was about to topple over.

Agnes said, "We were just complimenting Trudy on her wonderful wild rice stuffing."

"I make it with Rice-A-Roni," Trudy said.

"Rice, eh? Puts a little *ah-so* in the festivities, don't it now?" Ray said, though he passed on the stuffing entirely and shoveled half the bowl of mashed potatoes onto his plate. "Say, you know the one about the Chinaman and the working girl?"

"I'm not sure this is the time for that, Ray," Dolores said.

"The recipe's on the box," Trudy said. "It's nothing really."

"I'm sure no one's disputing that, dear," said Dolores.

"What about the Chinaman?" asked the Toad.

"Nothing, honey," Agnes said.

"Should get out the old chopsticks," Ray said, nudging Pop and causing him to drop his fork into his mug of gløgg, prompting Todd to laugh so hard he blew milk through his nose and Agnes to ask, "Is someone at the door?"

"Actually, wild rice isn't rice," Callie said. "It's a grass."

"Grass, ick," said Todd.

"Did you learn that from your Indians?" Ray asked.

"Callie's got an internship though her school," Jack said for my benefit.

Grey said, "She's working with the Chippewa Action Program—"

"'Bout time they get to swindle us for a change, eh," Ray said. "That's what I tell her, 'Bout time they get to swindle us for a change, eh Cal?"

"'Bout time they scalp somebody," Grey said, looking Ray's way down the table.

"The first thing we learn," Callie said, "is to avoid forming stereotypes."

"Sometimes we forget how much the young have to teach us," Dolores said, anxious to squash any conversation that would give attention to her daughter rather than herself. Her eyes scanned the table, looking for a target to zero in on. "Trudy," she said, "where's Dianne this holiday?"

"At her father's," Trudy said. Dolores knew this, and for a second I felt sorry for Trudy.

"Ah, yes, I should have thought."

"Would all grass look like rice if you cooked it?" Todd asked.

"Don't be stupid," Grey said.

"It's a fair question," Jack said. "Ask Callie."

"Ask me what?"

"Would it? Would all grass look like wild rice if you cooked it?"

"I don't know. I don't think so."

"I guess they can't teach you everything at college," Dolores said.

I said, "I've got a professor back at school who says—"

"Ray read in the *Weekly World News* that Satan is a college professor at one of those liberal universities," Dolores said.

The Toad asked, "What's the *Weekly World News?*"

"It's a tabloid," Callie said.

"You used to write for them, didn't you Dad?" Grey said.

Jack chuckled.

"I'm sure the devil has better things to do with his time," Agnes said.

"What's that supposed to mean?" Ray snarled and startled Agnes. Jack, too, looked up from his plate somewhat surprised and looked first at Agnes then down the table.

"Nothing," Agnes said. "I only just meant the devil could think of more destructive ways on earth than posing as a teacher."

"Or were you saying that I could find better things to do with my time?" Ray said, now looking at the table instead of at Agnes.

"What's a tabloid?" Todd asked.

"I'm sure that's not what she meant to say," Jack piped in.

"It's those papers by the checkout at the Kroger," Callie said.

Then everyone is talking at once and nobody hears Jack tap his glass with his fork and then he's saying, "Hey, hey," until finally he shouts it and everybody stops yelling at each other and looks. "I think a toast is appropriate."

"You want me to handle that, Dad?" Grey said.

"This is the day we count our blessings, and we are blessed to have Dolores and Ray join us for the first time"—we all lifted our glasses, except Agnes who lifted the gravy boat—"and to have Tom here to remind us of how much the joy of his return has made up for our sadness when he left us."

"In other words," Grey said, "how can we miss you if you don't go away?"

They were still going at it when Callie and Grey and I ducked out and walked over to Friendly's, which was hopping with refugees from other households around the island, many like us loosening ties and kicking out of pinched leather shoes. Greta waved from behind the bar and said something to Grey when she slid the two bottles of beer and a Coke across the bar that made him laugh.

"What's funny?" I asked.

"She said to tell you she knew they'd kick you out of college," Grey said.

"See," Callie said, "you could just stay here and no one would think anything of it."

"Grey doesn't need me around when he's got Natch."

"Shit, Tom," Grey said.

Callie asked, "Who's Natch?"

"She doesn't know him?"

Callie and Grey looked at each other. "Why would she, man? He's a customer."

"Who is he?" Callie asked.

"He's kind of a steer-er."

"A steer?" Callie said. "Like a boy cow?"

"No, a steer-er. He steers business my way."

"How about you?" I asked Callie. "You planning to stay here all your life?"

She looked at Grey and half laughed, "I like it here as well as anywhere else."

A Mac Davis song came on the jukebox, "It's Hard to be Humble," and all the regulars sang along. The song is funny the first time you hear it.

"You could at least stay a couple of extra days," she said. "Ellises are having a party on Sunday."

"Actually," I said, "I was thinking about going back tomorrow."

"How come?"

"I have to go back in a day or two anyway, so what difference does it make? Trudy doesn't want me around and Pop doesn't need me this time of year."

"Stay over at the Reeds'," Callie said, but Grey interrupted.

"He says he has to go," Grey said. "Right?"

"Yeah, that's what I said."

Pop and Trudy took the news better. The next morning—after falling asleep to the sounds of polka music and laughter vibrating from his room—I'd asked Pop, "Feel like going for a ride?" thinking I could borrow somebody's bike and we'd find enough dry pavement to make the effort worthwhile.

When I asked, Trudy looked up from her eggs, startled. My father noticed her movement out of the corner of his eye. He stared at me for a moment and shook his head and Trudy went back to eating.

"Anyway," she said. "It's snowing."

"Never stopped us before," I said, which was true.

"Well," Trudy said, "I can't be responsible for whatever foolishness went on here before me."

Pop lifted his eyes from the table for the first time all morning, and I looked into them for some sign of regret, but I didn't see it, only fatigue. "I guess I'll get going then," I said.

Trudy said, "Really, honey, already?"

Pop spoke, "You know when the bus comes?"

"Yeah," I told him. "If I'm on the 11:15 ferry I'll be able to catch it."

15

OR THE WONDERFUL LAMP

Ship drifted into the room, whistling Billy Joel. He'd been sullen because he was flunking Statistics. That was bad because Ship's major was Pre-Business, and from what he told me, if you were Pre-Biz, flunking Statistics was the one thing you didn't want to do. For all his talk, Ship was a bad student. You could attribute his incompetence to two factors: he was lazy and he was dumb. Normally he didn't let a bad grade get him down so the previous couple of days had been depressing, but now that he was back to his musical self, I missed the gloomy version.

He kept whistling, and I kept ignoring him, until he quit whistling and started to sing, and at last I said, "Shut the fuck up."

He smiled and dangled a manila envelope in front of my face. "I used the old yearbook ploy."

More than a minute went by while he waited for me to ask him what the old yearbook ploy was, and when he realized I wasn't going to, he said, "I went to the theater department and told them I was from the yearbook staff. I said we were going through our files and couldn't find a current photo of an actress, Drucilla—'Gordon?' she says. 'That's right,' I say."

I made a grab for the envelope, but he jerked it out of reach.

Slowly, he slid the black and white glossy photograph out of the envelope and, holding it tightly, dangled it in front of my face. "That her?"

It was.

Doing a lousy job of hiding his satisfaction, he put the picture back in the envelope. "Then I called administration and told them I was Dr. Whatshisname, requisitioning plane tickets for a show in Columbus and I don't have an ID number on one of my actors. She says, 'What's your authorization number?' and I say, 'Lady, I don't have a clue. This is the first time this has happened.' She says she needs it for the entry, will I call her when I find it. I say, 'Sure will,' and she gives me the ID number. After that I call records and say I'm verifying a scholarship on one of my actors."

"Do they give scholarships for theater?"

"Doubt it," Ship said, "but she doesn't know that. She says she'll send the transcript campus mail. I say, 'I need it today. I'll send over my assistant director Dennis Shipman.' When I get there, she doesn't get up from her desk. 'It's on the counter,' she says. 'Thanks,' I say. I take the transcript, and, in my carelessness, I accidentally get a copy of her application, too."

He waited for me to congratulate him.

"Let's see it," I said.

He tossed the envelope on my bed and read from his notebook. "Gordon, comma, Drucilla. No middle initial. Born 2-17. She'll be twenty in February—an older woman. Theater major, GPA 3.75—" he whistled, but then said, "Well, it's Theater. Parents Burt and Alice. Permanent address, Fox Valley Road, Windsor, Ontario."

"She's Canadian?"

"That's what it says."

"What's she doing down here?"

"Search me. She lives in Waters."

"How'd you find that out?"

Ship smiled. He tossed the directory on top of the empty envelope. "She's in the book, call her up."

I left the phone book lying where it fell.

Ship folded his arms across his scrawny chest. "Gonna call her?"

"Eventually."

"Why not call her now?"

"It doesn't work that way," I said. "You wouldn't just call her up."

"I wouldn't?"

"Well, you might."

"How're you going to meet her if you don't call?"

"Who says I want to meet her?"

"You don't?"

"I didn't say that."

"You going to stake out her dorm?"

"Oh jeez, you're bright," I said and kicked the directory onto the floor.

Ship went to pick it up, thought better of it, and headed for the door. "Bright enough to know you're yellow," he said and slammed the door on his way out.

As soon as he was gone, I ripped a page from the pad and opened the directory. Ship had circled the listing and number in red pen. I copied them out, tore the page out of the phone book, put a match to it and used the flame to light a cigarette. A burning ash landed on Ship's blanket. I whacked it out with the letter I was writing to Aunt Berthe about our happy holiday dinner.

It was after ten when I finished. Ship hadn't come back and figured to be in the TV lounge watching Leno. I stamped the letters, shut out the lights, and sat cross-legged on my bed, not sure what I should do. I smoked a cigarette, then lit a second with the butt of the first. I listened for Ship's footsteps in the hall.

I pushed a chair under the doorknob, so Dennis couldn't barge in, took the slip out of my wallet. I dialed six digits of the number and hung up. Then I dialed again. It rang. It rang a second time. Someone picked up on the other end, there was a silence, and before I could say hello, a girl said, "Dru Gordon doesn't live here anymore," and hung up.

That night I dreamed I was back on the island. It was just as it had been at Thanksgiving, only the table was outdoors and no one seemed to notice or care except me. The trees were bare. There was snow and a gale blowing from the north. Everyone was there, sitting at a long table. My father, Grey, Callie, the Reeds, Todd and Trudy, Dolores and Ray, his blazer now white instead of orange. We were dressed for a summer picnic on the beach. Everyone was talking at once. Or I should say that everyone's lips were moving at once. I couldn't hear a word over the wind, though I understood that what they were saying was horrible, full of hatred and regret. My place was at the head of the table, Callie sat at the other end. For a long time I stared at her, willing her to look at me. She leaned toward Ray to whisper something in his ear and as she did our eyes met for the first time. I said her name. She smiled and held her finger to her lips.

Waking in a state of dread, I lay in the dark with no idea of where I was until I heard air whistling through Ship's nostrils as he slept. I had an irresistible feeling that I should go home, that something hideous would happen if I didn't. I couldn't sleep the rest of the night and thrashed around until seven in the morning when I called the shop and let the phone ring for about twenty times without an answer.

I decided not to go home. Instead I would take Dooley's advice and fall in love with school instead of a girl.

"Take Edwards's class," he said, as I was filling out my registration form for the spring semester.

"He good?" I asked.

"He is a she, Pamela Edwards. No, she is not good. In point of fact she's dead awful."

"Then why would you want me to take her?"

"Don't ask the obvious question. It doesn't befit the scholar." He licked an envelope shut and held it up between two fingers.

"Even so I am going ask you to do something for me that you may thank me for and that I will equally likely come to regret."

"Do I have to do it?"

He looked at the envelope as he tapped it on his desk. "Yes, I imagine the powers of destiny are too strong for you to resist. Do you know the theater next to the church?"

"At the foot of the hill? Yes, sir."

"Take this envelope down there and give it to Harold Sing."

"Harold Sing, did you say?"

He smiled across his desk. "Yes, I believe you know him."

The front door was locked. I walked around to the side and tried the door there, which opened onto a dark corridor with a dim light coming from what turned out to be a small auditorium. As my eyes got used to the dark, I made out the familiar shapes of Crowder and Sing, another man with the sharp-featured good looks of a movie actor, Majors, he would tell me his name was, Mike Majors; and two girls, one tall and coat-hanger thin and the other not so tall. The not-so-tall girl was a familiar face around campus, dressed always in black mourning clothes, right down to the hat and veil, with her face caked with white makeup and black lipstick. She looked like a corpse. The tall coat-hanger I would get to know as Bea. The corpse's name was Harriette.

Downstage, Drucilla Gordon crouched on her knees, leafing through a pile of papers that lay on the floor in front of her. She was the only one who saw me coming down the aisle.

"Professor Dooley told me to bring this over," I said, croaking a bit.

"Dewey did?" Her black eyes reflected the gold light high above her head, in a way that gave her a look of willfulness, even willful willfulness.

"Dooley."

"Dewey to us. What'd he send over?"

Before I could answer, Sing called from upstage, "Is that our letter from Dewey?"

Drucilla Gordon looked at me. "Is it our letter?" she asked.

"I guess," I said

"He says he thinks so," she said.

"Then ask him to give it to you."

"I think he was going to—" and then to me—"you were, weren't you?"

"It's why I brought it over."

"Splendid," she said.

"You're making fun of me."

"Don't be silly," she said, tilting her head and talking to me like I was five.

It was a little humiliating. I handed over the letter and turned to leave.

"Wait." She called after me, "Want to see?"

"What?"

"We were just about to do a run-through."

I got the feeling that she was sorry about giving me a hard time, and I said, "Sure."

"Sit there," she said. She climbed the stairs to the stage. "Go ahead, Roy."

CROWDER: [standing against a semicircular rail that stands on top of a smaller stage or dais in the middle of the larger stage] Good Friday began with a third denial. General and Mrs. Grant had arrived in the capital on Thursday on their way to Philadelphia. They were hoping to meet with the Secretary of War and leave town before the Lincolns knew they were in Washington. President Lincoln was planning to go to Grover's Theater on Friday to attend a new production, *Aladdin, or the Wonderful Lamp,* with his son, Tad. But upon hearing that his general was in town, he canceled his reservation at Grover's and sent a messenger to the Grants inviting them to Ford's Theater to see *Our American Cousin,* probably thinking that an English drawing room farce was more suitable to the Grants' taste than a kiddie play about flying carpets and genies.

This fuss over the arrival of the Grants takes on the qualities of a farce, itself, if you imagine the hickish Lincolns scrambling around the White House to prepare for the arrival of le grand Général, Mrs. Lincoln dusting, the President dictating commendations and dispatching couriers. Just as plans appear to be set, a rider arrives with a letter conveying the Grants' regrets.

BEA: Stood up at the last minute, the President asks several of his cabinet members; all refuse. After declaring the theater outing off, the President inexplicably changed his mind and instead asked his military attaché Major Rathbone [Majors steps forward and clicks his heels] if he would like to attend with Clara Harris, his stepsister and fiancée.

DRUCILLA: Imagine, Henry, the theater with the President of the United States.

SING: We, myself and a small band of patriots, met at Gautier's restaurant on March 13. Over a dinner of oysters and cognac and fine cigars, I detailed my plan of abduction, one that outshone those previous in its boldness, desperation, and ingenuity.

Whereas in the past we had sought to stop the President's carriage in open country, like highwaymen, I thought instead to burst in upon his box, the next time he attended the theater. The plan, though well-struck, did not proceed well from its inception. Lee's surrender on Palm Sunday intervened, and the President's fickle nature when it came to public appearance also complicated our execution, when on the morning of the 14th of April 1864—

CROWDER: Eighteen sixty-five.

SING: Eighteen sixty-five, to be sure. I learned of the change in the President's plans when I went to Grover's to refamiliarize myself with the scheme of the building. Upon arriving I was informed that Tad Lincoln would be attending the performance that evening with his tutor, and the Backwoods Baboon himself would instead be going to Ford's, with the Grants. These developments suited me just as well. I went to directly to Ford's Theater on the excuse of picking up a letter I was expecting regarding my investment in the oil business. The previous month, I had performed there in *The Apostate,* which was a favorite of mine and a fitting play for my final role.

Then I proceeded to the stables where I rented a horse, a roan mare, a substantial animal, but hardly worth the five dollars I was charged by the liverer who must have recognized me from the stage and therefore thought I was of some means.

From the stables I rode to the National Hotel, and went to the desk where Merrick, a man I knew, was working behind the desk. I asked him for a sheet of writing paper and an envelope, both of which he produced, and—

MAJORS: He stood at the desk composing a letter. He seemed particularly agitated and distracted by the comings and goings around him and after a few minutes he asked me for a private room, at which point I directed him to the clerk's office behind the front desk. After another minute or so he called out to me,

SING: Hey, Merrick what is the date?

MAJORS: "The fourteenth," says I.

SING: Of what year?

MAJORS: He asked. "Surely you're joking," says I.

SING: I am not.

MAJORS: He said, annoyed with me at his error, he seemed. I informed him that it was 1865 and he resumed writing and left shortly after, though I was toiling at my desk and saw him not as he left.

SING: I was riding down Tenth in the direction of Ford's when I encountered John Matthews, a thespian with whom I had trod the boards a thousand times, and as recently as my farewell performance at Ford's in *The Apostate.*

MAJORS: Did you see Lee's officers brought in under guard?

SING: "I did," said I. Struck by the gravity of this moment, I put my hand to my head and cried, "My God! I no longer have a country." I then said, "Johnny, I wish to ask you a favor; will you do it for me?"

MAJORS: "Of course, John," said I. He extended a black-gloved hand which held an envelope and said—

SING: I have a letter which I wish you to deliver to the offices of the *National Intelligencer* tomorrow morning.

MAJORS: I told him, "Certainly I will."

SING: We parted.

CROWDER: Did you deliver the letter to the *National Intelligencer?*

MAJORS: No sir.

CROWDER: Do you have it in your possession?

MAJORS: No sir.

SING: From the hotel I rode directly to the Kirkwood House where Vice President Andrew Johnson boarded. A Negro doorman informed us that neither Mr. Johnson nor his secretary Mr. Wm. A. Browning were in, and I left him with my calling card upon which I wrote, "Don't wish to disturb you; are you in?"

HARRIETTE: *Why* was *that card* of Booth's found in Johnson's box? Some acquaintance certainly existed. I have always had the harrowing thought that they had an understanding. Did not Booth say there is one thing he would not tell? There is said to be honor among thieves. I have never heard of Johnson regretting my sainted husband's death. He never wrote me a line of condolence and he behaved in the most brutal way.

SING: That demented hag was only half wrong. As it happens I had had the occasion to meet Johnson, in Nashville, where he was serving as military governor, and I was serving as an adequate Richelieu, and had found him—as all who ever met him found him—a braggart and a drunk. I had given the task of killing him to George Azterodt, a German ferryman and known inebriate. This assignment was perhaps deliberate on my part, since Azterodt was almost certain to fail, and the one of those we had marked for death whom was known to me personally would be spared.

DRUCILLA: [climbs off the stool] Okay Harold, we get the idea. [pages through the script] Hey, you [points at Tom] get up here a second. [He points to himself to make sure she is talking to him, then reluctantly climbs up on the stage. Drucilla hands him a script with a line circled.] Follow along and when it gets to this line, say it—Roy he's taking your line here.

SING [annoyed]: At six I took the mare to the stables opposite the stage door of Ford's Theater. The play was scheduled to begin at 7:30. I would return around nine. I had seen the play more than a few times and never cared to see it again—

DRUCILLA: Let's go, Harold.

SING [more annoyed]: The performance began at 7:45. I read in the papers the next day that the President arrived around 8:45. At nine I retrieved my horse from the stables and brought it around to the stage door, where I asked Ned Spangler if he would hold the reins while I went inside. He said that he could not, that he would be needed inside to strike the first-act set in but a few minutes. He fetched for me another stableboy, whom I knew not.

MAJORS: This boy is later identified as Peanuts Burrows.

SING: Inside I encountered J. L. DeBonay.

MAJORS: He wanted to cross backstage. I informed him that this was the dairy scene and that there was no room but we could pass below the stage and we did.

SING: I exited though a side door that opened on an alley, and entered the Star Saloon through the back.

TOM: [noticing that all eyes in the room are upon him and reading at a level he believes will make him heard throughout the room, but is in actuality a good deal louder than the other performers] Yeah, he was in here—

SING: Thus fortified, I returned to the theater—

TOM: I wasn't finished.

SING: [as Booth—as if annoyed by a heckler] What's that you're saying?

TOM: I'm supposed to say, "If I had known what he was up to I could have killed him then and there with my bare hands. And even if I hadn't known, because I never liked him."—and then you go.

SING: Ur, yes, I had a bourbon to fortify me for what was to come, the most heroic and patriotic blow ever struck on these shores for freedom. I entered through the front door. The usher—a Mr. James E. Buckingham—reached out his hand for a ticket. "You don't need a ticket, Buck," says I and bounded up the stairs to the boxes, whistling a jig. If I had not known the layout of the theater so well I might have thought I approached the wrong box, for it was completely unguarded. Slowing the pace of my stride I timed the moment of my arrival at the door to coincide with the certain line when I knew but one actor would be on stage, tired old Lord Dundreary, calling off into the wings: "Don't know enough to turn you inside out, old gal—you sockdologizing old man-trap." At that I burst through the door of the box where the President sat in a rocking chair, roaring with laughter, like the rest of the mob. He must have noticed the change in lighting in the room, and I recall was just beginning to turn his head when I drew my pistol and fired but inches from his head. He lolled forward as though I had just sent him into a deep nap. His adjutant was slow to react. He stood and turned to me not thinking to draw his side arm, with my left hand I produced my dagger from my vest and thrust at him striking him in the arm. Mrs. Lincoln screamed.

HARRIETTE: [Screams, a fakey stage scream]

SING: Here I made my famous leap [he crosses to the edge of the platform and puts a foot on the rail]

DRUCILLA: Hold it, Harold.

SING: I have to jump [jumps]. I have to jump to the stage and cry, "Sic semper tyrannis." Shout, I say, for there were those who say I "hissed" the words or "spat them out," when the truth was that I used the projection and elocution befitting my skill as a tragedian. Of course, it is true that I had suffered some recurrent hoarseness, owing in large part to my despair and dissipate lifestyle, but when the time came—

DRUCILLA: [louder] Harold I said quit it.

SING: And I said I haven't finished.

DRUCILLA: But you have.

SING: I still have to escape. I was on the run for six days.

DRUCILLA: If you were, it was off stage.

BEA: It's not working Harold.

SING: Yes, it is.

BEA: No, it's not.

SING: Harriette?

CROWDER: Why not ask me?

SING: I know what you think.

DRUCILLA: It's missing something.

BEA: Like talent.

HARRIETTE: Hey, aren't personal attacks against our rules?

CROWDER: We have rules?

MAJORS: No.

BEA: Anyway, since when is it against the rules to criticize? I said what I thought. It's dead, it's *Spoon River Anthology* or something. [Sits firmly in chair, hands clasped in her lap] It's like, "I shot the President and now I'm dead."

DRUCILLA: Maybe, Harold, if you could tell us what you are trying to do.

SING [talking very quickly, as if to prevent interruption]: The point—if there has to be a point—is to situate the assassin at

the center of the history, rather than as an agent of the
victim's history, rather than as the Outsider, as Sandburg calls
Booth, the Strange Man, the American Judas. The Biblical
dimension of the proto-traitor is appealing for its grandiosity,
if nothing else. Yet Judas was a disciple and the one whom
Jesus favored of the twelve. On the other hand, Chapter 14,
verse 11 of the gospel of Mark, "And he sought how he
might conveniently betray him," that carries an echo of
prophecy for the conspiracy.

The more eerie echoes are of Shakespeare's *Julius Caesar*.
Consider that Booth's grandfather Richard Booth named his
first boy Junius Brutus Booth after the killer of Caesar.
Booth's father, like his father, was an anti-royalist. Booth's
second to last performance was in *Julius Caesar*, in New York
City, with his brothers, Junius Jr., and Edwin. Though in that
performance, John took the role of Marc Antony against
Edwin's Brutus. Neither comparison is perfect, Judas or
Brutus, yet it's the echoes of those two killers who were
seemingly driven by fate, that gives the man and his act of
violence something even beyond historical importance.

CROWDER: If you accept the view that Lincoln was predestined
to die, then who actually killed him is unimportant.

SING: I contend exactly the opposite: that Lincoln was not
predestined to die, Booth was predestined to kill. That's the
significant distinction.

CROWDER: By what standard?

SING: [reaches in his pocket and pulls out a small gun, a
derringer, which he places on the rail. All regard it silently
for several seconds.]

BEA: Is it loaded?

SING: Of course not. Don't be stupid.

HARRIETTE [amazed]: Where did you get it?

DRUCILLA: Mike got it.

MAJORS [nods self-consciously]: It wasn't that hard.

HARRIETTE: Is it the real one?

MAJORS: The real one's at the Smithsonian or someplace. This isn't a replica, but it was manufactured by the same company, several years later, there are differences, which sets us back in the sense of absolute realism, if that remains a goal but—

CROWDER: Where would you find the bullets?

SING: It's a .44 caliber. Not uncommon.

DRUCILLA: What we're looking for is like a cap, right?

MAJOR: A blank. That shouldn't be a problem.

BEA: Still, be careful.

DRUCILLA: Yeah, put it away, Harold, it's creepy.

They'd forgotten I was there so, before any of them had a chance to ask me why I was still hanging around, I stepped behind the curtain, up the aisle, and was actually out the door when Drucilla Gordon called after me, "Hey, wait."

"You're coming back, right?"

"Nah, I got some business."

"Not today. I meant you'll come to rehearsal again."

"Really? I wasn't good, was I?"

"What? God, no," she said. "That's not what I meant. But Dewey likes you and you seem to drive Harold nuts. It'll be fun. Trust me." Outdoors, her eyes were the purest black.

"When's the next one?"

"Next week actually. It's not a rehearsal really. It's a party, a party for us. Harold's just finished this play and he thinks he can get us a grant. Here, come here." She took my hand in hers, which was small, her fingers short and thin like a doll's, and wrote an address on my palm. "The door's around the side and don't knock, we'll never hear you."

I walked staring at the address on my palm, on air, but feeling like I'd been given something I wasn't ready for. I didn't know what to make of all the waving of arms and the yelling. The historical stuff was mundane. I didn't understand the argument and I seemed to be the only one who didn't. This was what I was thinking about, lying on my back and staring at the ceiling when someone knocked at the door of my room. "Get lost," I shouted, thinking it was Ship.

"I already am," a voice said.

I pulled the chair away and opened the door a crack. Over the course of the term more than half of the bulbs in the hallway had been broken, stolen, or burned out, and all I could see of the guy at my door was that he wore a heavy Army jacket and his head was shaved.

I said, "What's up."

He put his cigarette to his mouth backhanded, and I realized it was Grey. "Laertes," he said, "has come to Wittenburg."

THIS CARP OF TRUTH

He looked like shit and I'd never been happier to see anyone in my life. I went to hug him but he pushed past, dropping his jacket on the floor. Underneath he wore a blue filling station coverall, which was dirty and ripped at both knees, and his work boots were spattered with paint and varnish stains. His eyes were half shut and he'd shaved his head.

"Jesus," I said.

Grey jumped on Ship's bed and put his feet up. "This one yours?"

"No."

"Does it belong to Dennis?"

"Yeah," I said.

He sat up and looked for a place to flick his ash, which fell as he did. He ground the ashes into the bedspread, then found an empty Coke can on Ship's desk to use as an ashtray.

"How'd you get down here?"

"Hitched to Minneapolis and took a bus from there."

"Where's Callie?"

"Home."

"How come she didn't come with?"

"I didn't feel she should travel in her condition."

"Which condition?"

"Pregnant," he said. He said it in an offhand way, as though it was news I'd heard but forgotten.

"What?"

"She's pregnant," he said. "She's going to have a baby."

"When?"

"I don't know, six months."

"Do your mom and dad know?"

"Yes."

"What did they say?"

"Jack said I should tell you."

"Does Dolores know?"

"Yes."

"What did she say?"

"Get out."

"You're shitting me."

He shook his head.

"Where's she staying?"

"Our house."

"She mad you left?"

He took a long, two-part drag on the butt. "She didn't know I was coming."

I tried to picture Callie pregnant and couldn't, any more than I could picture Drucilla Gordon pregnant. "I'll go back with you," I said.

"I'm not asking."

"What'd you come for, then?" I asked, and he was about to answer when Ship popped through the door and looked sadly at Grey.

It was only after we convinced Dennis that Grey would be gone the next day—which we all knew was a lie—that he returned to his standard pallor. Grey slept in my bed that night. I couldn't remember how long it had been since we bunked together. We didn't say two words before he was asleep. The next morning Grey went to Dooley's class with me. It was hard to get used to him without the hair. It'd always been the first thing anyone noticed. I gave him a notebook to carry. If the campus impressed him, he didn't show it. Chewing on a wad of gum, he mostly looked straight ahead, except to turn his head occasionally to watch someone go by, never to look at the various landmarks I pointed out. I'd say something like, "There's the observatory," and he'd nod as though he already knew and say, "Yeah, great."

It was Dooley's last lecture of the semester, on Polk and the Mexican War. While he paced the western expanses of the map, tracing his pointer along the Rio Grande, Grey hummed to himself and doodled Fender guitars in his notebook. Dooley, who believed that history was made not in war but in treaty, skipped over the battles and talked instead of the Wilmot Proviso. We hadn't made it to the Civil War, which was kind of a bummer because I can only imagine what he would have to say about the dark enterprises behind that disaster. Nonetheless the students stood and cheered when he finished. He bowed and left the stage and the applause got louder, while Grey looked up from his drawing. "Do they do this every day?"

At lunch at the Plaza, a quarter-beer joint, Grey bought two bottles of Point and we played some pool. He knocked down two solids on the break and lined up a combination across the full length of the table,

"What are you going to do?" I asked him, hoping to mess up his shot.

He pocketed the ball and said, "About what?"

Grey was good at pool. I wasn't particularly. Grey was good at almost everything that I wasn't. I believed that there had to be something that I could beat him at, but I hadn't found it. "Get married, I guess." He put away the eight ball and held out his hand for more quarters.

I said, "You think you have to?"

"Break," he said.

The cue ball smacked the formation and sent the twelve ball flying off the table. He missed an easy side shot by striking too hard, and I ran three solids that were bunched in a corner before missing on a bank.

"So what's the problem?"

He didn't have a shot and circled the table twice before tapping the cue ball against the rail so I wouldn't either. "I need money?"

"How much?"

"How much you got?" he said.

I thought he was joking. "What does it cost to have a baby?" I asked and scratched. The question caught the attention of two girls sitting in the next booth and they stared.

Grey looked annoyed, missed his next shot, and watched me miss one as well before he said, "Not what I'm worried about." He tried to pocket the thirteen but succeeded only in kicking it out of the corner. I dropped the two and followed up with the eight on an easy shot and felt satisfied to have won, but Grey wasn't paying attention. He laid the cue on the table and dangled his beer between two fingers as we walked to our table. We sat. He leaned in close. "I'm working a deal," he said. "I talked to this guy at the marina."

"Local?"

"You don't know him."

"They own a cabin?"

"I said you don't know him. He's got a ketch—"

"He's got a catch?"

"A ketch, a twenty-two-foot ketch. Thirty years old, sixteen of those in dry dock, prime condition, he says."

"What does he want from you?"

"It's up in Canada. He wants five thousand dollars. It's worth ten times that. He says he'll give it to me for two grand if I sail it out."

"From where?"

"Up there."

"Where up there?"

"I don't know. The other side of the lake."

"What's over there?"

"I'm not sure we need to know," he said.

"He's got this boat worth fifty thousand dollars and he's going to give it to you for two."

Grey wiped the foam off his lips with his sleeve. "That's about it."

"How come?"

"I don't know. Taxes or something. You want another?" he asked, then lifted my bottle and saw that it was full.

"It doesn't sound right," I said.

He shrugged. If he was hiding something from me it wouldn't be the first time. He wasn't above a lie.

"How much can you kick in?"

Grey shook his head.

"I have it," I said. "It's about all I have."

He looked up from his beer. "It's okay," he said. "You'll get it all back."

"What do you mean?"

"That it's an investment. Look," he said. He set his beer bottle down on the far corner of the table, then with his left hand pushed the tin ashtray toward it. "They pay me to fly up to Sault Ste. Marie. I take a bus to Michipicoten, which is where the boat is. Hand over the dough, sign a piece of paper, and it's all mine—ours. Then it's a beam reach south by southwest home." The bottle left a wet trail on the Formica as he slid it back toward him and lifted it to his mouth. "It's a simple transaction. I bring the boat back. Fix it up. It shouldn't need much, from what he says, and whatever materials it does need I can cover on credit. I sit back and take bids.

"When it's all over you get the front money back and, say, twenty percent."

The more he talked the worse the deal sounded. "When would you go?"

"Soon as the thaw. End of March, I'm hoping. Might have to wait until April."

"I'll go with," I said.

"I'm not asking."

"I know," I said, "but I'll go."

"You don't get it," he said, "I'm not asking you."

When we got back to the room, Ship was on the phone, saying, "Yes, Mom, no, Mom, I don't, Mom. Mom—I don't." Grey flopped down next to him on his bed and Ship moved to the desk.

"When can you get it?" Grey asked.

"Tomorrow," I said.

"Cash."

"I'll get cash."

Ship hung up the phone. "What cash?"

Grey looked at me as if asking whether he should tell Ship the story. I shook my head. "Tom's been cheating on his tests," he said. "I told him I wouldn't say anything about it if he paid me off."

Ship looked like he was trying to decide if Grey was telling the truth. "Well," he said, pleased with the thought that just crossed his mind, "then I guess you won't be getting any money, then, because you told me."

"You know," Grey said, "you're right. I shouldn't get any money now that I told somebody."

On Saturday morning, we went down to the bank. You wouldn't have thought it was much of a thing for a student to withdraw his savings at the end of term, but the way Grey stood next to me—shoulder to the counter, casing the lobby—made the teller nervous, which got me feeling like I had something to hide. She held my driver's license for a long time, looking at the picture, at me, and at the picture again before she handed over the money, twenty-one hundred-dollar bills and change. I shoved the money into the inside pocket of my coat and held my arm tight against it so that I looked like I was packing heat or something. The white-haired bank cop watched us as we walked out.

It was one of those clear winter days that come with cold temperatures. Shivering, Grey held out his hand.

"What do you want?" I asked him.

He said, "Give it to me."

"That's okay."

The sun was in his eyes and he squinted the same way he did when he was looking to start a fight. "I said give it."

"I know and I said that's okay." People passing on the sidewalk were staring. I walked. Grey caught up and grabbed me by the arm. It's mine, I wanted to say, but he wouldn't have liked the sound of that. "What difference does it make who holds it?" is what I did say.

As he stared at the ground, I could see on his skull the inch-long white line where the hair didn't grow back, a scar from where I split his head open with a can of Lincoln Logs when we were eight. "Look," he said. "I don't think you're getting it. The people I'm talking about. They don't know you. They never asked me to bring anybody else in. Get it. I'm not asking you to come with. I don't want you to. Come on," he jabbed his knuckles into my belly and made a flicking motion with his fingers. "Hand it over."

I already knew I was going to give him the money, but I said, "What's the hurry if you can't go until April?"

He dropped his hand. "I left out a step."

"I figured that out."

He laughed sarcastically. "Yeah, well I hope so."

He smiled in a way I'd seen dozens of times but never aimed at me. There was hate in it. It said, You can't get where I am from where you are. "Fuck you," he said.

"Yeah," I said. "Fuck me," and slapped the envelope into his hand.

Grey ended up staying through exam week, which I didn't mind because Ship did. To get even for him conning me out of every cent I had (I already knew I would never see that money again), I told him I had to study. Every morning I sat at my desk, staring at an open book, until he threw on his coat and left the room. Most of the time I was too distracted to wonder where he went. My exam results weren't good, but nothing that happened could be blamed on Grey. I studied hard but exams were a lot like a field sprint in a bike race: you could go from first to last in a hurry. I blew my Trig final, a rookie error. The test was cumulative, which Professor Jeer might have told us and I forgot, or he told us and I didn't think to worry about it, reasoning that if I could do the problems from the end of the semester I could do the ones from the beginning. That turned out not to be true. By the time I finished the exam the room was empty, outside of me and the proctor, and I wasn't optimistic about how I had done.

On Tuesday, I had my German final, which consisted of a short-answer test and an oral presentation titled "*Auf den Strand.*" That should have been easy, except that Fräulein Menendez didn't care so much about how well you could talk in German as she did about if you used all the vocabulary words assigned. Since I hadn't bothered to remember which ones they were, it was pretty much dumb chance which ones showed up in my talk. I got nervous and substituted some of Pop's Frisian words—*wetter* for *wasser* and *seil* for *segel*, thinking, as I did, that it was a crazy world where someone like me who could speak the language like he had been born in Germany, wouldn't score as well as the captain of the girls swim team. This bothered me so much that I spent the rest of the afternoon feeling sorry for myself and forgot to hand in my final essay for English composition.

I still had my term paper for Dooley to write. I called my essay "The Betrayal of Tecumseh" because the word *betrayal* had been bouncing around in my head and I liked the sound of it. The problem is that I came up with the title before I did any of the research. Then I read three books on Tecumseh and couldn't find where he was betrayed by anybody. You could say that the tribes of the south and west betrayed him by not joining his confederacy, but they had never said they would in the first place. You could say that he was betrayed by William Henry Harrison, but to me betrayed means that someone you trust turns on you, and I doubt that Tecumseh ever trusted the general. You could say the betrayal was of the Indians by the white men, but, I thought, who doesn't know that? The betrayal of Tecumseh, then, had to be the fact that weak men can overcome stronger men if their only desire is to destroy those who are better than them. This came to me in my last paragraph. I didn't start over.

I typed the last of the bibliography at six in the morning while Ship wheezed underneath his blankets. I hadn't seen Grey since the previous afternoon. Blowing the last of the Wite-Out dry on the page, I threw my coat on over my pajamas, and headed down to Dooley's office to slide the paper under the door. On the way over to the Humanities building, the wind ripped through the fabric of my clothes and I shivered, but on the way back the sun was rising, casting a glare on the dome of the observatory.

A thought popped into my head, so odd that I said it out loud. "I go to college."

The words meant something to me. For four months I'd been lonely, scared at times, and angry, but I'd also been happy. I couldn't build a boat, but I'd learned a thing or two.

IN THIS SCENE

When I got back to the room, Grey was asleep face down on my bed with his Army coat still on and Ship was sitting at his desk watching him. "He just came in here and did that," Ship said.

"Did what?"

"That—he just walked in and fell over like that."

"Did he say anything?"

"He said, 'Bed.'—Where were you?"

"Turning in a term paper."

"How long's he going to stay?"

"I don't know, Ship, and I really can't talk about it. I'm wiped out."

"You can't sleep here."

"I wasn't asking."

"I said 'no.'"

"Listen, Ship, I'll sleep on the floor. You'll never know the difference." I yanked my pillow out from under Grey's head and lay on the floor. The pillow was wet from where he drooled on it, so I turned it over and was out before I knew it.

When I woke up, Grey was sitting at Ship's desk, smoking a cigarette and paging through one of Ship's business textbooks.

"Do you think this stuff would do me any good?"

"Sure, why not?"

"What do you have left to do?"

"That was it."

"So you're ready to celebrate?"

"Actually, I've got this thing I'm supposed to go to," I said and knew instantly I'd made a mistake.

"Great, where?"

"They just said me."

"That's only because they haven't met me yet."

Grey wore what he'd worn all week, and I dug out the yellow shirt I got from Howie who was going to throw it away. It was a perfectly good shirt, yellow chamois cloth, with steel buttons and red stitching on the pockets and cuffs, the only thing wrong with it being that Howie didn't want it anymore. Grey talced his head and the stubble on his face with Ship's baby powder and brushed his teeth with Ship's Crest.

I looked to see if my collar was twisted and saw that the months without sun had turned my hair the color of wet hay. "Look," I told him, "I don't know these people yet. Don't mess it up for me."

"Just going for the show," Grey said. "You look like a rodeo clown."

We walked east through the town. The sidewalks were wet. A hard chill made my teeth rattle. By the time we turned down Washington, my Chuck Taylors were soaked through. I meant to buy a pair of boots when it got cold enough. Now that it was cold enough I had gotten used to wet feet. Every few yards we walked I sneaked a glance at Grey, embarrassed to admit to myself that I was afraid he'd embarrass me, until he said, "Quit it, you're giving me the creeps."

When we reached the address Drucilla had written on my hand, I thought we had the wrong place. The building looked like a factory rather than a house or an apartment building. Grey looked at me and I shrugged. There were lights on so we pulled open the heavy outside door. Music throbbed in the wall, something rhythmic and repetitive, the same eight notes turning over and over. The stairwell smelled of dust and sweeping compound and was dark except for a single black-light bulb high overhead, which illuminated trails of fluorescent spray paint on the walls that zigzagged to the top in three parallel sets of right angles, hugging the contour of the stairs. In the ultraviolet light, Grey's dirty blue coverall looked suede black and his head a tarnished bronze, like the bust of some great man who'd gotten famous, gone bald, and died, all before he graduated from high school. He grinned, his teeth blue-white against the darkness of everything around them, and said, "I think I'm going to enjoy this."

At the top, a second door, the music was louder now, and I recognized the song as "Atrocity Exhibition." There had been something in *Rolling Stone*. The lead singer a suicide, his depression living on in the monotone voice.

We pushed through the second steel door and it opened on a bright and vast room. It was no warmer than it had been outside and the steam of our breath rose above us and fell in heavy clouds. To the left was a metal staircase leading to what looked like a catwalk. In front of us was a concrete floor in the center of this expanse, a room without walls: two old couches and battered armchairs, organized around an old Oriental rug and four or five space heaters with cords and extension cords spoking out toward the walls.

For all the space, the building was largely unused. On one of the couches sat Drucilla and the two girls from the theater, all done up like they were posing for the cover of a magazine—a magazine from forty years ago. Harriette was on one end, in mourning like always. In the middle sat Bea, in a beaded green dress that made her skin look yellow, and on the end, wearing a short gray dress, heavy black wool stockings, and looking like the last female of some exotic species smuggled in from the arctic, sat Drucilla Gordon.

Crowder appeared behind them, dressed in boots and lederhosen that must have taken an entire cow to make. Sing, behind him, wore a gold shirt of a shimmering fabric, and metal-flake pants and tennis shoes that had been spray-painted silver, so that he looked like one of those Greek messenger gods, one of the troublemaking kind, the sort that screwed up messages on purpose and started great wars.

When he saw us, Crowder's bulging eyes fixed on me. Suddenly he stepped forward and grabbed me. "Jesus! We're not doing this again!" he bellowed over his shoulder in a corny stage voice. "Run!" he said to me, "Run! Get out of here while you still can!"

Grey thought he was serious and stepped between us. Crowder looked at him soberly and turned to me, as though I'd been in on the joke all along. "Who's this?" he asked.

"Grey," I said.

Crowder released my lapels and straightened my collar. "Nice shirt," he said and pushed Sing forward against obvious resistance. "And this is Harold, whom you've seen before and no doubt discussed."

Harold Sing reached out his hand the way a woman would.

"That's Bea," Harold said, with a jab of his thumb. "We found her passed out on the front step one day, and no one had the heart to tell her to leave."

"Blow it out your ass, Harry," Bea said.

Mike Majors suddenly appeared. "Harriette. And that's Drucilla," he said. "Call her Dru. How do you like our little clubhouse? Crowder's dad owns the place. He told us he would let us hang out as long as we didn't rip him off."

"Where is everyone?" Grey asked.

"What do you mean?" Dru asked.

"I mean who else is coming?"

"Oh, no one, probably," Bea said.

"We're the only ones who ever come to our parties," said Harriette. The comment hung in the air, as they all seemed to be weighing the truth of it.

"Which is why we're so happy to have you here," Dru said. "Please take off your coats."

"That's okay," Grey said. "It's freezing."

"Yes, well we're afraid that can't be helped," Sing said.

"What do you major in, Gary?" Majors asked.

"Varnish," Grey said.

"What's that?" Harold said.

"He doesn't go to school. He fixes boats," I said, realizing after it was too late how insulting that must have sounded.

"Is that like a boatwright?" Crowder asked.

"Is it like a glovemaker?" said Harriette, who sounded quite normal underneath the eyeliner and pancake makeup, "because we were just talking about glovemakers. Roy was telling us that Shakespeare's dad was a glovemaker, because Dru lost her gloves and she was sad because it was an old pair that used to belong to her grandfather, and she could go buy another pair but they'd never be as good because it's a lost art, glovemaking."

"Nostalgic tripe," Majors said.

"No one works with their hands anymore. That's what we were talking about," Dru said.

"They do," Majors said, "but you'd never be able to afford anything they made—well *you* would. Gloves were cheap then because the workers were paid less than nothing to make them. Is that what you want?"

"I just want new gloves," Dru said plaintively.

I'd never heard people talk about glovemakers. The conversation struck me, not so much for what they talked about as the way they talked. They talked like people who were used to standing on stages, people who were used to being listened to. Their voices blended like a radio show: Dru's half-whisper and Crowder's bellow, Harriette's bland directness and Bea's sarcasm, Majors's cocktail stud rap and Sing's clicky patter.

Dru tapped on a glass and called out, "We've got to toast Harold's play."

I stood next to Majors as he put his arms around my shoulder and Grey's. "How about it you two?" he said. "Don't you feel lucky to be here?"

I looked at Grey and we both said, "Sure."

"So what's it called?" I asked Majors.

"What?"

"Harold's play."

"I'm sure I have no idea," he said. "That's Harold's territory."

Harriette flopped on the couch. Sing found a chair. Crowder walked around the perimeter turning dials on the heaters. Dru sat and curled her stockinged legs to her chest.

From beyond the reach of the lights, I heard a refrigerator door close. Majors appeared in the light with his index finger looped through the handle of a gallon jug of wine. He tossed a stack of paper cups to me. Once everyone had filled their cups, Majors tapped on the side of the jug. "A toast," he said, "to Dru, to Stovepipe Theater, to a new year, and—"

Crowder took a sip prematurely. "—And to wine," he said, "that comes in a bottle with a cap that screws on."

"Here, here."

The conversation grew louder as the evening went along. Everybody talked at once. Their voices rose and echoed through the lattice of steel support beams forty feet above our heads. Mostly they talked about people they knew, put-downs and rumors, ending with explosions of laughter. My attention wandered to the shadows just beyond the reach of the light. The railing that ran the length of the second floor and the glass windows of the abandoned offices beyond it. As my eyes became accustomed to the dim light I saw stretching across the floor rows of heavy machinery, drill presses and lathes arranged in rows. They reminded me of the dormant menace of the robots of Robot World.

We played games, charades and this one called "In This Scene," in which each team takes turns picking names of plays out of Harriette's hat. You decide which scene you want to perform from that play, the other team decides what twist the scene will take. "For instance," Crowder said, "if the play was *Hamlet,* and the scene was the play within the play, you'd do it just like it was in the dreary original, only the troupe only speak Lithuanian. Want to give it a try, Bea?"

She uncurled from the chair, walked over to the cap, plucked a slip, and read, "*A Doll's House.*"

"Okay," Crowder said, "in this scene, Nora, who has struggled for independence throughout the entire second act, must tell Thorvald that she crashed the Volvo."

Majors thought about it for a moment and stifled a laugh, Bea picked up a stained, crocheted shawl that was draped over the back of the couch and put it over her head. Majors straightened his blazer and stood upright until Crowder said, "Go," at which point Bea, looking worried and preoccupied, began rearranging items on the coffee table.

Majors strode into the light from down stage and said, "Honey, I'm home," in an accent like Ricky Ricardo on *I Love Lucy*, and everyone laughed.

Bea stood up with a start. "Thorvald," she said, "there is something I must tell you about the car. I was backing out of Thor's House of Cheese—where Jarlsberg is always on special—when Olaf who drives the cement mixer came down the road much too fast, as people will in such modern times as these."

With his head turned toward us, Majors stepped toward her and said, "What are you saying, Nora?"

"It was not my fault." Bea was rolling. I didn't like her, but I admired the way she could counterfeit such emotions. "How can I respect you as a driver Thorvald, if I cannot respect myself."

Crowder said, "Curtain."

"Our turn," Dru said and plucked a slip of paper from the hat. "Oh, great," she said, "Sophocles's *Electra.*"

Sing, Bea, and Majors huddled and then Bea said, "In this scene Clytemnestra suspects that Electra stole her vibrator."

I laughed, a little too loudly, and there was an awkward silence before Harriette laughed too. "How many do we need," Harriette asked, "two?"

"No three," Crowder said. "A chorus."

Dru leaned toward me, "You want to do that?"

"I'll watch this one," I said, not knowing the play and having no idea what to do.

They walked giggling to the center of the room like two high school girls who had been caught passing notes in math class.

Crowder stepped from the shadows behind them, carrying a push broom, bristles up, which he rapped on the concrete floor, "Behold Clytemnestra, queen of the house of Atreus"—with a wave of his hand he indicated Harriette, who curtsied—"wife of Agamemnon grown bitter at the absence of her warrior husband, who toils with sword and shield to return his brother's wife—and collect a deposit. He nightly breaching the nubile battlements of fair, unheeded Cassandra with his Trojan horse, while his wife remains behind, attended only by Electra, her daughter, in nature if not in name, or by any other available standard." Dru bowed quickly.

"Electra," Harriette called, "Electra come here this instant."

Dru stepped forward, her hand behind her back. "Yes mother—whore."

"Electra, where is it?"

"Where is what?"

"You know what I'm talking about."

"Do I? Then perhaps you are talking about the truth. In which case I do. It lies behind the mask of your sluttish lies."

There was laughter from the others sitting around. I thought to myself that this is a role, the spiteful teenage daughter, that Dru had played before. Harriette on the other hand seemed incapable of conjuring any feelings of spite or anger, her voice as it got higher only seemed less menacing, like that of a cartoon mouse.

She turned to Dru and said. "There may be truth in part of what you speak. And it may be also true that Aegisthus, in his fear of our master's return, has grown as limp as yesterday's olive salad. And still it would be well for you, who closes her eyes at night and dreams of her brother Orestes."

"I do not dream of my brother's Orestes. I dream of the day when your ears are deaf forever to the baleful hum of this artifice." At that Dru pointed toward Crowder, who made a low mechanical buzzing sound and held the broom at arm's length, hands shaking, like the broom was fighting to get away.

"For pity it comes," Dru shouted, "and so I fear shall I."

"Then it is done. You will impale thine mother." She shrieked and threw herself to the floor. Dru snatched the broom and raised it over her head like a spear.

"Curtain," Crowder yelled. Majors wolf-whistled and the rest of us applauded. Dru dropped the broom and curtsied, lifting the hem of her skirt with her fingertips, while Harriette fought her way out of the folds of her dress to get to her feet, her black hair streaking the powder on her face.

Harold Sing shifted in his chair with his hands clasped on his knee until he was facing Grey and me and said, "Now you."

He caught Grey gulping the last of a cup of wine. "What?" he choked.

"Yes, you," said Harriette. "We haven't seen you guys do anything."

A chill went up my back at the thought of picking a piece of paper out of the hat with the name of a play that nine chances out of ten I'd never heard of.

"Or maybe we've seen everything," Crowder said.

Grey wiped his mouth. "What's that supposed to mean?"

"You know," Dru said loudly and waited until she saw that everyone was looking, "I'm bored."

Bea looked at her and then at Grey and then at Crowder and Sing. "Dru's right," she said. "This is lame. I'm going. I'm your ride Harriette."

Harriette followed her to the door but with her head turned over her shoulder in case the show hadn't ended yet. Grey waited until the others were looking at the girls and nodded at the door. I hadn't thought to leave, but he was right. This was the time for it, if we were going to get out before we wrecked any chance I had with these people.

We pulled on our coats and fell in behind the girls, saying our goodbyes all around. Dru sat sunken in an oversized armchair, watching us through narrowed eyes. No one seemed particularly overjoyed or sorry to see us go. Though as we reached the top of the stairs, Majors grabbed my arm as Grey continued down and said in a low voice, "You should come back tomorrow."

"Maybe," I said, "I'm not sure he's going to want to."

"No," he said, *"You* should come back tomorrow. Leave your friend at home, huh?"

I looked down the stairway to see if Grey caught any of that, but he didn't even seem to notice I wasn't behind him.

Snow had started to fall and we walked through the still-dark morning with the streetlights reflecting off wet sidewalks. Grey wasn't talking and that made me wonder if he'd heard what Majors said or if I'd done anything wrong by not telling Majors to fuck off. "What'd you think?" I asked.

Grey made a face. "Little faggoty, the guys were, didn't you think?"

He disappointed me. "It's college people," I said. "You get used to it."

He looked at me like he wanted to be sure I was on the level. We were both freezing and still had a long walk ahead. "I suppose I could—if I ever believed a word that they said."

"You didn't?"

"You did?"

"What did they say that you didn't believe?"

"That's just it," he said, "I mean, Jesus, it's gloves and plays and what the fuck. It was nothing that made any sense."

I said, "So you wouldn't care if you went back."

"Why would I ever go back?"

"You wouldn't," I said, "Just asking," as the snow fell harder.

IN WHICH GREY PERFORMS ACTS OF DARING ON A CAFETERIA TRAY

By morning snow clung to the branches outside the window. Grey lay on the rug in the middle of the room in his clothes, like a homicide victim lacking only the chalk outline. Ship was gone and his bed was made, leaving me to suspect that it had been him slamming the door that had jolted me awake.

Maybe a half foot of snow had fallen on the grass and fields. It didn't stick on the pavement because of the warm temperatures, making for a picture-book landscape of white fields and wet slate sidewalks cutting through at straight angles. Grey and I pulled on gloves and scarves and trudged up to the observatory. I'd told him about Elise and wanted her to meet him, though truth be told I don't think either of them had cared much about what they heard about the other. A sign on the door said it was closed until the next semester.

Some kids were making a racket at the top of the hill that sloped toward the woods and the lake. We walked to the crest to see tracks fanning out in all directions and saw bundled figures scooting toward the bottom, then jumping off and rolling in a cloud of snow before they reached the trees.

"What're they sliding on?" Grey asked.

"Looks like trays," I said, "from the cafeteria."

His eyes glittered. "We have to try that. Do you think they'd let me try that?"

I saw Ship standing with a crowd of kids I didn't know. "Hey, Ship," I yelled. He didn't turn. "Hey Dennis, over here."

He nodded just slightly, enough to show he knew I was yelling at him. We went to him, high-stepping through the snow.

"Can Grey slide on your tray?" I asked him.

"I don't know," he said.

"Come on," Grey said.

Ship reluctantly agreed—not so much handing him his tray as letting Grey snatch it from him.

He pointed at the trees just beyond the base of the hill. "The trick," he said, "is to make yourself wipe out before you get to the trees."

Grey looked. "Screw that," he said. "If I can get through there"—he made a knifing gesture with his hands to show where he would cut through the one narrow path between the trees to a second hill beyond that ended at the water's edge—"I can make it all the way to the second hill."

"Not a chance," Ship said.

"Do you dare me?" Grey said, wiping snot off his nose.

"No," Ship said. "You'll bust my tray."

"Watch me," he said and jumped onto the tray so that the force of landing on it sent it and him sailing down the hill.

He paddled with his hands, until he was going faster than any of the others who had gone before him. As he neared the trees at the bottom, he seemed bound to crash into a thick oak and yet did nothing to change his course. I wondered if he intended to will the tree out of his way or hit it trying, but at the last second, he rolled off as the others had and the tray skidded harmlessly to a stop.

"There," Ship said, "now give it back," once Grey had grappled his way back to the top of the hill.

"No way. Almost had it," Grey said, huffing hard, and before Ship could lay a hand on him was on his way down the hill again. This time he seemed to have found the angle that would take him through the trees, until the tray drifted of its own accord, taking him toward the same oak that had caused him to abort the previous try. Instead of falling off though, Grey stayed on, leaning to the left, trying to coax the tray onto the right course, until he struck the tree, not quite center but glanced off, upending him and sending the sound of plastic striking wood echoing through the bare forest.

"Shit," someone said, but then Grey was standing and swatting the snow off his coveralls. He bent over the tray beside him and picked up two pieces of plastic cleaved in half.

"Man," Ship whined, "he broke it."

I slapped him on the shoulder. "Sorry about that."

"Sorry about that," Grey echoed, once he'd climbed back up the hill and laid the pieces of the tray at Ship's feet. He'd scuffed his chin and a trickle of blood ran down his neck.

Ship looked morose. "Why don't you go back in the cafeteria and get another one?" I asked him.

"They won't let us take them anymore since they figured out what we're using them for."

"Sucks, I almost made it," Grey said.

By this time maybe a couple of dozen kids were standing around. "You can take mine," one of them said. "I want to see this."

Grey's face lit up at this act of generosity. I wasn't as enthusiastic, as it seemed from their expressions that they looked at Grey as a kind of sideshow act, and were willing to see him kill himself for their amusement. But Grey, not noticing or not caring, gave them all the thumbs up, said, "See you at the funeral," and was gone again. There was something miraculous about this run from the start. We could see right away as he sped down the hill that he was aimed straight at the opening he'd pointed out and this time the tray stayed on course. Looking from the distance like a perfectly struck ball in bumper pool, he sailed among the trees, getting close but never so much as brushing their trunks, cleared the woods, and disappeared over the dip at the far end. Seconds later he reappeared, far down the hill, gliding at an ever-slower pace until the tray came to a stop just short of the rocks at the edge of the lake.

"Wow," said the guy who lent him his tray, "that was amazing."

"Jeeps," Ship said, before he caught himself and went back to looking sad again. I nodded, looking down the hill to the water's edge where Grey stood and raised his fist in the air.

"Never thought the thing would break, Dennis," Grey said to Ship as we walked down the path to Rosewalter.

Ship chewed on his mitten, not talking.

Grey tried to look him in the eye, but Ship turned away.

"You're crying," Grey said.

"I am not."

"You are, too. You're crying over a tray."

"Shut up. It's cold. My nose is running."

After what Grey had done I should've stuck up for Ship. Instead I said, "It was a fine tray," and felt bad about it the second I did because the last thing he needed was me adding to his misery.

When we got back to our room, Grey went to the bathroom to check out the cut on his chin and Ship took the opportunity to go down to the TV lounge.

"Where's Dennis?" Grey asked when he came back with a wad of toilet paper stuck to his chin.

I told him. I also told him the only reason Ship went was to get away from him.

"You think?"

"You do give him a hard time."

"I do?"

We played a few hands of gin. Grey turned the cards over and over, performing one-handed cuts and a shuffling technique he called the California Fan. I could tell he was in a good mood because I won as many hands as I lost. When he was mad enough to cheat, he shot the moon every time.

"We should head out around 7:00, if we want to get to the bus station on time."

"Whatever," Grey said.

"Can I ask you a question straight up?"

He knew that he wasn't going to like whatever it was and shrugged.

"Do you think you'll be able to get by on the level?"

He fanned the cards on the floor and flipped them over by turning the last in line and letting the others domino onto their faces. "What do you mean?"

"I mean how much of the money you got coming in comes from selling boats and how much comes from selling dope for Natch?"

Grey stopped shuffling. I thought he might go nuts. Instead he shrugged, said, "Screw Natch," and spread the cards with his fingers so that all of them were visible. "Pick a card, but don't tell me what it is." I drew the ten of spades. He gathered up the cards, patted them back into an even deck and tapped them on the floor. "Natch lacks all the necessary resources, except one. I have all the necessary resources, except one. It's a match of convenience. Once I'm fixed, I can tell him to get lost."

He held the cards endwise up and wiggled the fingers of his right hand over them, saying, "Rise . . . rise," as though he was hypnotizing them. A single card pushed upward from the deck.

"Go ahead," he said. I pulled it from the others and turned it over. "That your card?"

It was the ten of spades. "How'd you do that?"

"When we have a few years, I'll show you. What's going on tonight?"

"Tonight," I said. "Why?"

"Figure it's our last night down here. We should do something."

"I got somewhere I got to be."

"Yeah, where?"

"Just this thing. It's connected to school."

Dennis walked in, saw us sitting on the floor, and started to leave again.

"Come on back," Grey told him. Ship stepped delicately into the room, as though he thought the floor might be mined. Grey got up and locked Ship's head in his elbow. "I was just asking what Tom here was doing tonight and he said he had 'this thing' to do for school, and I said, 'It's okay. I'll stay here with my friend Dennis.'" Ship looked terrified and trapped, like a tagged caribou.

There was no music as I climbed the stairs to the second floor. I stopped at the door and listened. Hearing no sound from inside I thought maybe I'd got mixed up but remembered clearly that Majors had said, "Come back tomorrow," so I knocked. Crowder opened the door just a crack and peered around the corner, as though he wasn't dressed. "Yes?"

"Mike told me to come by."

"He's not here," he said.

"He's not?" I said. "Well, he just said to come by. Maybe he didn't mean come by to see him."

"So you're here," he said. He was still not opening the door, until Sing yelled out, "Who's there?" and Crowder stepped back and let me in. "One of those guys from last night. He's here for Majors."

"Did you tell him he's not here?"

"Yeah, he did," I said, stepping inside, determined not to play the fool.

Roy and Harold were the only ones around. Less of the room was lit than the night before. It was quiet enough to hear the wind piping through the cracks in the factory windows. I stood a minute, trying to think of what to say and if I should just leave, before Dru emerged out of the dark from the direction of the refrigerator, carrying a half-empty wine jug.

"I'm not sure how this will taste," she said. "Someone didn't screw the cap on very tight." She sat in the same easy chair she'd occupied the night before. "Sit down," she said. "Roy and Harold knew as well as I did that you were coming."

"Why'd Majors ask me?"

"Because I asked him to," Dru said. "I would have myself, but I wasn't sure how that would look."

"Dru worries about her reputation," Crowder said.

"We thought you might like us," Dru said. "It's not easy for us to mix with other"—she paused—"*peo*ple our age. They just don't seem to like us too much."

"They don't like us," Sing said, "because they don't *get* us."

"We're an acquired taste," Crowder said. "Your friend didn't like us."

"Grey? Actually, he did," I said, watching Dru fill a tall glass with wine and hand it to me.

"Really," she said. She sounded genuinely surprised.

I tasted the wine. It was sour, but I didn't really mind, not being a wine expert or caring about wine in any way except that if I emptied the glass I would feel less nervous than I had when I arrived.

"How do you know Dooley?"

"We had him for a class," Crowder said. "That was how we all met, except for Mike. He was a friend of Bea's from home, I think. We were impressionable and he made a great impression on us. Then, as you might have heard Dewey say, we got into a little trouble and he helped us out."

"That was nice of him," I said

"So he says," Sing said. "He's something of a tired queen."

"A queen?" I said, "like he's arrogant?"

"A queen like he's gay."

"He's gay?"

"You didn't know?" Crowder said.

"No," I said.

"You sound disapproving," Crowder said.

"I do?"

"Yeah you do," said Sing, "You're not a homophobe, are you?"

"No," I said and meant it, smug in my ignorance of what a homophobe was.

I thought Dru would step in, but she sat in her chair, staring through narrowed eyes as she had the night before, as Crowder and Sing hovered. Finally, she got up, walked to a metal stairway just within reach of the light and ascended into the darkness of the second floor.

Sing sat cross-legged in the easy chair opposite mine. Crowder fell backward on the couch, landing with such force that the wood splintered beneath him. He didn't seem to have noticed the crash and lay facing the ceiling, his snow-puckered boots hanging off the armrests. He put his fingers to his eyelids as if holding them shut.

"You must have taken a wrong turn somewhere?" Sing said, nearly a whisper, with the edge of a threat.

"I don't think so."

"You don't?" he said. He looked around the room as if for proof of his point and said, "Then what do you think?"

"Think of what?"

"Us," he said, gesturing to include the entire building and everything in it.

"I don't know."

"I'll tell you what you think. You think we're full of crap."

"No, I don't."

"You just said you don't know what to think."

"So?"

He moved forward in his chair and looked me in the eye. "Would you say so if you did?"

"Probably not."

"How come?"

"I wouldn't think I knew enough to say one way or the other."

He smiled and leaned back in his chair again. "Which proves my point."

"Which was?"

"That you're in the wrong place."

I laughed.

"What's funny?" he asked.

"I know someone back home who says the same thing."

"Well, then he's right," Sing said. "In this instance."

"Are you saying I should leave?" I asked.

"In one version you do," he said.

"What does that mean?"

"It means now that you are in a place where one wouldn't ordinarily expect to find you, what you do next is largely up in the air. Look at it this way: let's assume the universe is infinite, which by definition it has to be, right?"

"If you say so."

"Not because I say so. The universe has to be infinite because nothing can exist beyond the infinite."

"Makes sense."

"Of course it does, and if you accept that the universe is infinite, which you must because I've proven it, then you have to recognize that all possible outcomes of all events must not only occur somewhere but must also occur simultaneously. Which means in practical terms, in your case, that there is one outcome in which you are offended by what I say and leave and in other combinations, you remain."

"Do I know about *this* reality when I'm in these other worlds?"

"Sometimes. In some of them you are having this same conversation."

"Let's say I stay."

"Let's say you do."

"What happens then?"

"The stairs," he said, glancing toward the far wall.

I looked that way. "What about them?"

"There are a million outcomes in which you don't climb them and a million or so in which you do—aren't you hoping this is one in which you do?" He stared for a moment as though he were expecting me to answer.

I got up and climbed the metal stairway and stepped slowly so that my sneakers fell silently on the steel grating of the catwalk, as the concrete floor passed far below my feet, like the ground beneath a swing. All of the rooms I passed had been offices, with high windows and sturdy desks, most of them stacked with dusty office equipment. I reached an office whose window was covered with a blanket from the inside. The door was ajar, a blade of orange light sliced the catwalk in half. I looked inside. There was no furniture except for an office chair in the corner piled with clothes, a lit kerosene lamp on a wooden crate turned on its end that served as a sort of night table, and a mattress on the floor in the corner, on which someone slept under a pile of wool blankets. The room smelled of burning fuel and the stale oatmeal odor of an old furnace. I stood in the doorway until I heard Dru's voice from beneath the covers say, "What are you doing?"

"I just came to say I was leaving."

Dru pushed the covers away from her head and spoke to the ceiling. "You came up here to tell me?"

"Yeah," I said.

She sat up and pushed her hair from her eyes and squinted through the poor light between us. "Where are you going?"

"I guess I'll go back to my place, see if Grey's there."

"Who?"

"The guy from last night."

"The bald one." She yawned and clasped her hands across her knees, and said something I didn't catch.

"Huh?"

"Stay here," she said.

"Where?"

"In the bed."

"Where would you sleep?"

She laughed. "I'm starting to change my mind," she said, pulling back the covers, flashing a glimpse of a pair of black sweatpants.

Inside the room, the smell of the furnace was stronger, and comforting. Without bending over I pushed off my sneakers and slid under the covers, my feet feeling cold and wet against the flannel sheets, which smelled of moth balls and the lamp and something I couldn't identify that was all her. "You're sexy," I said and I wished I hadn't.

"At this point," she said, back-flopping onto the pillows, kicking up a screen of dust and lint that turned the light from the lamp into a solid amber field around us, "you should probably say as little as possible."

As I bent to kiss her she leaned toward me, smacking me square in the mouth with her forehead. There was a streak of white light like a photo-flash, a springing sound in my ear, and then the familiar tang of an old penny taste spread across my tongue. Dru rolled back on the bed holding her head and laughing.

"I'm bleeding," I said.

"Yeah, you are," she said, checking the palm of her hand to make sure she wasn't as well. She leaned over me, opened the drawer of her nightstand and came back with a bottle of rubbing alcohol and a roll of gauze. "Turn this way," she said.

The fact she kept field dressing in her drawer turned me on. I said, "Is this going to hurt?"

"Of course."

She saturated the cotton with the alcohol. The sting made my lip twitch. "Brave boy," she said, dabbing again at the cut. "You're such a big brave boy."

She kissed the unhurt edges of my mouth. I looked for her tongue with my tongue. She wrapped the fingers of one hand around my ear and pulled me on top of her. We fell into the deep scent of the mattress. She scissored my neck in an elbow lock and clenched her muscled calves to the back of my thighs. I had to push with all the strength of my legs, drawing leverage from my legs just to pull away so that she could pull me into her again. When I came, her biceps, hard against my cheek, trembled with the strain of her grip.

She broke free and rolled toward the wall. More than a minute went by before anybody said anything. Finally, I said, "I'll come to your show when you have it."

"You can if you want," she said. "I don't care."

I fell asleep trying to figure out what I might've done to make her mad.

I woke up to white light from the frosted window filling the room. My eye settled on a dark spot on the pillowcase. Lifting my head, I saw that it was a bloodstain, the shape of a small hourglass, left by the cut on my lip as I slept. Dru was still sleeping. Her cheek lay on the back of her hand. As I watched her eyelashes fluttering, it suddenly became important to me that she not be awake when I left. Feeling the cold of the floor in the bones of my feet, I snatched up my clothes and stepped out the door to dress on the even colder steel grating. I was relieved to see that Sing and Crowder weren't sprawled on the furniture. I grabbed my coat and ran like a thief for the door.

AGAMEMNON

The morning was bright and still. Days upon nights of freezing temperatures and cloudless days had turned the snow hollow and brittle and it crunched like Styrofoam beneath my feet. The wind blew through the loose folds of my coat as though it was hollow too, and me inside it a dried pea in a dead husk. The sun was a bloodless white, large and bright, but incapable of generating heat.

When I thought about home, it was always winter, in the three months when the ferry didn't come, and anything that we didn't have already had to come by plane with the mail. While the rest of the world carried on as always, we lived in a cryogenic suspension, subsisting on what we had put aside before the harbor closed. In the afternoons we played hockey on the frozen lagoon, measuring the days until spring by the dwindling supply of pucks lost in the dead underbrush along the shore or slid into holes newly left by ice fishermen. We knew if we lost the last one, there'd be no more until spring because cargo space on the plane was rationed and expensive.

Every year at this time, Ben Friendly got out the whiskey decanter that looked like a talking snowman, propped it up beyond the Beer Nuts display, and threw a Christmas party where the kids could come—his way of thanking the captive clientele. Being fat, he'd put on the Santa suit, while Greta wore stuffed antelope horns and played the Autoharp next to the artificial tree they put up at the at the end of the bar, with empty beer crates wrapped up to look like presents.

Even Pop liked those parties. When we went home, he'd let me watch the Christmas shows on television. That was our Christmas, and it was fine with me.

If I ever thought of my mother at the holidays, it was only to wonder what she was doing. I don't remember wondering if she was thinking of me. I wondered where she lived and did she have a new family with a husband and children and maybe a girl, which I think she would have liked. Once, two summers after she left, she'd sent a postcard from Houston. The picture on it had been of an oil well, but instead of oil, it gushed pictures of what must have been the local attractions. On the back she'd written,

Tomas,

Your father will have told you by now that I left because I don't love you. He knows in his heart that this is not true. He is a shit. I am safe.

—Mama

After that I had imagined her in Houston, which was easy, because it sounded like a nice place—cowboys and animals— and I wanted her to be happy. In grade school we watched a filmstrip, called "Christmas Around the World," which had showed an Indian boy in New Mexico (which wasn't Texas, but I figured was close enough) holding the reins of a donkey and hanging an ornament on a cactus. And that's what I thought her life must be like: Christmas warm and out of doors, hanging tinsel on the desert vegetation.

Campus was desolate. A freezing rain had cratered the snow, giving the ground a look of a planetary landscape—a dead planet formerly populated by a benign race of school builders. At the curb outside of Rosewalter station wagons and vans idled waiting for kids to come shuffling, sleep-addled and hung-over, out of the same gate they disappeared behind four months earlier. Hugs were exchanged, tinged with guilt from students, who sized up their parents for the right moment to confess their failed courses and their debts.

Howie was on the elevator, coming up from the basement with a load of laundry.

"Hiya, Howie," I said. All the guys on the floor addressed Howie thusly because we knew he hated it.

"How'd your exams go?" he asked. Acting like he cared came with the job.

"Well," I said. "You know."

"Tell me about it." He shifted the weight of the basket to his hip and held out his hand for me to shake. "Happy holidays, Zim."

"Yeah, you, too, Howie," I said.

From several doors away, I heard Mr. Shipman's voice echoing from our room. Shit, I thought, as Mrs. Shipman backed out of the door, directing Ship and his dad who followed behind with Ship's trunk. "Honey, slow down, you'll throw your father's back out."

The Mrs. saw me first and recognized me. She was wearing a pink snowsuit with pink fake fur around the collar that she had to blow out of her mouth to speak. "Darling," she said, "your roommate is here."

Ship looked up in time to miss the trunk getting dropped on his foot. He hopped on the good one with the grimace of a wounded ape. Free of his burden, Mr. Shipman swung his arm around in a bowler's arc to shake my hand. "Looks like so good, so far, eh," he said. "Ready for a little R and R?"

"Sir?"

"That's army talk," Mrs. Shipman said.

"I didn't know you were in the Army, Mr. Shipman."

"He wasn't," said his wife.

Mr. Shipman pulled on a pair of heavy leather work gloves

and clapped his hands together. "When we're through with Dennis's things maybe we can give you a hand with your stuff."

"He doesn't have any stuff," Ship said.

"That's right," Mrs. Shipman said. "You're a light traveler," looking critically at her son's trunk.

"Yes, ma'am," I said.

"This one'd pack for his own funeral," she said, a joke that was meant for me only. I wondered how many digs like that they expected Ship to take before he turned on them. Maybe he would pack for his own funeral, and maybe he'd take some people with him.

"Well," I said, "safe trip," and pushed past them into the room.

Ship's eyes had kept shifting toward his desk so I looked that way and saw what looked like a glossy folder with the picture of an East Indian girl with a pencil behind her ear and a notebook in her hand.

Ship snatched it up. "The calendar came," he said.

"What calendar?"

"The Faces of the Future," he said. "Remember, I told you?"

"Let me see," I said. He gratefully handed it over and stood shifting on his feet as I opened it. I paged past January, a girl standing in a room of green light holding a test tube, to February and there was the Shipper, standing with his hands on his hips—without his glasses—in front of a wall chart of what I guessed was supposed to be the stock market with a red line zig-zagging up and up.

"Looks terrific," I said.

"Really? You think so?"

"Sure," I said and meant it. Nobody'd come asking me to be on a calendar.

"Do you want one? I can get you one."

"Yeah, I would, Ship."

He smiled, not seeming to care, like he usually would, if I was putting him on. "Do you think Grey would want one?" he asked.

"Dennis," his mother called from the hallway, "I'm not carrying this thing."

"Okay, Mom," he hollered. I winced at the volume of it and he smiled. It was the first laugh we'd had together in weeks. "You living here next semester?"

"Yeah," I said, "you?"

"I don't know, yet," he said. "I have to talk to Howie about some things. It hasn't been easy around here, you know."

"Your mother is talking to you," his father shouted from the hall.

"I suppose not," I said.

He took his glasses off and rubbed the lenses with his scarf. "What'd you ask your dad for?"

"Huh?"

"Den-nis," his mother hissed.

"For Christmas."

"Your father is starting the car."

"We don't do it like that," I said.

He stepped backward into the hall. "They're going to leave without me."

"Can't have that," I said, pushing the door shut. When he turned to leave, I called after him, "Ship"—he stopped—"you're a good guy. Who cares what anyone says."

Howie was in his room stuffing balled socks into a gym bag. He didn't look happy to see me.

I said. "You know I'm staying."

"In town?"

"Here."

He cocked his eye and stared at me. "Can't," he said. "We're shut down until the second of January. Come to the floor meetings sometime."

"Sorry," I said. Howie had sent around one of his memos a couple of weeks earlier but I threw it away without reading it.

"They're putting a computer in the TV lounge," he said.

"What for?"

He shrugged. "I don't know. Homework."

"Cool, I guess."

"Hey Zim," he said. "Some of the frats rent rooms over the break. I could give you the phone numbers."

And I said, "That's okay." I went back to my room and filled my backpack with a pair of jeans, underwear, and socks, then scanned the shelves of the room for anything else I might need. None of the textbooks, the safety goggles from chem lab, the towels swiped from the natatorium were of any use. I pulled the drawstring and pushed my arms through the straps. Then I took my bike down and pushed it ahead of me out the door, and, without looking back as I usually did to see what I might have forgotten, pulled it closed and tugged at the knob to make sure it was locked.

As soon as I was out in the raw winter air, it hit me that I had three bucks in my pocket and no place to go. Rather than stand there looking lost, I got on my bike and coasted down the drive and turned west. With no destination in mind I pedaled into the wind, along the bay and the playing fields, into a wooded stretch along the lake, through wide-lawned suburban streets, and out of town, five miles and then ten. The two-lane highway I rode down sliced through snowy cornfields. Dead for the winter. Even rows of furrowed ground, frozen and black, their peaks rimmed with snow, like range upon range of distant mountains. Rows of stalks, slight and solid as bamboo, broken off a half a foot above the hard ground. The northwest wind blew snow across the bare road, each flake as small and hard as grains of sand. The sun was buried behind a solid sky of gray clouds and it was as dark as an autumn twilight. I rode until my hands went numb on the handlebars.

I thought about Grey back home, with two thousand dollars of my money in his pocket. For the first time, it struck me how hard it must have been for him to come looking for me. After all his talk of his business and the future, the thought that I didn't need him anymore must have scared him. As for the money, I'd given it to him. This is how my thoughts turned until, cold and tired, I turned back toward town.

The snow that threatened all morning never fell. The streets were dry and gave up no reflections from the streetlights, as I rode up State Street. I rolled down the steep hill on East Washington and jumped the curb.

Dru came to the door holding a fashion magazine the size of a movie poster.

"Hi," I said. "I'm kind of without a place to live at the present time."

She thought about that, her eyes scanning the distance behind me as if she was making sure the coast was clear, then stepped back from the door and pulled it open. "In that case," she said, "enter at your own risk."

20

THE PRINCESS MODEL

After the claustrophobia of Rosewalter, I liked walking the factory's catwalk at night—the feel of the cold grating underneath bare feet—but the first time it was creepy. The swaying lantern cast a circle of light on the far wall that raced across the floor and up the near wall and back again. The office that had the one good phone in the factory had no working lights, and I walked between the rows of sturdy desks and filing cabinets, with the lantern raised in front of my face, like I was exploring a wreck. The phone was an old two-line, white Princess model on the corner desk of the office, and the casters on the chair screeched when I put my feet up on the desktop. My breath flowed past the bell of the lantern in flaring streams, casting shadows of waves on the wall.

Across the desk was this brass paperweight: a micrometer mounted on an oval base with a shallow well, in which lay a pile of corroded paper clips. Reaching with a fingertip I slid it toward me. The scored knob on the micrometer turned smoothly. It was probably a freebie from some salesman, and yet as well-made as an Italian derailleur. I dumped out the paper clips and lit a cigarette. The perfect black print of a woman's right hand gripped the handset. With the tail of my shirt I tried wiping it off, but the stain was permanent. Not wanting to think too hard about what eerie phenomenon might explain this, I dialed our number back home. The ring when it came sounded far away, and I pictured the old black phone on the wall by the cash register ringing though the shop. We never had a phone upstairs. I could get to the one in the shop in three rings. Pop took five on a good day, when he heard it, which was hard when the door was shut, like it generally was in the cold weather.

The phone rang a fifth time and then a sixth. I stayed on long enough so that if Pop was there but not answering he would know it was me. As I counted the seconds between rings, Dru came in wrapped in a blanket and sat cross-legged on the desk, looking confused that I was listening so long without talking. I mouthed the word "ringing." She gestured to me to hand her the cigarette, which had burned down almost to the butt in the time I had been listening to the phone back home ring. She took it carefully to her lips and took a single short drag which she blew out without inhaling and made a sour face.

As I hung up, she said, "You know these aren't healthy."

"My father smokes a couple of packs a day. He's never sick."

"So you're saying they're medicinal?"

Taking the butt from her, I ground it out in the well of the paperweight. "In a way," I said and picked up the receiver again.

"Do you want me to go?" she asked.

"That's okay," I said, but she slid off the edge of the desk anyway and wrapped the blanket around her.

I dialed the Reeds' number, and this time Mrs. Reed answered on the first ring.

"Tom? Where are you?" she asked.

"Still at school."

"Is Grey there?" she asked.

"No, did he say he was?"

"He didn't say anything. We haven't seen him for a couple of days."

"He was here."

"He was?"

"But he left. I thought he'd go home."

"No," she said. "Callie's curious, as you can imagine."

"Where's she?"

"Right here. Do you want to talk to her?"

"I probably shouldn't stay on any longer," I stuttered. "This isn't my phone."

There was a silence and I got the impression that she was shaking her head to Callie. "You're not in your room?"

"No," I said.

"Are you coming home?"

"No."

"All right, then. Tell Grey to call if you see him."

When I went back to bed, Dru was lying on her back with her knees up, staring at the ceiling. "Who was it you called?"

"A neighbor," I said. "Back home."

The next day we took a shortcut along the frozen lake. The glare of the sun blinded us and the ice groaned under our feet. There was something about Dru in her leather jacket, her skin translucent with cold that made me want to possess her. I wrapped my arms around her waist and hoisted her over my shoulder. She laughed and slid down my back, swinging her legs around at the last minute to land on her feet like a bareback daredevil at the rodeo. When I turned she swatted me across the face. Then she went for my waist, taking me off my feet. I landed on my back, and she jumped me, pinning my shoulders with her knees. Her black eyes narrowed with determination, she cleared her throat loudly and let a glistening trail of spit drip from her mouth until it hung suspended just a few inches above my nose.

"Confess," she said, speaking through her teeth so as not to move her lips and let the spitball fall.

"Confess what?" I said, feeling the snow melt and tickle down my collar.

"Why did Dewey send you to us?"

"He told me to bring you the letter," I said and turned my head to the side so the glob of phlegm wouldn't land on my face.

She sucked it in and then spit it out well beyond my head. "Why didn't he come himself?"

"He was busy I guess."

"Have you ever seen Dooley busy?"

"I don't know. When he's teaching maybe. What difference does it make?"

"None really. We have a history."

"I know. He told me."

"What did he say?"

"Are you sorry he sent me?"

She whacked me on the cheek with her mitten. "Don't flirt." She got up and brushed the snow off her pants.

For a long time we walked with only the sound of the wind. Along the shoreline the spray had frozen into static crystal waves. Finally she said, "Sometimes I think we're all full of it."

"Why do you say that?"

"We just are," she said. "I mean don't you think?"

I said, "Sometimes when I'm watching you, I try to imagine what my father would think of you, but I can't."

"What's your dad like, then?"

"You mean is he stupid?"

"No, I meant is he a normal father?"

"To me he is."

"What's your mother like?"

"I have no idea."

Dru laughed. "I know what you mean."

"No," I said, "I mean I really have no idea. She took off when I was five."

She put her hand to her mouth. "Oh, I'm sorry," she said. "Do you miss her?"

No one had asked me that before and it occurred to me that I did, sometimes. "No," I said.

"Do you remember her?"

"Sort of."

Dru thought it over and said, "It might not be a bad thing. I mean if you don't remember then what are you missing?"

"I suppose," I said, "but I'd say it pretty much is always a bad thing."

"I guess," she said, but she didn't sound convinced.

"How come you're not going home?" I asked her.

"They get me once a year," she said. "Dad's fiftieth birthday was October. I went up for that."

Ahead of us, the Armory came into view, an ugly red brick menace built to look like a medieval castle. It'd been the National Guard armory until it got burned out in the sixties and turned into a gym. We climbed rocks onto solid ground, Dru refusing my hand so she could bound up the icy rocks ahead of me.

When I got to Dooley's office he was packing up to get out of town. His cracked leather bag was open on his desk and he was shoving papers in it without looking at them first. There was a bottle of scotch open next to his hot plate, where the kettle whistled. He looked at me and went back to his packing as though he hadn't seen me, then snapped his bag shut and went to the whistling kettle.

"Tea?"

"No thanks," I said.

"Sure?"

"Yeah."

He poured the water into the cup and dunked the tea bag up and down while pouring whiskey in. Then he raised the cup to me. "To the most wonderful time of the year."

He sipped, shuddered, and returned to the shelves behind his desk and began to take books down and set them in a pile on the floor.

I waited as long as I could bear before I said, "So did you get my paper?"

"I did," he said but didn't turn around until he had another armload of books. He put those on the pile, went to his desk, dug through a folder, and slid the paper across the desk.

I picked it up, suddenly worried about what I was going to find. I didn't worry in vain. Turning the pages, I found the margins crowded with Dooley's crabbed handwriting in green ink, words circled, arrows surrounding whole paragraphs and then shooting off the edge of the page and starting again on the next. My hands shook as I turned the pages, trying to get to the end to see what the grade was, but when I got there nothing was written.

"There's no grade," I said.

He grumbled something that I couldn't hear.

"Is it that bad?"

Dooley laughed. "Bad isn't the word for it. Unacceptable, pat, unambitious, trivial." He motioned to me to hand him the paper. I did. He scanned two of three pages, stopped, and read, "'Tecumseh returned from Greenville to learn that his brother had a vision and became a profit.'"

"That's right."

"P-r-o-f-i-t."

"Shit," I said.

"Quite," Dooley said.

"Anyone could make that mistake."

"Anyone careless. Which primary sources did you use?"

"Sir?"

"Which were referenced?"

"In the book?"

"Yes."

"I didn't see any."

"Did you find the spelling of names differed from one text to another?"

"Some of them."

"Which did you use?"

"Whichever I was looking at when I typed them."

"Was that your method?"

"I guess so."

He ran his fingers through the graying mess of hair on his head, got up, hiked up his cords, and walked to the bottle. Again he offered me a drink and again I turned him down, though I wanted just then to say yes, even if it was ten o'clock in the morning.

"You're putting me in a hard spot. This isn't passing work. If you were any other student, I'd fail you."

"Then do it," I said.

He stopped pouring and glared. "Don't say that if you're not prepared to accept the consequences. I'm not going to fail you. I'm going to do much worse." He stood looking out the window at the uniform gray sky of a winter afternoon. "I'm going to give you a C—but only after you've promised me that you will never disappoint me again."

"I won't," I said.

He held up a hand. "Don't answer so quickly. You'll be making fools of both of us if you go back on your word."

"I'll take the C."

He unscrewed the cap on his pen and I watched the tip trace a semicircle at the bottom of the page and then he slid the paper back across the desk. "I ran into our friend Harold Sing the other day."

"Did you?" I said.

"He tells me he's been seeing you."

I saw where this was going. "I guess he has."

"That wouldn't have anything to do with a love of theater?"

"I'd call it a growing appreciation."

"Yes."

"Where are you heading?" I asked just to change the subject.

"Majorca."

"Wow."

"Yes, there's a conference on the causes of the Inquisition."

I laughed. "Pop would say it was just a bunch of Catholics with too much time on their hands."

Dewey laughed. "Marvelous. I will submit that hypothesis."

When we got back to the factory that evening, I wrote the following letter to Aunt Berthe:

> *I did not go home for Christmas. I have made*
> *many attempts to contact Pop by phone and he*
> *does not answer. I have reported my absence to the*
> *Reeds and they have passed my message on to*
> *him.*
>
> *Your Nephew*

For the next three weeks Dru and I lived a fugitive life, hiding out from the morning sun on the dirty windows beneath a lead-heavy pile of blankets. Then, by some convergence of nerve, we'd dart barefoot to the only bathroom on the second floor. We got in the habit of showering together under a sprinkler head that hung over the drain in the corner beside a stationary sink, having learned that we could expect three minutes of hot water on the best of days, a brisk ballet of goose-pimpled pirouettes beneath the spray, one of us rinsing off while the other shivered in the raw air, then the sprint back to the room and the heat of the radiator, where we dressed from a single pile of clothes on the floor.

For breakfast we ate oranges or apples we bought by the bag at the warehouse grocery, generic yogurt, and day-old bread from the industrial bakery down the street. After breakfast, Dru sat cross-legged on the floor moving colored shapes around a model stage made of black construction paper or filling out the seemingly endless forms that the grant committee required of Stovepipe Theater, while I lay on the couch with my feet over the back, reading cycling magazines. At some point Dru would hoist her satchel to her shoulder, toss her scarf around her neck, and leave me alone until later, when Crowder and Sing and Majors came by, as they could be counted on doing more and more often.

The day of the show grew closer.

In Roy's old pea-green Volvo wagon, we made the rounds of the junk shops and dumpsters, and on trash days the curbsides of the richer neighborhoods, plundering clothes, furniture, and household machines—anything that might be useful in the future.

"Value shifts," Crowder said. "That which you may toss away today, might save a life tomorrow."

"Or kill someone," Sing said.

"As the situation dictates," said Crowder.

We drove to car graveyards scattered along the railroad tracks and to the industrial parks west of town where we'd be met at vinyl-sided prefab outbuildings by bored men with clipboards who'd wave us past to machine shops in aluminum storage sheds where some other bored man they had met somewhere or had found in the classifieds stood beside some piece of useless machinery, a broken down portable generator or a wrench the size of a softball bat with a crack in the flange. We would offer money that usually was refused. Usually they were happy to get rid of the object in question.

I liked these foraging missions for how they reminded me of some of the afternoons in the Reeds' truck, driving around the mainland with Grey behind the wheel, Callie on the hump, and me at the window with my right hand resting on the side-view mirror. Majors was in Vail with his family and I had the feeling that my seat in the Volvo might have been temporary, but I also had the feeling that when he did come back I'd be welcome to sit in back.

On the way back to town a clump of wet snow fell from a branch and exploded on the windshield. It would soon be time to go back to school.

SPY VS. SPY

Dooley came back tan and somehow even more slovenly in his appearance. His shirt was misbuttoned and his eyeballs looked sunburned. "I acquired a taste for paella and Balearic waiters," he said, and I laughed because I thought I was supposed to. Seeing him after a month, I knew my feelings for him had changed. I didn't revere him the way I had, and that made it easier to like him. I'd gotten to know my job and didn't have to ask any more if there were things he needed me to do. It got to be like back in the shop, the two of us in the same room without talking for hours at a time.

I didn't go back to Rosewalter until days after school started. Dru was happier than I would've hoped to see me go, and I wasn't back in my room for ten minutes before I wanted to leave. Ship had come back from Baraboo with no visible scars from four weeks of parental disapproval and with a new electric razor that he pointlessly propelled around his chin three times a day.

"Some girl's been calling for you," he said. He'd fieldstripped the razor and was cleaning the circular blades with a round brush.

"Who?"

"I don't know. She doesn't say. She asked for you. I said you weren't here. 'When's he going to be back?' 'I don't know.' Since then she just hangs up."

"How do you know it's the same girl?"

"I recognize her static." He held the blade on his finger and blew across the top. It grossed me out to think about microscopic fuzz from the Shipper's face flying all over the room.

"Quit it," I said.

"So you're going with that girl."

"Yeah," I said.

"What was her name, Sue?"

"Dru."

I crashed on my bed and realized I'd actually missed it. It was the first thing assigned to me when I arrived.

"That where you've been at night?"

"Yup," I said, picking a book and pretending to read. "What did you say the girl sounded like?"

"Just some girl."

"Happy, sad, mad?"

Expertly, he replaced the blades on their spindles, snapped the lid shut, zipped the razor into its fake leather case, and set it on his dresser, adjusting it a couple of times with his fingers so that the case lay parallel with the edge of the dresser top. "Sad," he said. "She sounded like a girl who was sad."

Just when I resigned myself to a life of Ship yattering in my ear, he went down to the lounge. I sat in the dark with my eyes open, appreciating silence on a noisy floor.

The next night I got delayed at the factory, helping Roy and Majors (back from the Rockies with his arm in a sling) paint some chairs. I stayed over and the next day woke up too late to make Edwards's class and skipped the rest of the day's classes to make up some extra hours of work. I helped with the sets at the theater and read books while the others rehearsed. It was fun. Fun enough to cut class. I had a job I liked. I figured I'd catch up on school later.

Then the CIA came to town.

It was Crowder who saw the notice in the paper. Recruiters were on campus looking for patriotic self-starters to join their outfit. I was sitting in the last row of seats, reading *Mill on the Floss,* where Tom and Maggie are about to get creamed by the wreckage on the river, when Crowder blew by, bounding down the aisle taking up feet of ragged carpet with each stride, yelling, "Did you see this? Did anybody see this?"

They passed a paper around. I heard Harold say, "This is interesting," and Dru said, "No, Roy, no way."

Bea said, "Remember."

Roy said, "This is different. We wouldn't be selling anything. Would we, Sing?"

"We wouldn't have to."

Then Roy called up to me, "Hey Tom, you in?"

I said, "Sure."

Dru stood with her hands on her hips. "I'm swear I'm going to kill all of you," she said.

Two days later, we loaded a barber chair that Roy had lying around the factory and had been looking to use for a long time into the Volvo and Majors, Roy, Harold, and me piled in front and we lurched off toward campus. There was already a line of students carrying signs and walking around in circles with signs that said, TORTURE THIS and CIA + $ = DEATH and like that outside of the Commerce building where the interviews were going to be. On a knoll nearby was another crowd, guys from one of the fraternities with their own signs that said things like, GO HOME QUERES. Plus there was a TV truck there. When we set up the barber chair, a crowd gathered immediately. Harold made for himself and me these baby blue smocks, with a zipper down the front and the name Harry stitched on his and Buzz on mine. Roy and Majors ducked behind the building, while Sing and I put up our sign that said, WELCOME SPIES—HAIRCUTS FREE FOR CIA RECRUITS. And Harold shouted, "Who'sa gonna go firsta?" in a bad Italian accent. Then Majors, who'd ducked into the building to put on a suit, walked up carrying a briefcase. With a flourish, Sing brushed the chair with a whisk broom and wrapped a sheet around Mike's neck, and I stepped up with a damp towel that steamed in the cold air and wound it around his face and Mike screamed like it was burning hot. As everyone laughed, Sing said, "So-a sorry," and shoved him back in his seat. Then I whipped up a muck of suds with a shaving brush in a cup and slathered them all over Majors's face, swiping across his lips with my finger to make a mouth hole.

I was supposed to shave him, which was a little scary, since we were using a real straight razor and with all the excitement my hands were shaking and while we had him in the chair Roy came creeping out from behind a tree, dressed in a spy outfit he made himself, like the cartoon in *Mad* magazine, with a black mask and black broad-brimmed hat and cape. He crept up on his tiptoes, which was hilarious to see because he weighed more than three hundred pounds and still he was really good at sneaking up on people. He pulled out this overstuffed envelope that said "Secret Plans" on it in red block print and slipped it into the pocket of Mike's jacket, while Harold gave Majors a truly awful haircut with a pair of electric clippers.

Then Sing whipped off the sheet, twirled it like a bull-fighter's cape. "Offa you go. You join the spies, make-a us proud," he said. And Mike got out of the chair, straightened his tie, ran his hand across his nicked cheeks and through his patchy hair, and walked through the door with the secret plans poking out of his pocket.

"Who'sa next?" Sing said, and one of the students who was walking the picket line handed his sign to the woman next to him and sat in the chair. He had very long hair, tied in the back with a rubber band, and when he pulled the rubber band out it fell on his shoulders. Sing looked nervous. "I don'ta know if you spy material," he said.

But the man said, "Cut it all off. I'm ready to join the war machine."

Harold looked at me. I don't think we'd thought through the idea of somebody actually wanting us to clip his hair. "He says, 'Take it off, Harry,'" I said, loud enough for everyone to hear, "we take it-a off." Harold plunged in with the clippers. Everyone was looking on—it had to be a couple hundred at this point—and hooting and cheering as this guy's hair fell to the ground in fat, brown clumps. Once again, Roy snuck up behind the chair, this time with a miniature tape recorder that he held up for everyone to see, while he put his finger to his lips. He made a big show of turning on the record button before sliding the machine into the pocket of the man in the chair who was into the bit enough to pretend he didn't notice. When we finished, his head was as bald as Grey's. He stood, felt all over his scalp with his hand, and raised a fist in the air.

"Your mama," Harold says, "she no recognize you."

The protesters were getting impatient about being upstaged and begin shouting louder and more often into their megaphone, *"Nunca mas,"* and "Hey, hey, ho, ho, the CIA has got to go." The police, seven or eight cops and a van, arrived but seemed willing to stand around the perimeter as long as the protest remained peaceful, which the picketers seemed content to do. Then one of the guys from the huddle of fraternity boys, this squat kid with a baseball cap turned backward on his head, pushed his way through the ring of onlookers, flopped in the chair so hard it almost toppled over backward, and said, "Do me," while his friends pumped their fists and barked like dogs. "And a shave," he said.

Harold didn't want him in our chair. He pulled off the guy's baseball cap, revealing a haircut that was already military short. "It-a looks like-a they already gotta you," but the guy grabbed Harold's smock in his fist, "Do it, faggot," he said.

If Harold was startled by the man's rage, he didn't take long to get over it. "You tell our secret to the neighborhood. That'sa no good. Buzz, you shave-a him good, eh?"

I brushed the lather on his square jaw, being careful to get as much as I could in his ears and nose. Then as I put the straight razor to his cheek, he said, "You cut me and I'll kill you," but as he moved his head to talk the edge of the razor skipped across his skin. As I drew back the blade the lather was tinted pink with blood.

"What did I say?" the guy shouted and grabbed me by the collar. As he did my first thought was that I had a deadly weapon in my hand, and as I was trying to decide whether to drop it or wave it in his face Roy jumped him from behind, knocking the chair over and tangling the two of them in his cape. At which point his fraternity brothers broke ranks and charged, reaching the pile at about the same time as the protesters who tried to head them off. I remember reaching for Roy's belt buckle, while trying to keep an eye on Harold and then the sound of cardboard whistling through the air and then black.

It was the second time Sing and Crowder made the cover of the *Daily Cardinal*, though this time all you could see of the two of them was Roy's huge ass, as the kid pulled his cape over his head, and Harold in character, with his hands to his face in mock horror, while I stood in the center of the frame—standing still amid the blur of fists and feet—in the second before the sign hit me.

The newspaper was on the corner of Dooley's desk. There was no doubt he had seen it, but I wasn't going to bring it up if he didn't. "Does it hurt?" he asked me of the black eye.

"Only when I touch it."

He smiled and picked up the paper. "You have chosen the path of the notorious," he said.

"It was just a gag."

"I should send a copy to Professor Edwards. I'm sure she'd like to know what you look like. She tells me she hasn't seen much of you."

"It's a big class."

"I told her to look."

"Why would you do that?"

"I was worried that you'd get lost. Not without reason, as it turns out." He put down the paper, laced his fingers together, and tilted his head back like he did whenever he was about to make a speech. "Historically the university—and you must remember and understand that when I speak about *the* university I am speaking of the institution, not of *this* university—has been viewed by the laboring classes as something between a country club and a sanitarium. The degree to which that was true at any point in history is irrelevant because what we're talking about here is perception. And nothing of what Harold Sing or Roy Crowder or Miss Gordon are inclined to undertake would go far toward changing that perception. It's their prerogative to do as they wish, as it is yours." He picked up the paper and turned the pages slowly. "However, you may have to suffer consequences that they will not."

"Like what?" I asked. If I'd known it was the last time I'd talk to him, I might've remembered his advice and not asked the obvious question.

"Ah," Dooley sighed, "but that is the nature of consequences— you can rarely predict what they're going to be."

ALLOW ME A FEW WORDS

[A stage, dark
Tom, Bea, Harriette and Majors occupy the front row of seats in the
otherwise empty theater with noisemakers and horns, layers of prop
clothes hastily thrown on: velvet period costumes of many periods, wigs,
boas, a fox stole with the head still on, crowns, tiaras, and a Robin Hood
hat with oversized feather protruding from the band. Harriette, as
always, in mourning.

In the background in colored lights, phrases punctuated by ellipses
seem to float in air ". . . **dazzling** . *.*." *and* ".* . . **pure**
entertainment . . *."* and *".* . . a **must-see** . . *."*

The lights come up on stage, revealing a wooden scaffold, a speaker's
platform, with a railing draped with flag bunting, red with white stars
upon intersecting blue stripes, the stars and bars of the Confederacy, and
in the center a portrait in an oval gilt frame, a bearded gaunt figure that
first looks like Lincoln but the lights reveal to be Jefferson Davis.
Standing on the platform with his arms on the rails is Roy Crowder,
dressed in a Lincoln costume two sizes too small, the buttons of the
waistcoat near popping, the stovepipe hat perched on his head like a
beanie. The audience cheers, whistles, blows their horns and spins their
noisemakers, a din barely audible over the sound of canned applause
piped in over speakers.] Friends of the Union, mothers, and loyal
Zouaves, it gives the Tahoe Holiday Inn the greatest pleasure to
introduce, direct from engagements in Richmond, New Orleans,

and St. Joseph MO, the greatest thespian of this or any age, Mr. John Wilkes Booth.

[ENTER HAROLD SING, WEARING A BLACK OVERCOAT WITH A FUR COLLAR, A NARROW-BRIMMED BLACK HAT, AND KNEE-LENGTH LEATHER BOOTS. IN ONE HAND HE HOLDS A LONG, BLACK CANDLE-STICK MICROPHONE. HE GUIDES THE CORD BEHIND HIM WITH THE OTHER. RECORDED MUSIC PLAYS, HE SINGS THE CHORUS TO "*IS THAT ALL THERE IS?*"]

SING: Thank you ladies and gentlemen, grand to be here at the Mary Chestnut Dinner Theatre in the Round. Of course, the way I feel it's great to be anywhere *[rimshot, scattered canned laughter]*.

I'm telling you the Union army chased me half way across Virginia, I said "Who do I look like? Harriet Tubman?" *[rimshot, no laughter]*

Wow, tough crowd. Last time I worked a room this tough the band played "The Battle Hymn of the Republic." *[delayed rimshot]*.

[ENTER DRUCILLA GORDON, FROM THE HOUSE, HER FACE FLUSHED WITH COLD AND ANGER].

Honestly, I didn't want to shoot the president. I sent him a letter that said, "President Lincoln, free the South and I'll call the whole thing off." Unfortunately, I sent it to his Gettysburg address. *[Silence]* I said, I sent it to his Gettysburg address.

DRU: Lights. [HOUSE LIGHTS COME UP] What's going on? Why didn't you wait for me?

ROY: We wanted you to see the opening without the psychological cue of a rising curtain.

DRU: Well, it doesn't matter anyway. We lost our grant.

HARRIETTE: What?

DRU: They pulled our grant.

BEA: How come?

DRU: Why do you think?

HAROLD: *[walks to the front of the stage]* You're not blaming this on us.

DRU: I don't have to, Harold.

ROY: In so many words?

DRU: It didn't have to be in so many words.

TOM: [FROM THE HOUSE] So what? Were you doing it for the money?

BEA and MAJORS: Yeah.

SING: Tom's right *[he crosses to the chair on the stage lit by the spotlight and sits with his legs crossed, turning the tip of his cane on the stage with his thumb and forefinger]*. Vanity, greed, and envy are the roots of plot. We have indulged in these vices, and we have been made to pay because of it. The play sucks. Roy knew it. I knew it. You all knew it, only you were too polite to tell me, except for Bea. If only I'd listened.

HARRIETTE: So what do we do?

SING: Nothing for now. When the time comes, we'll know what we have to do.

DRU: *[to Majors]* How'd you do the words?

MAJORS: We cut the words out of black construction paper and glued cellophane on the back.

DRU: Looks good.

Dru and I fought for hours, cross-legged on the floor in the living room, in the bathroom, while I took a shower, and in bed. She was angry at Harold and Roy. She took it out on me. We argued about expectations and responsibility. It all ended when I said, "If you feel that way about it why do you keep me around?" Walking through the stone gates of Rosewalter, I saw kids I knew. No one seemed surprised to see me or anxious to know where I'd been. The building felt even more unfamiliar to me than it had the first time I saw it. My mailbox door burst open, letting loose a solid rectangle of mail. Most of it was junk: flyers from the bookstore and offers for magazine subscriptions and credit card applications. Wedged among the litter was a small package.

It was wrapped in a brown paper bag. There was no return address on the package, which was postmarked Duluth. My address was scrawled on the brown paper in pencil and traced over several times. I recognized the choppy, almost hieroglyphic, scratchings as Pop's handwriting. Beneath the brown paper was a layer of wax paper wrapped in rubber bands—unquestionably the work of my father who prized the innovation of the rubber band as a technological contribution more valuable than fire.

Rolling off the rubber bands I found a small pine box, about nine inches long, three or four inches wide, an inch deep, and burnished into the wood with a hot blade were my initials TZ. I hadn't seen a pencil box in years, but it couldn't have been anything else, as confirmed by the six Ticonderoga No. 2s inside.

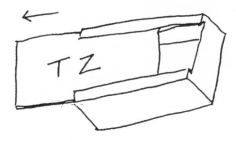

The letter that came with it, written on the back of an invoice, smudged and filled with words started and then scratched out and written in again, said,

Tomas,

The box that I sent is something I made that Jack said you would like and Berthe thinks you will have use for. She says you are doing well at school.

Just to look at the thing made me sad. It was hard for me to conjure Pop's vision of a university where we carried our pencils in homemade monogrammed pine pencil boxes. Still, he had taken the time to make it and that had to count for something.

I folded the note and put it inside the box and slid the cover closed.

I walked down to the observatory.

Elise looked up from her book and blinked.

"I've got to go away. How do I do that?"

"What do you mean?"

"How would I go away for a while without getting in trouble with anyone?"

"How long would you be gone?"

"I don't know, yet. Couple of weeks."

"I'm not sure, unless someone died—no one's died, have they?"—I shook my head—"that there is any dispensation available. What you would have to do is make arrangements with each of your professors."

"I don't have time to do that."

The look of worry she'd had on her face since I'd started talking softened a bit and she said, "Maybe you should tell me what's going on."

I must have been waiting for someone to ask me, because I let go with the whole story, which turned into the whole story of my life—not intentionally, but each time I started telling her about Grey and the Stovepipe crew and how that related to Pop, I got going so fast that I tripped over my words, and Elise would say, "Wait a minute. Back up," and I kept backing up until I was back on the cot in Uncle Karl's living room, hearing my parents threaten each other with murder in the dark. Then on the island and I told her about Callie, which led to Ray and Dolores, which led eventually to Professor Darling and the car wreck, to Jack, to the Mexican girl on the road, and back again to the afternoon in front of the telescope.

When I was finished, she took off her glasses, shook her head, and said, "Well."

"You can see my problem."

"Of course," she said. "I mean it sounds like a lot of the people in your life have problems, and they would like to make their problems yours, or maybe you do that—wow, I'm not sure."

"What would you do?"

"Wow," she said again. "I don't know. Nothing like this ever happened to me. That's the nice thing about the observatory: all I do is look at things and everything I look at is very far away. But if you're asking me, I'd go and do what you have to do. All this will be here when you get back. Look at the ivy on the buildings. It's not going anywhere."

A MAN CAN STAND UP

On the bus, I sat next to an ex-marine with the insignia of the corps tattooed on his forearm. He smelled like liquor and had some kind of white crust along the edges of a patchy goatee. Three times he asked if I'd ever been in the service. The first time I told him no. The second time I told him, No, like I told you already. The third time was fifty miles further down the road, when he asked, "So d'you say you'd been in the military?" I figured he was trying to start a fight and told him, "No, I haven't, but that's something I sure hope I get a chance to do."

"You fucking with me?" he said.

"No," I said.

"'Cause if you are I'll kick your ass."

"I said I'm not."

"Proud to have served," he said, tapping the tattoo.

I stared out the window looking for any landmarks to come into view that I might recognize, while knowing at the same time that places change in fourteen years.

Dru had said, "We kept you around to get to Dewey. It was Harold's idea. He knew Dooley's recommendation would carry a lot of weight with the committee. We couldn't risk applying without it and after what he'd been through, with Roy and Harold and the elixir, we weren't sure he'd say yes, and then well, there you were—"

"Well," I said, "you got what you wanted and it still didn't do any good, did it?"

"I guess not," she said, and I'd crawled to where my backpack lay propped against the wall and stuffed in a change of underwear and socks and my second pair of jeans and the yellow shirt I got from Howie and I left.

Only sleep had the power to shut the ex-marine up. Though I could still smell him. I turned toward the window and saw the skyline of Chicago, which sparked no memory in me.

When I left the station downtown, it was near noon and dark, which I blamed on the shadows of the building, until I saw the gathering clouds. I got directions from a cop—who looked at me strangely—and then made a chopping motion with his hand, "You want to go west and then north."

The rain *did* hold off—for nearly two blocks. Then it fell in sheets, sweeping across the pavement and filling the gutters instantly. The jacket I was wearing, a cotton windbreaker I borrowed from Majors, was soaked through before I reached the next intersection. Figuring I couldn't get any wetter I pressed on, walking for close to an hour before I reached California Avenue. I turned north and walked twenty-two blocks in the rain, through industrial neighborhoods and neighborhoods of black people and foreign-looking children who eyed me as I passed. Nothing looked familiar, until I spotted the Zimmermann Meats sign over Uncle Karl's butcher shop. Even that wasn't as large or as bright as I remembered it. Once through the door I knew from the smell that I'd come to the right place. There was a guy about my age behind the counter. He laughed when he saw me sopping wet the way I was and said, "What can I get you?"

"Karl here?" I asked.

He nodded at the small man sitting in the corner. Again memory had betrayed me. This wasn't the round, chuckling man I remembered. His clothes were loose on him and he didn't recognize me either. He pushed himself up from the chair with some effort and narrowed his eyes and tilted his head, giving me the once over. "Tomas?"

"Yeah," I said. "It's me."

"Is my brother dead?" he asked.

It wasn't a question I was expecting. "No," I said.

"Well, that's good."

"Yes."

"You want to be dry. Go, go back to the house and Berthe will throw your things into the dryer. We have a washing machine and a dryer now. Did she tell you that in her letters? One sits on top of the other. Make her show you when she puts the clothes in."

He pointed me between the freezers through the back door and along the narrow sidewalk I remembered riding a tricycle down to the kitchen door of the house. Through the gauze curtain on the window Berthe looked the same as I remembered and seemed not to have aged, though as she swung the door open, I saw a tiredness in her eyes that hadn't been there in the days she was tripping over me. Unlike Uncle Karl, she knew me at first sight.

The soup was pea—thick as oatmeal with fist-sized ham hocks. I ate two bowls at the kitchen table with the long tails of Uncle Karl's robe tucked modestly between my legs. As I blew on spoonfuls of soup and slurped it hot into my mouth, Berthe sat at the other side of the small, round table with a mug of coffee between her reddened hands. She wore a light blue housecoat with white daisies on it. This was not the Berthe I remembered who was dressed and at the day's work long before the rest of us

were up. But I took the changes—like the wallpaper peeling at
the corners and the chips in the green paint—as a sign of honest
wear rather than decline.

"You left school?" she said.

"Yes."

"Was this your choice?"

"Depends on how you look at it."

She took a cautious sip of her coffee. "Why would you be
smart with me?"

"I'm sorry."

"Did you quit your job as well?" she asked.

"I don't know if I can keep it. They give them to students."

"See if I understand." She pushed the mug away and crossed
her arms. "You are out of work. You have quit from your college,
and you have no plans of returning to your father. You are
running in the opposite direction, like your mother."

"I don't know."

"This is my fault. I ask too much of you. I will tell you that I
was not eager about you going to university. This was never
something that your father's family had much use for. I was
afraid that what has happened would happen. Now you have a
school you cannot go back to and a father who you wouldn't be
much good for if you went home to him. You are free to do as
you choose. I will have no more to say."

"I'd like to stay a few days if I could."

She poured a glass of buttermilk and set it in front of me.
"On the couch."

By the time my clothes were out of the dryer, Karl had come in
from the shop and taken his place in his easy chair. "What did I
say, eh," he said, pinching the warm flannel of my shirt between
his fingers. The pipe was long gone, he said. He'd had two heart
attacks that Berthe didn't think worth mentioning in her letters.

The girls came around for dinner. Hilde was twenty now and still round, with pink-dyed hair and black lipstick. She went to a Lutheran college in the suburbs but chose to live on campus for reasons that became obvious before dinner was even on the table. Silke was twenty-two and a beauty, with hair a darker blond than her mother's and long legs. She said she was a data processor for a bank downtown, and she had an apartment and a convertible and a Puerto Rican boyfriend.

Aunt Berthe was paralyzed with disapproval whenever the girls spoke, in their city accents full of slang and swear words and bad grammar. They were wary of me, probably remembering how I had been favored when I lived with them. I talked to Hilde about the clubs she went to and the bands she liked, pretending to know the ones I had never heard of. Hilde warmed to this line of talk when she saw how it annoyed her mother.

Silke left right after dinner, squealing away from the curb in her electric blue Mustang before the dishes were dry in the rack. Karl shuffled with his newspaper down the hall to the half bath. Berthe made up the couch with sheets and a down comforter. Hilde sat cross-legged at my feet talking for more than two hours, even though I was bone tired and longing for sleep.

She offered me one of Uncle Karl's German beers she swiped from the garage after her parents went to bed. "She doesn't want you to run a store. Trust me on that. As much as she might build your dad and our dad up, she looks down on them. Do whatever you think is right. She'll respect that. Even if she doesn't, what can anyone do?"

We heard the padding of rubber slipper soles down the hallway and Aunt Berthe called, "Hilde, go to bed."

"Jawohl," Hilde yelled back. She drained the beer and said, "You're cuter than your pictures. It's too bad we're cousins."

I pulled the covers up to my chin. "Get out of here. I'm beat."

The light over the kitchen sink cast a dim light over the living room that had been my bedroom for five years. I noticed that the row of bookshelves that had once run the length of one wall had been replaced with a console television. They had held my books, the books that Berthe read to me.

I stayed a week and spent the days helping out in my uncle's store. Karl, like the girls, always looked at me as Aunt Berthe's pet. We'd never been close. But he was a patient, generous boss and introduced me to his regular customers. "My nephew down from college in Wisconsin. He's a smart boy." And the venerable burghers were polite enough not to ask what the smart boy was doing behind a butcher's counter in the middle of a semester.

The work was dull. Karl viewed butchery as a profession and wasn't about to let me near the sides of beef with a bone saw. He'd only taught Marco the rudiments of meat cutting after three years of loyal gopherism of the sort I was assigned. The best I got to do was to mop the floors and rinse the blood from the wooden cutting tables and fetch sausages from the walk-in freezers. All of which made Marco happy because those were the chores he hated. He was a decent guy and if he worried I might steal his job, he didn't show it. He had nothing to worry about. As clean as they kept the place, the constant smell of dead flesh stuck in my nose.

The girls came over the first three or four nights, until the novelty of my presence wore off. We played Parcheesi at the dining room table, and it was easy to feel like part of the family, especially when Hilde brought her fist down on the table and sent the colored markers whirling around the room. Aunt Berthe offered me the use of Silke's room, which I refused, feeling comfortable in the only room in the house I'd ever slept in.

On the seventh day, I called Dru. The Princess Executive rang a couple of dozen times before she picked up. "What time is it?" Her voice sleepy and lost.

"Six."

"Jesus, Tom."

"I wanted to be sure I caught you."

"Well, you did. Where are you?"

"Chicago."

Pause. "How'd that happen?"

"Just kind of did."

"It wasn't true what I said."

"Forget about it."

"Do you believe me?"

"I don't. Doesn't matter."

"Are you coming back?"

"I don't know."

"You have to be back for the show. We're going to assass-inate Roy in front of the Board of Regents."

"Are you nuts?"

"It's just pretend," she said. "You have to see my dress."

"How's that going to work?"

"It's complicated. Come back and I'll tell you."

Berthe came into the kitchen and cast a stern glance my way, guessing correctly I was on long distance. "Why don't you come down here?"

"To Chicago."

"You could come for Easter dinner. Uncle Karl carves a mean ham." That for Berthe's benefit, though she was filling the percolator and didn't seem to hear.

"No way. We were never big on Easter in my house."

"Atheists?"

"Jewish."

"You're Jewish? Oh my God, you're kidding." That got Berthe's attention. She missed the filter with a full scoop of coffee and it scattered on the Formica.

"Come back for the show," she said. "I want you to see my dress."

When I hung up, Berthe set a full cup in front of me and returned to her soiled counter. "I've got to go," I said.

She swept the spilled coffee into the sink and, without turning to look at me said, "Good."

24

BESIDES THAT, MRS. LINCOLN

April thirteenth was bright and cold. I got off the bus in front of the student union and walked west in the direction of Rosewalter, blending in with the flow of students that were heading up the hill to class. I had a hundred and twenty bucks in my pocket (six day's pay from Uncle Karl that I hadn't asked for and didn't expect) and clean clothes.

The room stunk of cologne, explained by the half-empty bottle of Williams Lectric Shave on Ship's dresser. My old mattress was bare and piled with books. His Faces of the Future calendar on the wall was still on February. The course schedule he'd taped above his desk said he was at something called "Business Lab." I dropped my stuff, stripped, and yanked one of Ship's towels off the closet door. In the empty shower room, I turned the hot knobs as high as they would go and sat underneath the rising steam until I started to doze off. Then I shuffled back to the room, shoved Ship's books on the floor, and hit the mattress.

I was asleep when Ship came in but woke up when he turned on the light and howled, "Holy crap."

I rolled over and saw him standing in the middle of the room arms down, palms out, like the human body chart on the wall of a biology lab. "You scared the shit out of me," he said.

"Sorry."

"What are you doing here?"

"Kind of in a bind. I need a place to crash for the night."

"Well," he said, pacing to the window and then back again, "you can't stay here. It isn't even legal. Don't think I don't know you dropped out."

"Who told you?"

He tapped his pocket notebook. "Nobody has to tell me anything."

I felt around on the floor until I found my jeans and pulled a twenty from the pocket. "Here," I said. "Think of it like a hotel."

He paced back to the window. "Forget it. No way."

I dug around for a second bill. "Forty, then."

"What is that? Drug money?"

"Actually, it's meat money."

Not even knowing what I meant, he laughed, in spite of himself, and that was the end of the discussion. "Just for tonight. Give it over," he said.

"You mean you're actually going to take it?"

"You said."

"All right." I handed him a bill.

"You said forty."

"Jeez, Ship."

"Okay, twenty," he said. "But you got to put your clothes on."

I did and was asleep again before Ship put out the lights. In the morning, I woke to the sound of him pacing the floor. I waited for him to go and jumped out of bed as soon as he was gone. I headed straight for the factory.

The door was unlocked. I pushed it open and heard the steel catwalk ringing with the sound of footsteps. Dru was standing at the top of the stairs, leaning, arms folded, against the rail in black tights and an oversized green sweatshirt that said NIAGRA FALLS. Her hair was wet from the shower and mussed from a towel and she stood there for a good half-minute, letting me take in the sight, her eyes, from a distance, black as pinpoints. Then she ran down the stairs at a pace that would have tripped anybody lacking an athlete's balance, and with her hands balled into fists launched at me and caught my neck in an elbow lock.

"You can't see the dress until tomorrow," she said. "It's bad luck, but this is it in the wrapper. You're going to die."

"I can't wait."

"Bea found it. She and Mike have been running all over the place. He found a costume for you. Harold wants you to be James E. Buckingham, the boy who asks Booth for a ticket when he's on his way up to commit the dastardly act. Do you want to?"

"How am I going to know what to do?"

Dru laughed, "You don't have any lines. Harold walks in. You reach out your hand. He says, 'You don't need a ticket from me, Buck.' And bounds up the stairs whistling a tune."

"Then what happens?"

"We do everything according to history. We're going to show up forty-five minutes after the meeting starts. I'm playing Clara Harris, Mike's Major Rathbone, Harriette's Mary Todd—dressed as herself, Bea couldn't get her to wear anything else, but it's kind of appropriate when you think about it—Harold and Roy, you know. The regents meet in the Union Theater. There's a box. Harold knows a guy who can get us in. When our grant comes up on the agenda, Harold's going to burst in and *bang*. Then Mike pretends to try and stop him, then Harold pretends to stab him, and then leaps on to the stage and yells, 'The Stovepipe Foundation grant application procedure is arcane and unfair!' and dashes out the door to the waiting Volvo."

"Kind of a mouthful, isn't it?"

"Yeah, well, the real line is *sic semper tyrannus* but since, as a company, we haven't established a position on tyranny, we thought it would be preachy. Then Bea—who's planted in the front row—gets up and screams, 'Heaven help the republic!'"

"And then what?"

Dru shrugged. "I guess we run. It's against the law to yell 'fire' in a crowded theater. This has got to be worse."

"Some prank," I said.

Dru smiled and shrugged. "We're deploying the term *event*."

"When would I have to decide?"

"Before tomorrow afternoon. Nobody knows you're back. They're not expecting you. They'll be so thrilled. Harold's been wearing his Booth outfit ever since you left. When he sees us on campus he pretends not to know us and will only communicate through coded notes that he slips into our hands. Very sinister. He's got all these girls following him around, which is a first for Harold and a waste of time for them. And he's making Roy wear his Lincoln suit, but Roy says he got the short end because everybody thinks he's some minimum wage guy passing out flyers for a new bank."

She smiled. It was a grin I'd never seen before from her.

"Okay."

"Oh great. God, I'm happy. I'll call Bea and have her bring over your clothes. And I should get word to Harold—but how?" The melodrama of the phrase struck and she laughed. "If only there was a way."

"I'll look for him," I said, "I've got to go get my stuff."

The door was unlocked. I pushed it open far enough to see a girl's feet, brown and scuffed with dirt. There was the smell of cigarettes, and then someone slammed the door shut pinning my shoulder against the jamb. "Ow," I yelled, "what the fuck, Ship?" and then a voice I knew said, "Tom?" The door swung open and there was Callie lying on my bed.

"Hey, Tom," she said and then Grey caught me in a bear hug before I saw him coming at me from behind the door. "Brother," he said, "Man, we're glad it's you."

"Bottom line is we're on the run," Grey told me, once we were all sitting on my bunk.

"We're not on the run," Callie said. Her belly strained at the bib of her overalls. Her arms were as thin as handlebars. There were circles under her eyes and her nose was running. She seemed to have forgotten the carton of orange juice in her hand. "The deal was we'd come here and talk to you, and we'd all figure what to do next."

"What'd you do?" I asked Grey.

"I sank the boat," he said, which explained why his hair, which had mostly grown back, was matted and his coveralls smelled.

"Which boat?"

"The ketch. The one the guy wanted me to sail over from Canada."

"How'd it sink?"

"A fire," he said.

"Did you start it?"

"I might have—when I poured gas in the cabin and shot it with the flare gun."

"What you do that for?"

"Long story."

There was the sound of a key in the lock and, before Grey could get up and hold it shut, the door swung open. It was Ship. "Aw, no way," he said the second he saw us. "You've got to be kidding me. I'm going to go tell Howie."

"Can't let you do that, Shipper," Grey said, getting between him and the door.

"You said one night," Dennis said to me forlornly. "And you didn't say anything about him. Oh hi," he said to Callie, seeing her and her condition for the first time.

"Hi," Callie replied.

"Like you can see, this is an unusual situation, Dennis," I said. "You're going to have to be a little flexible."

"What's going on?"

"Callie's having a baby."

"Now?"

"Yes," Grey said.

"No, not now," Callie said.

"But soon," I said.

Ship inched toward the door. "I have to pee," he said.

"I told you you got to stay here," Grey said.

"But I really got to go."

Grey looked at me. "Let him go," I said.

"All right," Grey said. "I'll go with you."

"You're going to go to the bathroom with me?"

"Sure," Grey said. "Pretend we're girls."

The second they were out of the room Callie started to cry. "Tom, you've got to get him to stop."

"How much trouble is he in?"

"I don't know. He won't tell me."

I got up and stood by the door to hear when Grey and Ship came back. "We'll go back tomorrow night," I said. "I got a thing I have to do and then we can go."

"But what if Grey won't?"

"Don't worry," I said.

"I feel like throwing up," she said.

"Is that what they call morning sickness?"

She laughed over the tears. "I was over that a long time ago. I just feel like throwing up."

Grey pushed Dennis back into the room with a grip on his shoulder.

"That wasn't so bad," Grey said.

Dennis said, "I've got glee club in an hour."

"You got to miss that one," I told him.

"They'll come looking for me."

"It's just till tomorrow, Ship," I said. "Callie and me talked it over. We're leaving tomorrow. Till then you have to stick this out with us. It'll mean a lot."

Ship looked at Callie, who was blowing her nose for the fiftieth time. He was in love, no question about it. As long as he believed he was helping her, we had a chance. "We get no unexcused absences. Someone's going to have to write me a note."

At dinnertime, I went down to the cafeteria and got sandwiches packed in plastic triangles and Cokes and milk for Callie. Twice I called the factory to tell Dru that I wouldn't be over until the next day, but no one answered. Callie fell asleep before eleven, curled on my old bed and Dennis said we should turn out the lights.

Grey and I slept on the floor using our coats for pillows. Before long we heard Ship's whistling adenoids and figuring he was sleeping, lying on our backs in the dark, Grey told me the story of his sail across Superior.

"I got to the docks at dawn. There were two guys there, fisher types. One stays in the pickup, the other meets me at the boat. I give him the cash, he gives me the key and a sail bag with the jib in it, tells me the rest of the suit of sails is on board. He says, 'You know what you're doing?' I say, 'Yeah,' even though I'm thinking I don't have a clue what I'm doing. My only rule was I wasn't going to run the motor unless I absolutely had to.

"The first day out was fantastic. Wind out of the northwest, maybe ten knots. The boat handled like a skateboard, quick and easy on the changes of course. It was like God was looking out for me personally."

"Did you think that was likely?"

"Why not? What beef's he got with me? I ran a beam reach, all three sails, straight for my mark, which was the Keweenaw Peninsula. From the charts, I made the distance to be 180 nautical miles, maybe twenty-two hours, less if I stayed that lucky. The sun was out, which was good because I found out before long that it got very cold when it wasn't. Chunks of ice were smacking against the hull.

"At night, the winds slacked, the sails luffed, and I couldn't work the winches and steer at the same time. The jib fouled when I tried to lower it, and I had to cut it down. Then I find out the global positioning gear is out and I'm up all night, trying to stay on course and freezing my ass off, even in long johns and my parka. In the morning, the winds pick up again only now it's cloudy and winds are maybe twenty knots this time out of the southeast—which is okay because I can keep my heading—but then I find out that she didn't handle worth a shit without the jib. It was like trying to keep a spinning top on course. By then I'd been out twenty-four hours and I haven't touched any of the peanut butter sandwiches, which was all I brought to eat, but the gallon jug of water I brought was almost gone. The only other thing I got to drink is some whiskey I found in the cabin, and I don't want to drink that 'cause I got to stay awake but I don't know how long till I reach land and I can't spare the water, so there I am eating peanut butter sandwiches and washing them down with liquor at seven in the morning.

"I thought I'd be on the water a day and a half. But by dark on the second day, I saw no sign of land and a lot of freighter traffic and so I said, Fuck it, I'm not going to get rammed by twenty thousand tons of iron ore in the middle of the night. So I take down the sails and crank up the motor, which works great for an hour before it runs out of gas. But I don't panic 'cause I see two other cans below. So I grab the handle of the first of the spare cans and pull as hard as I can to lift it and end up almost throwing it over my shoulder because it's empty. I go to the second one, and it's not totally empty. I can hear the gas sloshing around in the bottom. So I hook that one up to the fuel line but there's not enough left to get the thing primed, and so there I am adrift in a shipping lane at night. At which point there's nothing much to do outside of jumping overboard, so I went to sleep and prayed to Jesus I wake up in the morning."

"Which you did."

"Obviously. And when I did I saw land. Man, Tom, you'll never have that feeling. I felt like Commodore fucking Perry. I got the mainsail rigged about halfway and figured I'd follow the shoreline the rest of the way."

"So what happened"

"The Coast Guard."

"You must've been glad to see them."

He laughed. "So glad I scuttled the boat."

"Christ. What'd you do that for?"

"That would be largely due to the fifty kilograms of powder taped in the hull."

"You're kidding?"

"I'm not."

For a minute I lay in the dark listening to Callie and Dennis breathing, hoping they hadn't heard any of this.

"You knew about it?"

"Hell yeah, I knew about it. I knew about it when I came down here. I just might've forgot to mention it."

"Man," I said, "Who were you getting it for?"

"People," he said, "Even some people you know." I heard him roll over and then he was breathing on my cheek. "Remember Natch?" he whispered. "This was his gig. I met him last year at a cookout at Rossmeier's and he got to talking about what he called these designer drugs. He said that the drugs people are doing now are all obsolete. And that these new drugs that are custom made were what everyone was going to be doing, at least the people who had the money to pay. The problem was procuring the necessary materials. That's where we came in."

"But it sank, right? They can't bust you because your boat sank."

"I don't think you're hearing me. The Coast Guard isn't exactly my problem right now, or at least they weren't until I took off on them. I think they wondered why all of a sudden when they show up the boat goes up in flames. When they hauled me out of the water, the officer said, 'Son, how come your clothes smell like fuel?' He was from the south. You wouldn't have thought they'd have southerners in the Coast Guard."

"Why not? They've got coasts. What'd you tell him?"

"I had a fuel leak. That's what started it. Just a good thing they happened along. Believe me, I played that up big. I said, 'Man. If it wasn't for you guys I'd be dead.' They took me to the station in Black River, and said, 'Don't go nowhere.' I said, 'Where am I gonna go?' and first chance I got I went. Walked home forty miles because I didn't want to hitch and run the risk of getting picked up, got home, got Callie, got Jack's truck, and here we are."

"Kind of a mess," I said.

"Yeah but for a while there it was something. I was master of my ship and the sea. You think anyone around here will ever know that feeling?"

"No, they won't," I said. I said it without thinking. But he was right.

"Then that's something I have on them. Remember when we swam the channel?"

"It's funny you ask."

"I saved your life."

"Yeah, but I think the time you knocked me out of the tree in the Talbotts' yard with a football kind of evened us out."

"That was before."

"It was?"

"Had to be."

"Then I guess you're right. I do owe you."

PART III

LAST SEEN
WANDERING
VAGUELY

USELESS, USELESS

When the phone rang the next morning, Ship made a dive for it, but Grey got there first. It was Dru.

"Look," she said, "Can you come over? Roy was just here and told me something, and I think he might be nuts."

The phone woke Callie. She sat up, listing to her right, and clutching at her abdomen below her stomach. She walked out the door. I wondered what the girls on the floor below had made of a pregnant girl they don't know appearing in their bathroom every hour. Probably honored. It was the kind of thing they talked about but never got to see.

"What happens when the baby comes?" I asked Grey when I hung up the phone. He was lying on his back, placidly blowing smoke rings at the ceiling.

"Got me. Our college fund's at the bottom of Lake Superior."

Either Ship was still asleep or he was faking it. I told Grey to come out into the hall with me and he did, keeping a firm grip on the doorknob. I told him, "I've got to go somewhere. Let's let Ship go and you and Callie come with me."

"We can't do it. What if he tells someone?"

"Who's he going to tell?"

"The cops."

"What's he going to tell them?"

"Doesn't matter what he says. Just that he talks."

"Come on."

"I'll end up floating face down on the Mulberry River."

"Tell Natch what you did. It must've been the right thing, under the circumstances. They got to expect something like that's going to happen."

"I don't know," Grey said. "We didn't review the guidelines before I left with fifty thousand dollars of his cash."

Callie came scuffling up the hall and put her head sleepily on Grey's chest. "Are we going home now?" she said.

"Yeah," I said, "we're all going home tonight."

"Okay, okay," Grey said, "but we'll do it this way. You go do what you have to do. We'll stay here and sit on Ship. Then it won't matter who he tells because we'll be on our way."

While Grey was talking I noticed Howie tacking a flyer on the bulletin board down the hall. I turned my head but not before he saw us.

"Zimmermann," he said. "Thought we'd lost you."

"Looks like I'm going to be taking a semester off," I told him.

"Hardship?"

"Hardship in a big way," I said.

Just then Dennis yelled out from the room. "Howie, help."

Howie shook his head. "What's wrong with Shipman?"

"The usual."

"Tell him to keep it down," he said and walked off in search of the next bulletin board.

"See what I mean?" Grey said.

"All right," I said. "You can watch him. But just until tonight. Have Callie tell him. He likes her."

Dru came gliding down the metal stairs of the factory. The dress was lavender and decorated with lace and silver beads and went all the way to the floor so that she had to lift it as she descended.

"Does this look like a gown befitting a debutante going to the theater with the doomed president of the United States and my fiancé and stepbrother who years later will go mad and murder me in Germany?"

"If that's what you're going for," I said. Her shoulders were bare in the style of dresses you see in Civil War movies and around her neck she wore a necklace of blood-red stones that the light shone through like wine.

"They're garnets," she said. "It belonged to my grandmother. Oh, Tom, isn't this magnificent." She touched her fingers to the necklace and her expression darkened. "I'm worried about Roy."

"Why?"

"He came here last night and said he wanted to go for a walk. He was out of his head and talking a mile a minute about what Harold was saying about an intersection and about what he called the triumph of art over history."

"What's that?"

"I don't know. It's the sort of thing Crowder says that sounds cool, but when you think about it it doesn't make any sense. Then he told me he wanted to switch the blank in Harold's gun with a real bullet."

"Harold agreed to that?"

"Harold doesn't know. Roy says this is re-creation, not reality, so he can't be hurt."

"That's nuts."

"I guess," she said.

"I'll go look for him," I said.

"Maybe he's not serious. Maybe he knows what he's talking about. Here. He gave me these. These are the blanks." She opened her fist and dropped the two shells in my hand. They were warm from her holding them and looked like regular bullets, except that they were flat at the end. It struck me that if Crowder had given Dru the blanks, then he'd been doing more than thinking about switching them.

"Maybe we should call the whole thing off," I said.

"We can't," she said, "Like Harold said, we're at an inter-section."

"Where is he?"

"Harold? Nobody knows. Lurking about. Roy and Harriette are spending the day together. They thought that would be appropriate. Mike's coming over around six and we're leaving for the theater. The meeting starts at 7:30. Bea and you are the only ones who have to be there on time. Here, come upstairs and I'll get you your suit."

I didn't like it. The fabric was a thick corduroy and an ugly brown, to say nothing of the knee pants. "Bea guessed about the size," Dru said. "Do you want to put it on now? The rest of us are."

"That's okay," I said. "I've got people over."

"Who?"

"Grey and Callie. They just got in last night."

She raised her eyebrows at that. "Are they coming to the show?"

"I don't know yet."

"They should. We can all go someplace after."

I couldn't tell her I was leaving. Instead, I tried to think about what it was going to be like for us when this was all over, but I didn't have a clue. All I knew for sure was I didn't want to wear the brown corduroy suit.

When I got back to the room, Callie was gone and Grey had gagged Ship and bound him to a chair with masking tape. Ship stared at me with bug eyes and breathed hard through his nose.

"Holy shit, Grey."

"After you left he started yelling, and I couldn't get him to shut up."

"Where's Callie?"

"She's waiting downstairs?"

"In the truck? It's freezing out."

"I don't know. She said she couldn't watch me tape him up."

"Let him go."

Grey gave me the kind of look of violence that I'd always backed down from when we were kids. "Not until we're out of here," he said.

"Then we're out of here." He didn't stop me as I took a pair of scissors and cut the tape and yanked it off of Ship's face along with a good bit of his hair. "Cripes," Ship yelled as soon as his mouth was free.

"Dennis," I told him, "you got to shut up, or I'm going to put it back on."

"Okay, okay," he said. "You got to let me loose. I've really got to whiz."

I cut him free from the chair and he bolted out the door toward the bathroom before Grey could do anything to stop him.

"Are you insane?"

"What was I supposed to do?" Grey said. "He started screaming. You heard him."

"It's time for you to think this through," I said. "Callie's in no shape and you're on the run and tying people up. What we should do is go back home."

"No way," Grey said, "I do that and I get killed."

"We'll tell Spires."

"He'll lock me up, and he'll probably lock you up too."

"Think about it. We'll tell him what we know. They'd much rather get a guy like Natch than us. If they get him, he can't touch you if he wanted to. Tell them you just thought you were buying a boat. It wasn't until you got out on the water that you found out. Who's he going to believe? You or some pusher?"

Ship came back from the can, and Grey told him to get lost.

"I want you to leave," Ship said. He was as mad as I'd ever seen him, which I guess was understandable. "You should go to the hospital with your girl and see if she's still okay and then you can't come back here." As he was talking, there was the sound of hurried footsteps in the hallway and Callie appeared in the doorway, out of breath. "The cops are here," she said.

"You little—" Grey said and made a grab for Ship, but he made it out the door.

"Okay," I said, "Go. Take the stairs to the second floor. Turn right and go to the end of the hall. There's a second set of stairs that go out back."

"Aren't you coming?" Callie asked.

"They don't care about me. I'll stick around and talk to them while you get on the road."

Callie looked as though she would cry again. Then we hugged.

Then Grey and I hugged. "This was fun, wasn't it," he said.

"Sort of," I said, and they went.

The police were cordial. There were two, an older officer, Tremble, and his partner, a woman, Officer Parker, who did most the talking, with her elbow resting on the handle of her gun. She asked to see my student ID and said, smiling, "We had a report of a kidnapping,"

"Huh," I said, then saw Ship hovering in the hallway.

"This gentleman said you tied him up."

"He's my roommate," I said. "He lives here."

"Why's he got tape in his hair?" Officer Tremble asked.

"We were goofing around."

"Was this a hazing incident?" Officer Parker asked.

"Something like that," I said.

"Hazing is a violation of university policy," she said.

"Is it against the law?"

"Depends on the action," Tremble said.

"Ask him where the other ones are," Ship said. "The guy who sells drugs and his pregnant girlfriend."

The officers stood blinking at me.

"These friends of mine just left," I said. "But it's not like he says. She's pregnant, but he's no drug dealer."

Tremble looked at me as Officer Parker said, "Would you empty your pockets for us?"

"How come?"

"If what this gentleman says is correct," Tremble said.

I said, "Sure," because I knew I had nothing to hide. When I turned my pockets inside out the blanks Dru had given me for Harold fell on the floor.

Tremble collected them. "Tell us about these," he said.

"They're props," I said, "for a show."

"What show?" Parker asked.

"At the university regents meeting."

"You're just full of surprises," said Tremble, at which point they took Ship down the hall and talked to him. I couldn't hear what they were saying but I could see that he was all excited and waving his arms and when they came back, Officer Parker said, "Mr. Zimmermann, at this point we're going to ask you to come downtown with us, if you wouldn't mind."

"Are you arresting me?" I asked.

"No, we'd like to clear up the matter of your friends," Tremble said.

"Can I say no?" I asked.

"You could," Officer Parker said, still smiling, "But then we probably would have to arrest you."

"For what?"

"Try us," Tremble said.

My reception at the police station was something different from what I might have expected from watching the cop shows. I wasn't handcuffed or put behind bars. I was issued a can of Coke and a key to the washroom connected to a six-inch-long piece of laminated plastic with the city's logo on it. I told Officers Parker and Tremble about Grey and Callie (leaving out the part about what went on on the boat). I told them the first time

Grey came down he had some pot with him, and we'd smoked some of that and Dennis, prude that he is, assumed that anyone who smoked marijuana was a dealer, but the truth was that Grey wasn't and if they wanted to arrest everyone in the state of Wisconsin who blew the occasional doob they'd have to build more jails.

They were mostly concerned with Callie and her baby. They asked when she was supposed to have it. I told them as best I knew. They asked if I thought Callie was at risk traveling with Grey. I told them that Grey was the father and that they had been together for five years and that he had never harmed her and wouldn't. I told them I'd stake my life on that. They asked if I'd ever had any trouble with the law and I told them no (which was true as far as they would see from any records they could look up). They asked me again what the two blanks were for and I told them exactly (leaving out the part about the real bullets). Whatever I told them they seemed to believe or did a good job of pretending. I wouldn't have worried all that much about my detour to the station, except that all this took more than three hours.

In between asking me questions, Officer Parker and Officer Tremble came and went, sometimes disappearing for a half hour at a time. I'd see them down the hall, drinking coffee from Styrofoam cups and shooting the breeze with the other police. And I got the idea that all the time they had somebody, like me, down for questioning was time that they didn't have to be driving around their beat, which meant they weren't in any hurry to let me go.

With nothing better to do with my time, I worried. I worried first about Callie and her baby and then about Grey and Howard Natchell. I worried about how I was going to get my corduroy James E. Buckingham suit out of Ship's room. Then, as it got too close to 7:00, I worried about if I'd have time to get over there at all, even if Ship would let me in. And finally I worried about Harold and the loaded derringer he carried in his pocket.

And then it was 7:30 and I didn't see either of my officers and I decided I couldn't wait any longer. I put the restroom key on the counter, tossed my Coke can in the trash and headed for the door, reasoning that I wasn't under arrest and that I could just get over to the show, make sure that nobody did anything stupid and come back and turn myself in again, which would have to score me points as being above the call of the ordinary citizen. I had my hand on the handle of the glass door, an inch from the anonymity of the street, when somebody yelled, "Hold on."

I had seen a lot of this officer in the time I spent at the station, carrying stacks of manila folders from one desk to another, making time with Officer Palmer by the fingerprint machine. "Where do you think you're going?"

My knees shook. "I thought I was done," I said.

He said. "Has anyone signed you out?"

"I guess so."

"Sit there," he said, pointing at the bench I'd just left.

I sat and waited for him to come back with Tremble or Parker, who I figured would bawl me out for not asking permission to leave then let me go anyway. For fifteen minutes, I waited for Officer Parker or anybody to return, then thirty minutes, and when still nobody came, I got up and, looking both ways this time to make sure the coast was clear, made a second run for the door.

It was ten blocks from the station, up past the capitol building and down State Street to the auditorium. I made the distance running flat out in five minutes. Forty-five minutes into the meeting, the lobby was deserted. I heard the shot clear as thunder above the silence of the hall.

Then there were shouts and screams. I distinctly heard Bea cry out, "Heaven help the republic!" and what I thought was Harold delivering his line from the stage, but couldn't be sure with all the chaos. I ran the rest of the way up the stairs. As I got to the box, I might've paused a second, afraid of what I was going to see. Pushing back the curtain to the box, I first saw Dru, standing and staring in my direction but not seeing me, then Majors, in his blue officer's uniform, leaning out of the box, screaming, "Doctor, somebody get a doctor." Harold was gone. He'd fired the shot and jumped over the rail onto the stage, exactly like the script said, leaving Roy, with his head in the lap of Harriette, his wife for this drama, the white makeup on her face, plastered on even thicker for the occasion, now wet with Crowder's blood.

26

GRAVITY

We drove the back roads all night in Crowder's Volvo, turning what would have been five hours by Interstate into eight. Dru slept in the passenger seat, still in her gown, curled against the door with her hand on the lever, ready to bail out at the first danger that woke her. The yellow line ticked by like stitches, flowing into solid ribbon at the hills then back to dashes at the crest. It was rearview-mirror driving all the way, looking for headlights coming up on us from behind. We touched backward all the spots I'd stopped at on my way eight months before—the Dells, Lois's drive-in, and the stretch of County Highway M where I'd bought a bag of peaches off a Mexican and his daughter for a hundred dollars—like it was a celebrity map tour of three days of my life that I'd never told anyone about.

The Volvo handled like a tin box on steel wheels. Doors rattled and the steering wheel vibrated between my hands. The back seat was piled with odd junk, plastic milk crates overflowing with extension cords and paint brushes, a case of empty beer bottles, coils of copper wire, and a two-foot-long muskie stuffed, lacquered and mounted on a plaque, with a brass tag that read *Clement Odegaard, Lake Wingra, April 3, 1974.* The interior smelled of mildew and rot. Roy was proud of the state of his vehicle. "It's organic," he said. "It heals. It thrives. In spite of us."

Dru stirred, shifting in her sleep and pulling her knees up under her dress. I turned the radio lower but not off, thinking that would wake her up, and if she woke up we could talk. The scene in the theater box had been as real as anyone could've contrived a tableau to be: Majors in his uniform leaning out over the rail calling for a doctor, Harriette with her hands to her face shrieking, torn in her gestures between pushing Roy's bleeding head off of her lap and cradling him to her chest. People crowded past me from behind, shouting credentials. "I'm a nurse," said one, "I'm a doctor. I'm an EMT." It was touching how ready people were to help. I headed down the stairs in search of Drucilla and found her leaning against the car.

"Where's Harold?" I asked.

"I don't know."

"Why didn't he take the car?"

"I don't know."

"What should we do?"

"Get out of here."

"Should we wait for the others?"

"Don't you think they be down here by now if they wanted to come?"

At four in the morning I stopped for gas in Butternut.

As I was pulling up to the pump, I heard the rustle of taffeta. Dru rubbed her eyes. "Where are we?"

I told her, knowing the name would mean nothing to her. Just another one-tavern snowmobile town in northern Wisconsin. "Does it remind you of Canada?"

She looked around, but there was nothing to see but pumps and the yellow light from the station. "No."

The kid behind the counter didn't look up from his textbook, as I slapped down a five for gas and two Styrofoam cups of coffee. Dru sat cross-legged in the seat, holding the cup between her fingers so it didn't spill on her dress. The coffee was burned and sour-smelling and steam filled the car. I put the car in gear and she said, "Don't drive just yet."

"What do you think happened?" I said.

She shook her head and dipped her lips toward the rim of the cup.

"So what should we do?"

"What do you mean?"

"I mean we can go to my house. Then what?"

"We'll go to your house—then we'll see." She took a sip and her whole face wrinkled, showing the first sign of the disgust I'd been looking for. "God, this is awful," she said.

The black sky turned gray with the morning, making the familiar landscape of the peninsula seem unfamiliar. I pointed out landmarks, all of them mundane, the national forest, the Washburn Dog N Suds, the Chevron station. She kept her eyes turned toward the black pane of the passenger window. I thought she was afraid of what the next day would bring.

As we rounded the bend on Highway 13, where I'd first seen Lake Superior from the back of Uncle Karl's Ford wagon, I saw a vehicle on the shoulder. I realized it was Grey's truck.

"How come we're stopping?" Dru asked.

"Some people you have to meet."

The surprise Grey and Callie might've felt at seeing me was blown away by their surprise at watching Dru tiptoe across the gravel, holding the hem of her gown in her fingertips. Callie sat in the open passenger door with her feet on the ground and Grey stood in front of her, his hands on his hips.

"Trouble?" I said.

"No," Grey said.

"Yes," Callie said.

"This is Dru," I said.

"Hi," Dru said.

"Hey," they answered, looking at her the way you might a toddler on a ledge.

"What's going on?" I asked Callie, hoping to get the straight story from her. She looked half asleep, the dark skin under her eyes even darker with exhaustion.

"We're just trying to figure out how to work this," Grey answered for her.

"He won't get on the ferry," Callie said.

"I didn't say that."

"What did you say?" I asked him.

"Listen," Callie said to Dru, "do you want a sweater?"

"Would you mind?" Dru said.

While Callie fetched the sweater from the truck, and while they clucked and cackled like girls do when they try on each other's clothes, Grey and I walked to the edge of the bluff. The rising sun turned the eastern sides of Otter and St. Raphael Islands from black to green. It'd been a cool night and the light glittered on the frost like quartz. Below us was the beach that we'd pushed off from in Grey's blue canoe just months before.

Grey put his hand on my shoulder and I flinched, thinking he was going to pull the kind of stunt that he used to, trying to scare me into thinking he was going to push me off the bluff.

"You can't leave," I said, "not before Callie has her baby. And if you stay that long you might as well stick it out."

"Easy for you to say," he said.

"I trust Spires. I always got the feeling he liked us, no matter what he said, more than he liked any law-abiding FIB anyway."

"I guess we'll see."

"We had a little trouble of our own."

Grey looked over his shoulder at Dru, who was smoothing her necklace over Callie's brown sweater. "Like what?"

"Long story. When I tell you, you won't believe it." I looked over the edge of the bluff and said, "I remember this being higher."

"Still high enough," he said and gave me a shove.

I caught myself before I got close to the edge and took a wild swing at his arm. He jumped out of the way and laughed. "I'm still smarter than you."

"Head wounds bleed a lot." That's what the trauma doctor told a waiting room full of bewildered Stovepipe Theater members, to explain how Roy could be sitting up in an emergency-room bed with a turban of gauze around his head, drinking juice through a straw. This information Dru got from Bea's roommate after dialing her way through nearly every number she knew. She hung up the phone and threw herself against my chest, crying for the first time since the incident. I assumed she'd heard for certain that Roy was dead. "He's going home tomorrow," she said between sobs. I thought, in my own grief, "That's a nice way to put it," until, out of nowhere, she added, "I wonder if he'll transfer."

"What do you mean transfer?"

"To another school," she said.

I asked, "Are you saying he's not dead?"

She laughed and pushed away from me, leaving my shoulder soggy. "Of course, silly. What did you think?"

"That he was."

Around us the shop, crowded with the first repairs of spring, looked much the same as I'd left it at Thanksgiving, though I noticed the picture of Pop and my mom had been taped back in place on its broken mount above Pop's bench. Dru turned the metal dial on the phone, with her hand on the lever. "This is cool," she said. "Where'd you get it?"

I knew by the handprints on the curtains above the kitchen sink that Trudy was history. The house was otherwise tidy, if not spotless. "Pop, it's me," I called, as though I'd just come back from an afternoon at the Reeds'. There was no answer.

"Kitchen," I said to Dru, by way of a tour. "There's the living room."

"Great," she said, "where's the bathroom?"

When she emerged, smelling of soap, carrying Callie's sweater over her arm, and looking like she'd come from the ball rather than ten hours on the run, I showed her my room, as pristine as I'd left it.

"You're neat," she said.

"Thanks," I said. "So are you."

"I meant the room."

The kitchen door slammed, and we walked to the kitchen to find Pop in his riding clothes, red-faced from exertion, reaching for the cane to beat down the intruder whose footsteps he'd heard coming at him down the hallway.

"Eh?" he said, looking first at me, then at Dru, then at me again, determined to keep staring until he understood what he was seeing. The sight of him without Trudy and back on the bike gave me more comfort than I ever would've dreamed, and I wanted to hug him except for the fact that I never had. Dru stood beaming, a little uncomfortable and anxious, I think, to make a good impression, which surprised me because who was he to her? Or, more to the point, who did she want to be to him?

I said, "Pop Dru, Dru Pop"

She reached out her hand and he shook it, saying, "How do you do." Swear to God, just like that: How—do—you—do and clicked his heels together.

At dinnertime, Pop pulled his easy chair up to the head of the table so that Dru and I could have the two kitchen chairs. We had buttered noodles, green beans from a can, and beer. Dru had found a sweatshirt and jeans I hadn't worn since junior high that fit well enough and sat cross-legged, watching Pop out of the corner of her eye each time he leaned forward and extended his arm as far as it would reach to put his glass back on the table.

Dru went to sleep before dark in my bed. I lay on the couch in the living room as Pop reclined in his chair. I told him the story of why we'd come home. I left out my failing grades. Grades were irrelevant.

He sat in his chair with his legs crossed, smoking and watching me as I talked. "Roy," I said, "you'd've liked him"—I said that a couple of times, "you'd like Mike, he's a good guy" . . . "That's Bea I'm talking about, I don't think you'd like her," and on like that. He watched and listened and just when I was wrapping up and was going to ask what he thought about the whole mess—though I have no clue what I would've done with that information—I heard him snore.

The next morning Dru and I went out for a walk, west through the state park. We came out of the woods, which had been damp, into a clearing, which was bright. This was Sitwell land. By then almost all of the undeveloped land was Sitwell land. Spring had come late, but it had come, and the ground was soft and the air filled with the stench of turned up mud and rot. We held hands and that felt strange because I'd never held her hand like that before. I guided her across the field.

When we reached the bluff, she hesitated because the path leading to the cove was steep and the dirt was loose. She gripped my hand tighter, the sweat of her palm mingling with mine, as we descended a stairway of exposed roots. At the bottom I let go and we hopped the stones to the water's edge.

She pulled off the sneakers she'd borrowed from Callie, rolled up my jeans, and waded into the icy water, her calves white against the onyx surface of the lake. There was the sound of laughter in the distance and the ferry rounded the bend, its rails lined with day tourists scuttling off to the outlying islands for the afternoon. They waved. Dru waved back, as though she'd lived here her whole life.

27

WATER

I wonder if Crowder had died whether we would've had the guts to show up for a hearing in front of the same board of regents we'd spattered with his blood. Luckily, we'll never have to find out.

Of course, in spite of Roy's fortunate survival, those of us who hadn't been expelled already were expelled now. Only Bea (four credits from her BS) objected. She said, in front of all of us, that this had been Harold's fault, and mine. She said that if she'd known anyone was going to get hurt she never would have gotten involved. The Chancellor—give him credit—looked Bea square in her cold, hazel eyes and told her he hoped we all felt that way.

It was funny seeing them all in their clothes. Bea in slacks for the first time I'd ever seen and a yellow sweater and white blouse underneath. Majors was dapper as ever in a blue blazer, though on his face was something I'd never seen, something that looked like remorse, but could have also been doubt. Harold wore an aquamarine polyester suit that might have been meant as a gag, but no one was in the mood and so the gesture lost all effect. And most surprising of all was Harriette, without the makeup and pink and looking too young for anyone getting kicked out of college her senior year. She looked to me, more than anything, like a bank teller.

Dru wore the same black number she'd worn at that first party. It was wrinkled at the hem.

Afterward there was nothing to do but retreat into the protective custody of our permanent addresses and let our parents pull whatever strings they could to steer us back toward lucrative professions, except for me, whose father had no strings to pull. This, I realized, was what Dooley had meant about consequences.

I told Dru I had to pick up my things at Rosewalter. She said she'd be at Bea's.

The day was warm and humid. The semester was coming to an end and, unlike the fall semester, when nerves over exams combined with bleak weather for a pathological mood on campus, the warmth of spring defused the anxiety and the students looked complacent and content. The ivy on the walls of Rosewalter was turning green. Girls lay in halters on the grass.

I knocked on Ship's door once, then twice (not calling his name because I figured he'd never answer if he knew it was me) before I gave up. I was heading down the stairs when I saw him coming through the double doors. He saw me, stopped, turned back and ran. He beat me outside to the courtyard, but I caught him by the arm when he made the mistake of turning to see if I was still following him.

"Come on, Ship," I said. "I'm not going to hurt you. I just need to get my stuff out of the room."

He squinted in the sun and thought about it.

"You're going that way anyway. Don't make me get a court order."

"That's good coming from you," he said.

We made a deal. I'd wait in the hall while Ship packed up my stuff and handed it to me. I leaned against the wall, looking down a couple of times as floor mates who might've recognized me came out of their rooms. I heard slamming dresser doors and the sounds of Ship's footsteps and then after about ten minutes the door opened again, and I saw my blue Bellwether backpack hanging from the end of Ship's chicken claw fingers. I took it from him, saying, "That wasn't so bad. Now will you let me apologize?"

He slammed the door.

"I'm saying I'm sorry," I said through the door, "and asking you to forgive me."

"Go away," he said.

I waited for him, but he wouldn't come out. "All right, but you're going to regret this," I said, having no idea why he would. I was halfway up Observatory Drive before I remembered that I'd left my bike behind.

The shuffling of sneakered feet echoed through the observatory. Elise Winters stood in front of a school group, second graders from the size of them, trailing their hands along the curved rows of books and stumbling as they tilted their heads up to look at the domed metal roof. "Can anybody tell me," she asked them in a singsong voice, "what word you can find in 'observatory'?"

A girl in back said, "Servant."

Elise tilted her head, as she thought of what to make of that and said, "Yes, 'servant' and what else?" A long silence and then she said, "Observe, right? Can anyone tell me what observe means?" This time she didn't wait. "It means 'look,' doesn't it? That's what we do here. We look at things with the big telescope behind me."

She saw me, smiled, not especially surprised, and made a gesture with her eyes to all the kids standing around, meaning I'd have to come back. I nodded that I understood, waved, and left. I'm sure she thought I was coming back. I wondered how long she'd wait.

By the time I got to the lecture hall, Dooley was already into the announcements that he started every class with. I stood in back by the doors, scanning the rows for a seat. "Papers are due on Thursday at four," Dooley said, speaking softly as he always did when he began. "That means on my desk. The department's secretaries have been instructed to indicate papers that are late. This is done by drawing a skull and crossbones in the upper-right-hand corner.

"After Monday's lecture my attention was called to a book that was left behind by a student." He held it up, a paperback with a glossy cover like you buy at the grocery store checkout line. He studied the cover and read, "'*Slugs*—they crawl, they mate, they crave human blood.'"

"Oh, my God," a girl's voice called out, "that's mine."

There was a soft ripple of laughter as she stood in the middle of a row, climbed over knees and backpacks to the aisle, and jogged to the front. Standing on her toes, she reached up toward the lectern. Dooley looked again at the book and then down at the girl in mock disapproval. Scarlet with embarrassment, she took the book from him and walked back to her seat, cradling it to her chest.

"Before the advent of electronic communication, it was routine for the presidents to pursue what they perceived to be national interests without explaining their intentions to their citizens." Dooley's voice filled the room without the need for amplification, the increase in volume the signal that his lecture had begun. "With the coming of radio and television, it became necessary for the executive branch to either inform or deceive its constituents. In matters of war, this nation's leaders would always choose the latter. Truth became a commodity, hoarded by intelligence agencies, concealed from the public and—as demonstrated by the Pentagon Papers—ultimately from the leaders themselves."

Not seeing any seat other than in the first row, I waited until Dooley turned to the map, then I retraced the same route taken by the girl with the misplaced potboiler and sat in the aisle seat.

"The encounter of the destroyers *Maddox* and *C. Turner Joy* with phantom North Vietnamese patrol boats in the Gulf of Tonkin was not an incident of war exploited to justify the commitment of US military forces. It was a fabrication whose need was determined in advance to prod an ignorant public into embracing a foreign policy whose ends they were forbidden to know under the power of executive secrecy"—he turned back from the wall and spotted me immediately, as if he'd been scanning the crowd every day for my face, maybe he had. He paused, sorted the papers on his lectern, opened his mouth to begin, shuffled the pages in front of him again, before saying, his voice somehow louder than the volume of his lecture, "Mr. Zimmermann, what did I say about sitting up front?"

"What did you do?" Dru asked. We were sitting on the porch of Bea and Harriette's house on Williamson Street. A couple of doors down, a father was throwing a Frisbee with his daughter.

"I didn't know what to do," I said. "First I laughed, like he was making a joke, but he just stared, until I realized he wasn't going to start talking again until I moved, so I got up and I left."

The father and daughter stood on opposite sides of the street. Before he threw, the man pantomimed the gesture of throwing and each time the girl, who might have been ten or eleven, raised her arms to be ready, but never caught the Frisbee. Always it bounced off her hands or chest or, once, her forehead.

"I talked to my folks," Dru said. "Dad says he'll pay for me to go to law school."

When she said that, I was watching the girl wind up to throw the disc back. "Don't you have to take some test?"

"I already did."

"When?"

"Before the show. When you were in Chicago."

"How come you didn't tell me?"

"Why would I have?" she said, with a teasing intimacy.

"Is there one around here?"

"One what?" Now she was watching the girl. After twisting her body until her back was to us, she let go of the Frisbee. It fluttered a few feet and fell to the grass. The father, looking both ways for cars, jogged across the street and back to his original spot, as he'd done four or five times since we'd been watching, before throwing the Frisbee again, seemingly thinking if he was patient enough and determined she would reach him with her next throw.

"Law school."

"The way it works is you don't just go to one. You want to go to a good one. You want to go to the best one you can get into."

"Which one would that be?"

She looked at me. All the potential for deception I'd seen in her eyes the first time we met now showed for real. "In my case that would be in Philadelphia."

"I can't go there," I said. "Not with Pop—"

"I know," she said and waited for the significance of the sentence to penetrate my thick skull. When she saw that it had, she said, "You should come and see me, you know. I wouldn't mind."

"I'd like to," I told her. "But I don't think I ever will."

I think she'd expected me to argue with her, and when I didn't the energy she'd reserved for the fight to come had no place to go and turned into a doe-eyed pity. "It's my fault," she said.

And I said, "I know."

Callie was wrong that night at Friendly's over Thanksgiving vacation when she said I could come home and nobody would think anything of it. I wasn't shunned, but no one was particularly glad to see me. On the other hand, Grey and Callie, with the arrival of Baby Freda (after Callie's father Alfred)—because of the child's beauty (she had her father's jet hair, her mother's wide brown eyes) and because they'd increased the island's ever-dwindling population, if only by one—became Island Royalty.

It didn't bother me much, being the town pariah. I'd been one of them once, I would be again, whether they liked it or not. I wasn't going anywhere. People would forget how I'd let them down and others would get the chance to fuck up worse than I had.

I spent a rainy afternoon pulling together discarded components and bolting them on an old Raleigh frame a FIB had left behind to settle a bill. A battered, dull silver, the bike was a sad substitute for the one that for all I knew still leaned in a corner of Ship's room, but I wouldn't be testing it the way I had the other. I didn't have to. Pop had little of the old spring left in his legs. Whether it was the accident, or the cigarettes or the liquor or the lethargic months with Trudy in the house or just the withering of passing seasons, we never talked about it.

One afternoon in August, Grey came home from taking Freda to the pediatrician in Ashton to find a calling card of a familiar design wedged in his screen door.

"'Just stopped by to see if you were in town,' it said."

"Wow, what'd you tell Callie?" I asked him.

"Some siding salesman."

"Have you seen him?"

"Natch? No."

"Do you think he'll come back?"

"Fifty grand of his money and a boatload of drugs are missing. I'm thinking he might drop by the house again, when I'm home."

Two weeks later Grey's hangar burned.

It was after dark. Pop and I were working late. Grey had gone home hours earlier. I said, "Do you smell smoke?" Pop looked at the cigarette burning in his ashtray and shrugged.

Thinking there might be a fire in the state forest, I walked out on the porch but saw no flames rising above the ridge, though the smell was stronger. I walked around the side of the house, noticed an amber glow through the window of the hangar, and ran back into the shop.

"Call Grey," I told Pop. He looked at me and blinked, so I went to the phone myself and called him.

The fire trucks got there before Grey did, though not before the flames had breached the windows.

Grey pulled up in the pickup, with Callie, and Freda wrapped in a blanket. He cursed and ran for the sliding door.

"Don't open that," one of the firemen yelled, but Grey was opening it up as he did.

"I got to get my boats out. Tom," he shouted as I ran after him. The far half of the building was in flames, swallowing boat hulls as it came toward us. Rolling waves of heat slapped at us as we both stepped through the doorway. Grey grabbed the handle of the cart with a new dinghy on it and dragged it toward the door. "Get that stuff," he yelled, pointing at a tool belt and some tubes of diagrams. I did and leaned into the back of the boat as he pulled, until I felt the night air cool the sweat on my neck. Grey went in again and came out seconds later, choking and empty-handed. Callie pulled the blanket over the baby's face to shield her from the floating embers. The airport firemen had run a third line up from the lake and were hosing down the side of our house, where the heat had already blistered the paint.

"Give me a wet rag or something," Grey said, hands on knees, breathing hard, his white T-shirt stained gray with soot, his hair smoky. Jack had arrived and yanked Grey by the shoulder and said, "No, son," just like that, and Grey sank to the ground, knowing everything he had was gone.

The fire burned so hot and fast that by the time word had reached Friendly's and the patrons had made the walk up the hill, still carrying their drinks, the flames were already letting up. As the hoses got the better of the blaze, a dozen or more people stood watching as blankly as if they were staring at a test pattern on TV.

The next morning, Spires drove by in the patrol car, his eyes shadowed by the broad brim of his trooper hat. In the daylight the damage looked many times worse. The air smelled like a doused campfire. Ultimately the heat had melted the steel roof at the center, and it settled in the middle like a whale with a broken spine. The Sarge stood with his hands behind his back in military at-ease position and asked, "Anything combustible inside?"

"Shit," Grey said, "I refurbish wooden boats. It's all combustible."

"Did you tell him about the card?" I said.

"What card?" Spires asked Grey.

"Some guy came by the house and left a card. Tom thought it was weird."

"What did you say to him?" Spires asked.

"To the guy? I didn't see him, just the card."

"Can you show it to me?"

"I tossed it."

"What makes you think he'd do this."

Grey looked my way, warning me with his eyes not to contradict and said, "No particular reason. Like I said, Tom thought it was strange."

Spires took his cap off and wiped the sweat from his forehead with the back of his hand. "Well—I'm awfully sorry, Grey. This is just terrible. You insured for fire?"

Grey laughed.

Spires shook his head. "That's a lesson some people learn the hard way."

Grey sold the twisted steel for scrap. A truck with a giant mechanical claw came over from the mainland to load metal onto a flatbed and cart it away. When it was gone, what had been

Grey's business was a scorched rectangle on the grass. The rescued dinghy sat in our back yard under a tarp through a week of overcast days. Then one morning the sun came out and Grey poked his head in the back door of the shop and said, "I'm putting her in the water."

I walked out on the porch and Pop followed, wiping his hands with a rag. Grey pulled the cart behind him, bracing himself against the incline of the street, so it didn't roll away from him.

I helped Grey roll back the tarp. The varnished white paint of the hull reflected the noon sun like a mirror.

Pop smiled and squatted to inspect the workmanship. "Very fine," he said to Grey, which was unusual because he normally spoke to him through me.

Grey hoisted the sail. "Brand new," he said, "it's canvas. The nylon didn't seem right. Even if it did weigh half as much." He backed the cart halfway into the water and led the boat off with a line.

"Up for a sail?" he asked me.

"Can't," I said. I probably could have. We weren't backed up, and I doubt Pop would've objected, but I figured there'd be other chances.

Grey hopped over the side, coming to rest seated at the tiller. "See ya, then, I guess." He drew the boom sheet tight and a breeze caught the sail. The dinghy heeled and Grey shifted his weight up onto the gunwale to straighten her out. By the time he was a hundred feet away the dinghy looked no larger than a washtub on the vast lake, but she handled smoothly. Silhouetted against the sun, Grey turned and waved, a broad sweep of his arm. We waved back, the two of us, and we watched until he disappeared beyond the point.

They found the boat two days later beached at the headwaters of the Mulberry River, the new canvas sail fouled on a fallen tree.

There was one sign of hope.

"No life jacket," Callie said.

"He didn't take one with him," I told her.

Her posture sank and she propped Freda, who was twisting the strap of her mother's tank top in her fingers, on her hip. "You sure?"

"He never did."

So just as she had with her father, Callie was left waiting for word. She hadn't gotten any better at it. I'd had experience waiting for somebody who never came back and still I had nothing to tell her except that I was certain that there was nothing anybody could say that would mean anything.

"When should I give up?" she asked me a week after Grey went missing.

"Doesn't matter to anybody but you when that is."

"And maybe Grey."

"Maybe." I wasn't the one to tell her there wasn't a chance. The Coast Guard had done that, and it had made no difference.

"He really jerked us around, didn't he?" she said.

"Yeah, he did," I said, "But we let him and we didn't mind."

Callie looked at me and said, "I mind now. And if I ever see the son of a bitch again I'm not going to let him anymore." Then after waiting to see if I had anything to say about that, she asked, "Did you ever wonder why it was me and Grey and not me and you?"

I thought about that. "Nope," I said, "I never did once."

The days got shorter without me noticing, until one night I looked at my watch and saw that it was 5:30 and dark already. I walked down to the lake and stood at the water's edge long enough to see the constellation Orion rise above Otter Island.

It was colder than the paper said it was going to be, and I didn't know how much longer I was going to want to be standing around outside. If Harold was right, then out beyond the quasars and the plasmatic clouds of space gas, Tomas Zimmermann was living a life I'd ridden my bike south to lead, just past the reach of my imagining, of love and wealth and no remorse. Good for him.

ACKNOWLEDGMENTS

I would like to thank the Ragdale Foundation for a residency during which a significant portion of this book was written. Thanks also to the following people for their invaluable professional or personal support during the writing of this book: Susan Hahn, Fred Shafer, Gail Hochman, Donna Seaman, Mark Heineke, Linda Manning, Donna Shear, Rudy Faust, Stephanie Freirich, Joanne Diaz, Susan Herro, Esther Spodek, Michael Thomas, Richard Fox, Eileen Favorite, Enid Barron, Rochelle Distleheim, Ruth Smith, Gwen Ihnat, S. Kirk Walsh, Katherine Deumling, Louise Farmer Smith. Wilma, Sean, Clelia, and Marya Morris. Mary Zerkel, Joanne Zerkel, Ann Zerkel, and Zelda Zerkel-Morris.

Of the many sources that were instrumental in the writing this book, I wanted to hold up two that were particularly useful. *"Right or Wrong, God Judge Me": The Writings of John Wilkes Booth* (University of Illinois Press, 2000) and *We Saw Lincoln Shot: One Hundred Eyewitness Accounts* by Timothy S. Good (University Press of Mississippi, 1996).

IAN MORRIS grew up in a household filled with the sounds of opera and folk music. He played the cello, then the French horn, before settling on the bass guitar. In high school, he played in an album-rock cover band but was kicked out when he suggested they play songs by The Clash and The B-52s. In addition to *Simple Machines,* his second novel, Morris is the author of the novel *When Bad Things Happen to Rich People* and coeditor, with Joanne Diaz, of *The Little Magazine in Contemporary America.* He lives in Chicago with his wife Mary and daughter Zelda.

GIBSON
HOUSE
PRESS

GIBSON HOUSE connects literary fiction with curious and discerning readers. We publish novels by musicians and other artists with a strong connection to music.

GibsonHousePress.com
Facebook.com/GibsonHousePress
Twitter: @GibsonPress

For downloads of reading group guides for Gibson House books, visit
GibsonHousePress.com/Reading-Group-Guides